THE DEVIL'S
CODE

THE DEVIL'S
CODE

COLIN WADE

The Book Guild Ltd

First published in Great Britain in 2023 by
The Book Guild Ltd
Unit E2 Airfield Business Park
Harrison Road, Market Harborough
Leicestershire, LE16 7UL
Freephone: 0800 999 2982
www.bookguild.co.uk
Email: info@bookguild.co.uk
Twitter: @bookguild

Web: www.colinwade.com
Twitter: @CPWADE1
Facebook: @colinwadeauthor
Instagram: @colinwadeauthor

Also by Colin Wade: *The Lost Years*
Also by Colin Wade: *Plutus*
Also by Colin Wade: *Deadly Connection*
Also by Colin Wade: *The Sins of the Father*

Typeset in 11pt Sabon MT

Printed and bound in the UK by TJ Books LTD, Padstow, Cornwall

ISBN 978 1915853 257

British Library Cataloguing in Publication Data.
A catalogue record for this book is available from the British Library.

For all my amazing readers, especially my 'super-fans'. You know who you are.

1

Grief. It consumes you. As Joshua stirred from another troubled sleep there was a split second when his brain tricked him into thinking that everything was alright. That his mother was still alive. The moment passed all too quickly, and the gut-wrenching pain returned. His mouth was dry, and he fought back the rising bile. His brain did what it always did. Flashed images of his mother, in and out of his mind. He buried his face in the pillow, stifling more tears. People said that time healed, but the two weeks since her sudden death had done nothing to ease the agonising pain he was feeling every hour of every day.

Today was as bad as it got. Today she was being cremated. Given back to her God. Joshua shook his head at the thought. He loved her more than anything in the world, but he hated how she thrust God and her faith down his throat at every opportunity. Forced to pray. Forced to read extract after extract of the Bible. Where was her God now? Why had he taken her from him? He never understood her faith.

He knew he had to move but the car accident that had caused his mother's death had also left him with injuries that made getting up a Herculean task. He had little

1

feeling in his left leg and limited mobility in his right. Scans had been inconclusive; doctors giving him all sorts of empty platitudes about temporary paralysis and how things would improve if he kept up the physiotherapy. For now, the wheelchair that sat by his bed, and the pair of crutches leaning against it, were his only way of getting about. The ground-floor flat they lived in was a small oasis of goodness in the shit storm that was his current life.

He managed to shower and shave. Mechanical, boring actions that used up time. Time that he didn't want or need if it meant he was sat thinking about his mother. As he opened the fridge to have some breakfast, he cursed. No milk.

He grabbed his coat and wallet and wheeled himself outside. The shop was across the park but as he entered, he knew there was going to be trouble. The local gang of youths was milling about near the children's playground, shouting and swearing and drinking strong lager even at this early point in the morning. Joshua urged his wheelchair on, hoping to sneak past without them noticing. Fat chance.

The ringleader, a six-foot tattoo-covered skinhead, jumped up and headed straight for Joshua, hurling his can of lager in his direction. It hit his chair's right wheel, exploding in a mess of metal and fizzy liquid. The gang roared with laughter as they bore down on Joshua. The ringleader spoke.

"Well, if it ain't the retard on wheels."

Joshua tried not to make eye contact, urging the wheelchair on. "Just leave me alone."

The thug jumped in front of the wheelchair, straddling Joshua's legs and gripping the arms of the chair.

"Now that ain't very nice is it, Mr Cripple. You wanna have more respect than that."

"Leave me alone."

The thug looked at his gang. "Should we leave him alone?" They laughed as he started to spin the chair around as the rest of the gang punched, kicked and showered Joshua with lager. By the time the attack was finished, Joshua lay on his side, half in his wheelchair and half on the ground. He watched as the gang ran away. Laughing.

It only took a few minutes for 'concerned citizens' to come to his aid but as he let them fuss over him, his mind inevitably turned to his mother. She wouldn't have let that happen. Joshua was thirty-five, but all his life he had been a target. His lank, greasy hair, odd face and rotund shape were magnets for bullies. Everywhere he went people pointed and sniggered, calling him *weird* or *mental*. His mother was the only thing that had kept him safe and sane. His life was nothing without her. Worthless.

Several hours later his neighbour, Mrs Robertson, sorted him out. Patched him up, helped him buy his groceries and made sure he had all he needed for the funeral. He dismissed her as quickly as he could. A classic busybody who meant well but just wanted the latest gossip. Joshua was sure he would be the subject of her inane chattering at bingo or whatever *sad old person* activity she was doing that night.

The hearse arrived and the staff from the funeral directors helped him into the car. He was the sole attendee.

3

They had no friends and no family. This is how Joshua wanted it. Just he and his mother, in one final act.

The celebrant made the best of the service, banging on about God and how he was taking one of his precious souls back to him in heaven. Prayer after prayer made the bile rise once again, but Joshua knew his mother would have approved.

The final act was unconventional. He had begged the funeral directors to let him see his mother's coffin going into the fire. They had eventually relented with the agreement of the crematorium staff. He was the only one attending the funeral and they all could see that it was Joshua's way of achieving closure.

Joshua, on crutches, was led into the room to watch from behind glass as his mother's coffin entered the large kiln. As the doors opened, the roaring flames made him squint. As he watched the flames engulf her coffin, he clawed at the window, his body convulsing as uncontrollable sobs made it hard for him to breathe. He began to fall as he relinquished the support he'd been getting from the crutches.

The staff saved him from falling over and helped him to a chair, giving him a glass of water. They left him alone in his grief. He wrapped his arms around his waist. He was still shaking with the shock of seeing his mother's last moments. "We'll be together soon, we'll be together soon," he muttered as he slowly rocked back and forth. He closed his eyes, trying to shut out the vision of her last moments, but it wasn't working.

Nothing would stop the pain. So deep, so profound that it turned into rage. A rage, that started in his gut, quickly rose to his chest, up into his neck and finally to the top of his head. An all-consuming rage that made him grip his head and screw up his face. "No, no, no," he said as the rage grew so strong that he thought his head would explode. He let out a scream, so loud and so sudden that the crematorium staff rushed back in to see what the noise was about. They fussed around but he told them to leave him be. The tears started, the rage getting worse, his gut tight, his chest tight. He collapsed on the floor.

The next thing he knew he woke in a hospital bed. As he looked around at the bland, lifeless room, he suddenly knew what he had to do. He had to be with her, but he was not going to go quietly. Exiting this world, like she had done, with no one around and no one caring one jot about his life, was not going to happen. For once in his miserable life people were going to take notice.

He grabbed his bag and found the one thing that still made sense to him. He turned it over and over in his hand, allowing himself a brief pained smile.

A plan was forming.

2

ONE WEEK LATER

Matthew McCallum sat in St Cecilia's Hall waiting for the classical concert to start. The Hall was Scotland's oldest purpose-built concert hall, dating back to 1762. The Georgian architecture was beautiful and the acoustics the best he had ever experienced.

Matthew took every opportunity he could to support the burgeoning talent that flowed through the musical undergraduate programmes at the University of Edinburgh. The Hall had been a second home for more years than he cared to remember. He was an accomplished tenor himself but work often got in the way of pursuing his passion for classical music.

He shuffled in his seat, trying to get comfortable as the formal black-tie attire seemed somehow tighter around his belly than the last time he'd put it on. He was the wrong side of fifty and, whilst his work consumed lots of nervous energy, he never had enough time to properly exercise and indulge in his other passion of hill walking. He was a few months away from potential retirement and he resolved to sort out whatever was causing his growing waistline when he had more time on his hands. He smoothed his hand over his hair, another thing that always seemed to be out of control. It still had body, but the greyness belied his years, and he cursed every time he looked at the unruly mop in the mirror. Something else he would do when he had more time on his hands. Get a proper haircut.

The orchestra and vocalists did their final preparations as the conductor addressed the crowd and called for silence. The orchestra started with Beethoven's fifth. This was followed by a breathtaking solo from a young undergraduate singing *Nessum Dorma*. Pieces from Handel, Liszt and Wagner followed. Matthew stood with everyone else to give the students a standing ovation. A real triumph.

As he left the building, he turned his phone back on. It immediately started to beep with what seemed to him to be a disapproving tone. Numerous messages flashed up. His heart sank. He was supposed to be on a night off, but crime didn't respect free time. He was a detective chief inspector for Police Scotland, responsible for major crime in Midlothian, East Lothian, the Scottish Borders and the City of Edinburgh. The messages were from his regular partner, Detective Sergeant Louise Cookson. An attempted murder had been called in from a house on the outskirts of Edinburgh. He called her back, getting exact details of the location. He ran to his car and took off his dinner jacket and dicky bow, replacing it with an Arran jumper. He didn't need any more remarks about his unusual interests for a police officer. The McMorse jibe was wearing particularly thin.

The initial investigations were concluded quickly, statements taken and a warrant issued for the main suspect. It was true that, more often than not, a murder is committed by someone the victim knew. In this case, the victim had survived and was able to identify the perpetrator. Matthew thanked his lucky stars that his night off had not been disrupted by a difficult case.

3

He approached the door, his presence shrouded by the growing darkness.

Go on, knock on the door and remember he is a bad man. He hurts children. Remember that.

He knocked. A tall, muscular man answered, his impressive frame blotting out large parts of the light that was now streaming onto the porch. "Ahh, Mr Reynolds. You're right on time. Come in." He turned to lead the way.

Get the cloth ready. Come on. Do it now, while he's off guard.

He moved fast, attacking from behind. He was a big lad himself, which gave him an advantage as the other man's brain slowly reacted to what was happening, and he tried to struggle free from his grip. He held firm, resisting the man's efforts to free himself. Within seconds the man was unconscious, collapsed on the floor.

Is it done? Is it done?

"Yeah," he said.

Good, good. Now stand on a chair and screw the hook I gave you into the ceiling.

He struggled at first but managed with the help of a lever from his backpack.

Now get the rope out of your backpack and tie it on the hook.

He tied it securely and let it hang loose.

Get the chair and place it underneath the rope. Now lift the man and put the noose around his neck. It should be the perfect length.

He did as he was told. The man was heavy, but his strength allowed him to haul the man up into a standing position on another chair, right next to the one he had used to secure the hook. The rope length was perfect. The noose was tense around his neck, whilst the tip of his feet just about made contact with the chair seat.

Now get out the picture I drew and scrape it onto the floor with the knife. Place the skull where I said.

He worked slowly and diligently.

Now get the phone out and press the red button on the screen.

They waited.

It was only about twenty minutes, but it seemed like an eternity. The man's eyes began to open. As the man realised what was happening to him, he began to scream.

4

After the brief interruption to his night off, Matthew sat listening to some Brahms as he digested an adequate fish pie that he had heated in the microwave. He tried to empty his mind using the rise and fall of the music as a stress reliever. As the first track came to an end his attempt at a calm and relaxing few minutes were rudely interrupted by his phone ringing.

"McCallum."

"Sir, I'm sorry to bother you again. It's DS Cookson. We've had another murder called in from a house in Musselburgh. It looks a bad one. I'm on scene but I think you need to come."

Matthew sighed. "Jesus Christ. What is going on tonight?"

"I know. I'm sorry, sir."

"Don't worry. Criminals never respect a night off. I'm on my way."

It was past 10pm, meaning traffic was light and he arrived at the house within twenty minutes. The house was along a narrow lane bordering the western edge of the golf course. *Remote enough for the perpetrator to get in and out without too much risk*, he mused. The house was surrounded by numerous police vehicles, the blues flashing.

Matthew parked and walked towards the crime tape. He was met by DS Cookson. She was a model copper. She had just celebrated her thirtieth birthday and had been a police officer since leaving university, becoming a response sergeant within five years and moving to CID a couple of years after that. She had been with Matthew for a year. At five foot six with blonde hair that was always scraped back into a ponytail and a pretty round face, she was often taken for granted by colleagues and criminals alike. Whilst Matthew had always felt quite protective over her, he soon realised she was not one to be messed with and quickly stopped exhibiting any patronising gender stereotypes towards her.

"Evening, sir. I'm sorry to disturb you, but we have a rather grim one here. I thought you would want to see it first-hand."

Matthew gave a resigned sigh. "I'm sure you're right. You'd better show me what we've got."

They walked in the front door and turned left into a large sitting room. Matthew stopped the second he walked into the room. A man was hanging, the rope around his neck secured to a large hook in the ceiling. An overturned chair lay to the right of the hanging man. Underneath the victim, a star-shaped symbol contained in a circle was scratched into the wooden floor next to an animal skull.

Matthew looked at Louise. "What the hell is this?"

"We're not sure, sir. We wanted you to see the scene before we let the forensic team in."

Matthew took a careful step into the room, trying not to compromise any possible forensics. He eyed the scene intently.

"Why did you decide this is a murder scene? This could easily be a macabre suicide ritual."

"We have a witness – a neighbour – sir, who saw a man running away from the house about three hours ago. She didn't think anything of it until the victim's wife ran from the house screaming for help. Seems she was working a late shift in the bar at the golf club and found him about 9.45pm."

"Where is she?"

"She's in one of the ambulances outside being treated for shock."

Matthew stepped back out of the room. "Right. Let the forensic team in and do as much door to door as you can this evening, without upsetting the neighbours at this late hour. Get someone to confirm what that symbol is. It looks like a pentagram, but let's not jump to conclusions. Work out the significance of the animal skull. Make sure the wife is looked after and get her statement as soon as you can. I'd better phone the chief constable and let Gold command know what is going on. I'll get the incident room set up back at the station and I'll need debriefing from you and the forensic team in the morning."

"Yes, sir. I'm right on it."

Matthew stepped out of the house and walked towards the ambulance. He introduced himself to the widow and made all the right noises. She was largely incoherent, and he did not push it. He stepped back under the tape and walked a little further along the lane. He opened up his phone. There was no signal. He cursed and grabbed a cigar from his pocket. The spring night was cool, but the winds were light, and he managed to light it with limited fuss, revelling in the sharpness of the tobacco taste.

He eventually made his way back to his car and started to drive back to the centre of Edinburgh, making the phone calls he couldn't make earlier.

The weariness began to consume him. He had a feeling this was going to be a tough one.

5

It was a little after 10am as the team of detectives assembled in the newly formed incident room at Edinburgh police station. Matthew saw some weary faces, as many of the detectives had worked through the night collecting as much information and intelligence as they could. There were a couple of detective constables he hadn't worked with before, so he took the opportunity to introduce himself.

"Right, my name is DCI Matthew McCallum. I'm the DCI responsible for major crime in this area and will be the SIO on this case. I can see that some of you have been working through the night so I will get this briefing done as quickly as possible so you can get some sleep and be back on shift later tonight. DS Cookson here will be managing your shift patterns on my behalf and should be your first port of call for any issues. That said, I adopt an open-door policy. If you've got something to say, I want to hear it."

There was a murmur of agreement from the room.

"OK. Murder or suicide? DS Cookson, can you give me your preliminary findings?"

"Yes, sir. The victim is Gareth Wilson, a thirty-four-year-old personal trainer. He has a wife but no kids. As you said, many of the team have worked through the night completing the initial investigations and we are working on an assumption of murder."

"Why?"

"Firstly, there is no suicide note and his wife is certain that he had no reason to kill himself. Secondly, we took a fuller statement from the neighbour, and she has given us a good description of the man she saw running away from the scene. Although she couldn't see his face, as he was wearing a hoodie, we have a good description of an athletic-looking man, about six feet tall wearing a distinctive pair of yellow trainers."

"Hmm, I think I will reserve judgement until I have heard all the evidence. What else have you got?"

"You were correct, sir, that the symbol under the body is an inverted pentagram and the animal skull is a goat. Both these are symbols normally associated with the devil."

"Yes, I did think that when I saw the scene. Did you ask the wife about it?"

"She was clear that there was nothing in her husband's life that would show any connection to these symbols. In fact, she said he was a committed atheist."

Matthew nodded. "Interesting. These symbols are clearly at odds with this man's beliefs. Anything else?"

"We have the preliminary forensics report."

Matthew turned to Jed Spencer, the lead CSI on the case. He always chose Jed to be on his team, if the opportunity was there. A dogged forensic specialist, with a nose for the minutest detail, he was lovingly referred to as Sherlock for his incredible ability to solve cases with the smallest amount of evidence. A Mohican haircut, numerous nose and ear piercings and a penchant for Iron Maiden T-Shirts seemed to be at odds with this job, but Matthew didn't care what he looked like if he kept delivering results.

"OK, Sherlock. What have you got?"

"Thank you, sir. We processed the scene and have a fingerprint on the hook in the ceiling, which is not the victim's or the wife's. Unfortunately, no matches on our systems. There are no other non-victim prints around the scene so assume if there was a perp, he or she used gloves the rest of the time. The abrasions around the victim's neck are interesting. If someone is hung in one swift act, you would expect the marks to be in a consistent ring around the neck. The marks on our victim are erratic, suggesting that the rope was around his neck for a while, and he was struggling against the restraint. We think the chair, that was tipped over on the floor, was underneath him for a time before the final act."

Matthew rubbed his chin. "Couldn't that evidence also suggest a man who had got himself into position to commit suicide but was racked with doubt as the reality of what he was doing hit home?"

"I guess it's possible. Apart from the fingerprint that doesn't belong to anyone in the house, there is little forensic evidence to suggest there was another person present. The post-mortem should be done tomorrow and that might give us a few more clues."

Matthew turned his gaze to the wider room. "What about this scene? For me, it fits a suicide scene much better than a murder scene. If we do believe it's a murder scene how did this go down? You say this man was a personal trainer and I could tell from my own observations that he was well toned. If there is a perp, how did they overpower such a strong, powerful man? Does this suggest we are looking for a man, if I indulge your theories?"

DC Harry McDonald, a regular on Matthew's major crime investigation teams, piped up. "I da na, sir. Some of the women I pick up in Edinburgh are big, strong lassies."

Harry was another officer who had been on Matthew's team for a while. In his late twenties, he was the joker of the group. Despite his young years, he already had a rugged, well-worn face, supplemented by a severe skinhead haircut. Brought up in the Highlands he was the most Scottish person in the team, with a deep, growling accent that many found hard to understand. He'd moved to the 'big city' when he became a probationer and never looked back. Matthew often winced at some of the stories he heard about Harry's off-duty antics. A heavy drinker with a penchant for the ladies, he somehow managed to turn up for work at every shift and do a good job.

Matthew let the chuckles subside. "Thank you for that sparkling insight, DC McDonald, but I think we'll stick to collecting proper evidence, rather than using your questionable approach to meeting women."

The discussions carried on for a while but nothing else really engaged Matthew. He brought the meeting to a close, doling out the next tasks.

"OK. I can't say I'm blown away with how far we've got, so we need to keep at it. I want several lines of inquiry pursued across the team. Firstly, I want a fuller picture of our victim. Look at his clients and whether there is anything relevant linked to his atheist beliefs. I want someone to look into this devil angle. See if there are any satanic cults in this area that could be linked to this crime. Make sure we have all the witness statements we can get and that all the door to doors in the local area are done. Have a look at traffic cameras to see if there is anything we can use in the local area. Sherlock, can you chase up the post-mortem report and get it to me as soon as it's available. For my part, I want to go back to the scene with DS Cookson. I want to try and work out how this could be a murder scene with such a physically fit individual."

The team began to disperse. The night shift detectives left to get some sleep and the day shift were tasked out by DS Cookson.

As the room emptied, Matthew turned to Louise. "Come on. We need to sort out this MO. I can't tell the chief super and the big cheese that we don't have the first bloody idea how this went down."

6

A week had passed since the funeral. Joshua had never experienced sadness like it. The moment he watched his mother's coffin enter the flames was the worst of his life. It seemed so cruel, so full of damnation.

He'd been plotting all week, trying to contain the grief, thinking about everyone who had wronged him and his mother. The bullies, the ignorant arseholes, who had made his life a living hell. What he hadn't been ready for was the realisation his mother had been hanging onto one of the most traumatic incidents in their lives. A box hidden under her bed contained all the press cuttings. Day after day, the same story. Their story. She told him to forget about it. Never to speak of it, but there the memories laid. In that box. He was angry for a couple of days but as he stewed on it, the need for revenge against everything bad in their lives galvanised him. He started to research the story beyond the press cuttings. He couldn't believe what he found. In his current state of immobility, it was perfect. He had found the goose that laid a golden egg. His path to redemption was set. It was showtime.

As he accessed the video storage vault the adrenalin began to kick in. He fought back tears as he glanced briefly at the picture of his mother on the desk. His head was pounding. The bottle of pills had stayed on his desk, untouched. It would have been so easy to down the lot, to end the pain, but he was determined to follow his newly set path. He opened up the only file that was there. He watched the action with a cold detachment. Step one was done.

He downed a shot of vodka, wincing at the sharpness as it hit the back of his throat. It was time for step two. He navigated back to the colourful welcome screen of the chat room he had just joined. It kept flashing up images of happy couples in various nauseating settings. He fought back the rising bile in his throat.

He shook himself out of the disgust and felt a flutter in his stomach. Now he had the taste for this. Being back with his mother was driving him on. A mania was gripping him.

He watched the general chat, where people tried to entice each other into the private chat rooms. His skin prickled as he read the abhorrent language.

@Babycakes2000: I'm wet for you baby. Come and join me in the private chat and we can go all the way

@Pigtailsandshortskirts: I'm so horny. Let's meet up soon or I think I'll burst with lust

There it was. Lust. A sad human emotion that his mother never stopped preaching about. Lust was not God's teaching, she would say. It led to what she described as 'lying with the devil'. It wasn't that his mother objected to the act of sexual intercourse, as long as it was within the sanctity of a heterosexual marriage. That was God's teaching. At least that's what she preached. A dark memory flashed into his mind, which made him shiver. He was so confused.

He shook off the turmoil in his mind and watched as more and more explicit messages flashed on the screen. He had to do it. He had to hook up with someone or his journey could not continue.

He chose @Pigtailsandshortskirts. He logged on with his username:

@Lucifer: Do you wanna private chat @Pigtailsandshortskirts

There was a brief pause. Just as Joshua started to think she was ignoring him, she replied:

@Pigtailsandshortskirts: ooooh, a horny devil indeed. Let's do this

They moved to the private chat area.

@Pigtailsandshortskirts: tell me what your gonna do to me, you beast

Joshua almost vomited at the brazenness of this person. He powered through it.

@Lucifer: wouldn't you like to know

@Pigtailsandshortskirts: I would, stop teasing me

@Lucifer: I'm gonna lick...

@Pigtailsandshortskirts: What? Tell me? I'm rubbing myself just thinking about you

@Lucifer: Do you deserve my attention?

@Pigtailsandshortskirts: What? I need to earn your attention?

@Lucifer: Oh yes, if I'm gonna grant you my sexual favours, I need to know you're worthy

@Pigtailsandshortskirts: F-me mate. I'll suck your cock till I've drained your balls. Is that worthy?

@Lucifer: it's a start. What are you wearing?

@Pigtailsandshortskirts: Nothing

@Lucifer: Do you have pigtails?

@Pigtailsandshortskirts: Oh yeah. I can be whoever you want me to be

@Lucifer: OK, you're worthy. Let's meet up tonight

@Pigtailsandshortskirts: I'm ready. Just tell me where

Joshua wheeled himself quickly to the bathroom, retching into the toilet. Over and over. He eventually controlled himself and breathed deeply.

He looked in the mirror at his pale, drawn face and tired complexion. He had to hang in there. His journey had only just begun, and he needed to complete each step if he was going to be truly absolved of all the hurt and pain.

He splashed his face with water and applied some deodorant. He brushed his teeth and fussed about with his hair. He was ready for *@Pigtailsandshortskirts*.

7

It was just gone 8pm as Matthew once again stood in front of his team of detectives for the evening briefing, the handover between day and night shifts. He had agreed with the chief super that they would put the detective team on a twenty-four-hour shift pattern for the few days after the murder, so as not to lose any opportunities to catch this killer, if indeed there *was* an actual killer. It was a fact that cases could get cold very quickly if they didn't maximise their investigative tasks in the early days after an incident like this.

He had made little progress himself. The second review of the crime scene with Louise had not helped Matthew piece together what had happened. They were treating this as murder, but he was still less than convinced that this wasn't just a suicide.

He was met with the same mix of tired and alert faces as one batch of detectives were finishing a busy shift and the rest were about to start.

"OK, team, I'm still concerned about the lack of progress on this case, and I still haven't made my own mind up what this actually is. Can we start with your updates?"

As Matthew's sentence drifted off, Jed crashed through the door, looking sheepish as all eyes turned to look at him.

"Oh shite, sorry for being late, sir, but I've just got the post-mortem report. I think we can now confirm this was murder."

"Oh. Why?"

"The ME said that there were traces of chloroform around his mouth and nose. There were no signs of a struggle and no defensive wounds on the victim, suggesting that he was taken by surprise."

Matthew nodded and looked at Louise. "We didn't find any evidence of forced entry at the property, did we?"

"No, sir. This evidence would suggest that the victim either knew his assailant or was comfortable letting him into his house."

He turned his attention to Harry. "DC McDonald. You were looking into his client list. Given what we now know, are there any possible suspects?"

"I'se afraid not, sir. He had twenty regular clients and the team checked on every one of 'em. They all had alibis for the time of the murder."

Matthew cursed under his breath. "Right, who was looking into this devil angle?"

A DC that he hadn't worked with before raised her hand, enthusiastically. "I'm DC Morag Williams, sir. Our team has been looking into this and does have some interesting news."

"Do tell, DC Williams. I could do with some good news."

"Well, it seems that there is one main group of devil worshippers in Edinburgh. They run an online forum for like-minded individuals, and it seems they can be regularly found in the forest doing their weird rituals. Having checked our systems, it seems they've had a number of run-ins with us when people complained about them congregating at Roslin Glen, which is a wooded area about seven miles outside the city."

"Have you been able to interview their so-called members?"

"We're working on it but, understandably, they ain't being too co-operative, as they have a wee problem with authority."

"Keep at it. They sound like an interesting line of inquiry."

"Yes, sir, and it gets better. It seems our victim was very vocal about his atheist beliefs, regularly blogging about how the concept of God and the devil were a global conspiracy to supress people's beliefs and freedoms. We found evidence of him clashing with members of the devil-worshipping group online and with other people with strong religious views."

"Well, well. This seems like our best angle at the moment. Please make sure your work is handed over to the night team. I want us all over this group."

The briefing carried on for a bit longer, as jobs were tasked out and handovers were completed. As the team dispersed, Matthew's thoughts turned to what he was going to eat that evening, along with a couple of pints of Best Bitter. His musings were rudely interrupted by a gasp from Louise, closely followed by a deep frown.

"What is it?"

"Oh, shite, sir, there's been another one."

8

After a rushed sandwich in the car and with the hopes of a nice beer dashed for the evening, Matthew arrived at the crime scene with Louise, closely followed by most of his night shift and Jed.

A woman's body had been found in a detached house in Wyvern Park, an apparently quiet street in the southern suburbs of Edinburgh. The first responders had secured the scene and called it in.

Matthew spoke to the sergeant in charge of the cordon. "What have we got?"

"We had a nines call about three-quarters of an hour ago. The owner of the property, who was renting the place out, came round to check if everything was OK with the new tenant and found the dead woman. It's really horrible in there."

Matthew gestured to Louise and Jed to join him in reviewing the crime scene. They donned their forensic coveralls and went over the threshold. Laying in the middle of the main living space was a young woman, multiple stab wounds evident over her body. Her blood-stained clothes were sexy and provocative. She was wearing a tight white blouse, with a school tie draped over her ample cleavage.

A micro skirt and pigtails in her hair completed the whole schoolgirl fantasy persona. The most disturbing thing immediately evident was the word 'whore' scratched into her forehead.

Matthew watched as Jed began to inspect the body, regretting the decision to wolf down a sandwich on the way. He fought back the nausea. "What are you seeing?"

"I think it's fairly obvious she was killed by multiple knife wounds, something with a slim, pointed end. Based on lividity, I would say this happened within the last couple of hours. There's no sign of the murder weapon and on first inspection, I can't see any obvious forensic clues. I would say that the word on her forehead has been carved post-mortem as there is limited blood loss in the area."

"OK, keep at it and let me know if you find anything else."

Matthew turned and walked back out of the property, leaving Louise to oversee Jed's work. He spoke to the sergeant and the team of DCs. "Let's try and get some immediate statements from the neighbours and check any CCTV or traffic cams in the area over the last three hours. Our perp must be on something." As they began to task out, a woman was gesturing from behind the cordon. Matthew walked over. "Can I help you, madam?"

An elderly lady, with a stern expression and piercing brown eyes, fixed her attention on Matthew. "Is yoose in charge round here, laddie?"

"Yes, ma'am, I'm DCI Matthew McCallum. How can I be of assistance?"

"What's going on? Has summat happened?"

This was always the difficult bit in dealing with initial incidents. How much could you really say without alienating the public? He decided to go for the basic truths.

"We have a suspicious death in this property and my team are completing the initial investigations."

"Is the lassie dead?"

"Oh, you saw her?"

"Oh aye, dressed like a common tart. Not the sort of person we expect round here."

"Did you see anyone else?"

"Aye, I saw a young laddie going in that hoose earlier today. Big strapping lad. Looked like a rugby player. Ghastly yellow shoes on his feet."

Matthew quickly gestured one of his DCs over. "Can you take a statement from Mrs…?"

"Miss, laddie. Miss Amelia Hanley."

"…sorry, Miss Hanley. She has some critical evidence on this case."

Matthew thanked the lady and checked in with the rest of the team. Door to doors were being done and some of the team were checking the routes into the close to see if there were any CCTV or traffic cam opportunities. Even at this late point in the evening, the crowds were gathering, and Matthew desperately needed to get the 'circus out of town'. As he stepped back under the crime scene tape, he noticed the arrival of the first TV crew. He cursed under his breath and phoned into gold command. This would need some comms support, and quick.

As he finished his call, Louise gestured him back into the main scene. "What is it?"

"I think Sherlock better tell you."

Matthew looked at Jed, expectantly.

"I think we may have a link to our previous murder."

"I agree. There's a woman outside who's just described the same man that we saw running away from our first crime scene, entering this house. What has made you think there is a connection?"

Jed pulled the woman's blouse up. "It's this, sir."

Matthew stared at three numbers that had been scraped into the woman's stomach. 666.

"Holy shit. More devil symbology. The number of the beast."

With that, Jed closed his eyes and started to nod his head furiously.

Matthew frowned and looked at Louise, mouthing, "What is he doing?"

Louise shrugged as Jed re-engaged in the scene, a mischievous smile over his face. "Oh shite, sorry, sir. It's just whenever someone says *the number of the beast,* I immediately start rocking the Iron Maiden song."

Matthew wasn't sure whether to laugh or reprimand him. He mused that only Sherlock could go off on an Iron Maiden tangent whilst in the middle of such a disturbing murder scene. He went for calm authority. "Let's just get this crime scene processed, shall we."

9

As the preliminary investigations came to an end Matthew pulled Louise around the side of the house, away from the prying eyes of the press and public. He got out a cigar and Louise offered him a light as she tapped out a cigarette from her packet. He took a minute to revel in the bitter taste of the tobacco.

"What on earth have we got here? Two murders committed by the same man with a devil complex."

"Aye, sir, it's certainly a strange one. Do you think one of these devil worshippers are responsible?"

"It's the best lead we have at the moment, especially as DC Williams found they had contact with our first victim. But I can't see what the link is to this victim."

"I was thinking about that. Scratching the word 'whore' on her forehead suggests some deep-seated disapproval of her way of living. Certainly, that outfit left little to the imagination."

"Hmm... OK but why would a bunch of devil worshippers disapprove of a bit of debauchery? Isn't that what the devil is all about? Being bad?"

"Yeah, I suppose you're right, but there are definitely some sort of religious connotations with these two murders."

Matthew took another drag. "I hate to say it, but the way this is going it looks like we might have a serial killer on our hands. If we can't find some better connection between these two murders, some reason why both these people were killed, we might just have a psychopath out there killing random people. The press will have a field day with this, and the chief will be all over us like a rash."

"I guess the DCS will want a report soon, as well."

"Oh, feck me. I was trying not to think about that. Alexander is a proper wanker. If ever there was someone that brown-nosed his way to the top, it's him. A fatuous pretty boy with his public-school education and 2.4 children. Christ, what have I ever done to deserve him as my boss?"

Louise chuckled. "You don't like him then!"

Matthew grunted a resigned laugh. They both took another long drag of their nicotine fixes and stared into the night. Matthew's mind was full of noise, none of which was helping him form a clear opinion on what was going on. He sighed.

"Come on. Let's get this wrapped up for tonight and get some sleep. I have a feeling this killer isn't finished."

*

Joshua sat at his desk, watching the local news on his laptop. The headline story was running. A young girl had been murdered in a quiet suburb of Edinburgh. He cocked his head to one side as he listened to the story, like a child trying to understand what they were hearing.

The report switched to a copper reading a statement. *Need the public's help... man seen at the property... blah, blah, blah.* Joshua eyed him curiously. The tag below his name said DCI Matthew McCallum. Next to him stood another grim-faced copper. A woman. Could these be the people that he could engage in his journey?

As Joshua listened some more, he was disappointed at the lack of detail about the murder scene. Why were the police holding information back? The report flicked back to the copper. He quickly grabbed a screenshot of DCI Matthew McCallum, his face slowly appearing on the paper as his ancient laser printer produced the image, one line at a time.

The report finished and he pulled the printout off the printer. He stared at his face. A properly grizzled Scottish copper. Joshua started rocking slowly, the copper's face going in and out of focus. He eventually stopped and placed the printout flat on his desk. He picked up his letter opener and slammed it down hard. It stuck in his desk. The point of the letter opener, right between the copper's eyes.

As he surveyed his handiwork, he glanced at his mother's picture. She seemed to be looking at him. Disapprovingly. He swiped the picture frame off the desk, smashing it against the wall.

"I'm done grieving for you, Mother. Is this what your God wanted? Is this what your God planned for me? Well, it's my time now. All your preaching means nothing to me now. You left me like this. It's your fault that people are going to have to die so that I can be truly redeemed. I will be heard."

He picked up the one thing that made sense to him in all this madness. The thing that was guiding him to his salvation. His heart rate slowed down and he allowed himself a brief smile. It was time for the next one.

10

Matthew called the morning briefing to order, a load of weary faces staring back at him. "OK, team. I know we are all feeling a bit *wabbit*..."

Matthew's attempt to engage in a bit of the Scottish dialect, *wabbit* meaning tired, drew a number of amused expressions from the audience. Matthew's Scottish father, English mother and Oxford education had left him with a weird hybrid accent that added fuel to the McMorse jibes. His attempts to sound more Scottish just didn't work.

"...but our killer doesn't seem to want to slow down. We're gonna keep the twenty-four-hour rota system on for now, so we can maximise our inquiries. Right, Sherlock, can we have your preliminary forensics report from last night's murder?"

"Yes, sir. The victim is Lauren Robertson, twenty-three, a nurse living and working in Edinburgh. She was stabbed eleven times with a sharp, thin blade. The word 'whore' and numbers '666' were scraped into her skin, post-mortem. We picked up a number of DNA samples throughout the house and are currently working through them, eliminating both the victim's and owner's samples. I'm pretty certain that we will get a hit on our perp."

"That's great. What about the interviews with the satanists, DC Williams?"

"Yes, sir, we are continuing to contact all the people in the group. We should have broken the back of this by the end of today."

"Good. We also now have a really good description of the man seen at both crime scenes. DC McDonald, can you work with the comms team and get this description out on all the normal channels? I want everyone looking for this man."

"Oh aye, sir and will make sure Ops know so it can be in everyone's daily briefing pack."

"What about these yellow trainers? Are they a line of inquiry?"

DC McDonald picked up the question. "We've checked on the brand and whilst they are freely available, they isnae cheap. If nothing else, it's a distinctive part of the perp's get-up which should help us with the witness appeal."

"OK, for my part, I'm gonna work with DS Cookson on victimology and profiling our perp. I want to explore more about any connections between our victims and how the killer may have been in contact with them. I'm gonna procure some profiling support from the behavioural analysis unit, to see if we can get a better fix on our killer. Finally, I have a meeting with the chief super to discuss how much we tell the public about this devil angle and the messages that our killer seems to be leaving at the scenes. Let's get to it and meet back at the same time tomorrow for our next briefing. I want this *bawbag* lifted ASAP."

The detective team filed out of the briefing room, once again amused at Matthew's attempts to engage them with a bit of Scottish dialect. As the room emptied, Matthew and Louise stood staring at the growing incident board. "Come on, let's grab a ciggie and a coffee. We've got a lot to do."

*

Joshua scoured the internet. He knew what he was looking for but the groups he was targeting had to be meeting tonight. He had to keep the journey going. He had to keep the pace up.

He had no sense of who his victims were. It was their actions that defined them, not whether they were male or female, straight or gay, married, divorced, alone, with loads of bairns running around their depressing houses. If their actions caught his attention, Joshua was their judge, jury and executioner. It was necessary to tell his story. He idly doodled on his notepad. *The Devil's Code.* He smiled at the words. He liked that. It would frame his journey.

He searched some more, becoming irritated as he failed to find what he was looking for. A glint of light caught a smashed piece of glass from the photo frame that was still strewn on the floor. The reflection shone briefly in his eyes, and he winced at the interruption. It was like his mother was still goading him, blinding him with her nonsensical preaching. He adjusted his position.

Finally, he found something. A meeting in a local community hall near Craigentinny. Nice and remote. Perfect.

*

The coffee and ciggie had quickly turned into a lunchtime beer and chip butty at the local pub, just a stone's throw from the police station.

"Right. Let's talk about victimology."

"Well, sir, the second victim, Lauren, was using a popular chat room to meet men. The tech guys went through her laptop last night and found loads of provocative chat about meeting up for no-strings sex. Seems she played on the whole schoolgirl fantasy persona. Her username was *Pigtailsandshortskirts*."

Matthew raised his eyebrows. "Dear me. I'm never gonna understand the youth of today. What's wrong with good old traditional courting. Going down the flicks, having a fumble in the back row and a chip supper on the way home."

Louise tried to stifle a pitiful laugh. Matthew picked up on her mirth. "OK, I know I'm a dinosaur. Carry on."

"Anyway, it seems she arranged to meet a person with the username *Lucifer*."

"Interesting. Another devil link."

"Indeed, but unfortunately all attempts to trace this person through their profile failed. It was completely fake with no trails we could follow."

"OK, but still a clear link to this devil thing."

"Agreed."

"What about links to the first victim?"

"Nothing so far. The tech guys trawled through her laptop but couldn't find any links. She certainly had not accessed or commented on the first victim's blog, and there was nothing in her profile that suggested she had any sort of religious leanings."

"I don't get it. When you compare this with what DC McDonald found about the first victim, there are simply no connections. Are we sure these murders are connected?"

"We have the same man at both scenes."

"Yes, that's all we have. I hope we are not chasing wild geese just because of that one piece of evidence."

11

The beer and chip butty lunch lay heavy as Matthew sat waiting in the chief super's office. He desperately hoped that it didn't manifest itself as arse gas any time soon. Stinking out the boss's office was never a good move.

"Ah, Matthew, good to see you. Sorry I'm a bit late. Had the chief on the phone asking me about these murders. What have you got for me?"

Detective Chief Superintendent James Alexander quickly sat down, fixing Matthew with an attentive, expectant expression.

"Well, sir, as you can imagine, two murders in as many days is stretching the team, but we do have a number of active lines of inquiry."

James's expression didn't change, a sign for Matthew to carry on.

"We have two seemingly unrelated victims that are connected by witness descriptions of the same man at both crime scenes, wearing distinctive yellow trainers. We also seem to have a devil connection."

"Devil connection?"

"Yes, sir. Devil imagery was left around the first victim, and the second victim had the numbers 666 scraped into her skin post-mortem."

"Macabre."

"Indeed. We are currently investigating a devil-worshipping group that are active in Edinburgh, some of whom made contact with the first victim on his blog site. Unfortunately, we can't yet find any link to this group with the second victim."

"Apart from the 666 scraped on her body."

"Well, yes of course, but no obvious links to this group apart from that."

"What else?"

"We have two very good descriptions of the man seen at both crime scenes, and we are going to be putting this out on all the media channels. The yellow trainers should be a key part of this appeal."

"OK, what do you need from me?"

"Apart from signing off the overtime budget, I wondered what you thought about telling the public about this devil angle. Do you think it would spook them too much?"

James rubbed his chin. "See what we get from the public appeal. If that doesn't work, we may have to think about releasing more details about the murders, such as this devil thing."

"OK, sir, I'll hold off for now."

"Good. What are your next steps?"

"We'll obviously respond to any leads from the public. The team should have finished interviewing these devil worshippers today; we'll finish off the door to doors, look at the forensic reports, and I'm going to get some profiling done."

James had the ability to keep his face emotionless, making it hard for Matthew to decide whether he was happy with what he was hearing. He left a short pause for the reaction.

Eventually, James stood up, making no comment for a few seconds. He turned his back on Matthew and gazed out of the window.

"The chief doesn't want this to turn into some sensational serial killer story. She's under enough pressure as it is without something like this getting the press and public all excited. Keep at it and get a result quickly."

James still had his back to Matthew and the pause after his statement made it clear to Matthew that he was being dismissed. He walked out of the office. The stress was beginning to build.

*

Marjorie Blakemore sat in front of the semicircle of chairs that had been arranged in the middle of the Craigentinny community hall. An array of faces stared back at her.

"OK, ladies. Welcome to this week's session of Weightbusters. In a moment, we will do the weekly weigh-in, and I hope that we have all made progress with our diet and exercise regimes."

She could see straight away that there was a mixture of optimism and guilt showing on the faces of the group. Marjorie could immediately tell the ones that were not going to like what they saw on the scales.

She decided to start with one of the faces that had seemed optimistic. "OK, Erica. Let's start with you. Pop yourself on the scales."

Erica was what the professionals called morbidly obese, and she took a minute to get up and waddle slowly to the scales. As she was about to step up, she stopped and let out a blood-curdling scream.

After recovering from the initial shock of her sudden scream, the ladies realised Erica was pointing at the window. Marjorie took the lead. "What on earth is wrong with you, Erica?"

Erica was shaking. "The window... oh my, it was horrible... a face at the window... inhuman..." she struggled to catch her breath.

Marjorie got up and looked out the window. The darkness around the remote community hall made it difficult to see anything, with only the light from the hall providing any sort of help. She looked left and right. There was nothing there.

She turned back to the group. "I'm sorry, Erica, there's nothing out there. Probably some local kids messing about." Erica had sat back down, hands in her face, trying to calm her breathing. Marjorie decided to leave her be and called up the next lady. "Come on, Jane, we'll give Erica a minute to recover. Let's get you on the scales." Jane stood up and got on the scales, a satisfied smile appearing on her face as she saw the reading.

"That's good, Jane, now..."

Marjorie's sentence trailed off as she caught a movement by the windows on the opposite side of the hall to where Erica had been pointing. She stood up and quickly went to the window. Her sudden movement was met with gasps and worried faces stared at each other. She once again strained her eyes against the darkness looking left and right along the sides of the hall.

Marjorie turned and shook her head. "Sorry, ladies, Erica's got me all spooked. I thought I saw someone outside, but there's no one there. Anyway, Mary, you're up next."

As Mary made her way to the scales, the tension in the room had ramped up. Everyone kept glancing nervously at the windows, desperately hoping not to see anything or anyone.

A few minutes passed and nothing else happened. Three more ladies were weighed, the results mostly good and the room began to return to its normal jolly, chatty vibe.

The weigh-ins finished, and Marjorie gestured for them to form a circle in the room to start the exercise portion of their evening. As they started to complete the light exercises and stretches, Marjorie noticed that Erica was not moving. She was staring back at the window, a look of terror on her face. Just as Marjorie was about to ask her what was wrong, Erica collapsed on the floor.

As the group reacted, all moving toward Erica's stricken figure, an orange glow seemed to be lighting the area. Very slowly, a few ladies began to cut away from the chaos and turned towards the origin of the light. Multiple screams filled the room. As the whole group reacted, they looked on in horror at one of the windows. A figure was stood in the frame of the window wearing a goat skull over their face, holding a lit torch in their hand. Everyone was paralysed with fear as the person in the mask just stared into the hall, the flames of the torch lighting up their macabre get-up.

The women looked at each other, waiting for someone to make a decisive move. Marjorie shouted for one of them to phone an ambulance, simultaneously striding purposefully towards the window, making a dismissive gesture with her hands like she was shooing a dog.

As she got nearer the figure moved the torch down, seeming to sweep it at their feet. As they did, they turned and walked away.

Within seconds the women could all smell the acrid scent of smoke and burning wood. Marjorie immediately realised what was happening and gestured for everyone to get out. As they walked towards the exit, the door that had been previously open was shut tight. Marjorie reached for the door handle, recoiling with the heat that was now emanating from the growing fire.

They rushed over to the only other way out. The fire exit. The door was jammed from the outside.

They were trapped.

12

Matthew sat in his favourite armchair, listening to a Duke Ellington album on vinyl. It was another reason the younger officers called him an old fuddy duddy, as they listened to their music on their mobile devices with their endless downloads. To Matthew, it epitomised that generation's obsession with immediacy. No one took the time anymore to find their music amongst a stack of vinyl, taking in the interesting covers, sliding the record out of its inner sleeve and gently placing it on the turntable as the needle arm slowly moved to the start of the record, followed by the unique scratchy sound as the song began to play. Old before his time? He didn't care.

As the melodies washed over him, his eyes began to droop, a symptom of a crazy forty-eight hours. Mentally and physically exhausting. He hoped the team would get a breakthrough soon, especially as he now had the chief constable watching his every move.

The needle moved onto the next track, 'Take the "A" Train', as Matthew began to lose the fight between awake and asleep.

He wasn't sure how long he'd been out when he was woken by an insistent banging on his front door. "Sir,

sir!" It was Louise. He jumped up from his semi-slumber, trying to shake off the disorientation of being suddenly awoken.

He opened the door, rubbing his eyes. Louise spoke without any prompting. "Sir, there's a live incident at Craigentinny. Someone has deliberately set fire to the community hall. There are loads of people inside and the fire service is trying to rescue them as we speak."

Matthew's brain was beginning to catch up. "What's that got to do with us?"

"One of the women inside the hall, who called 999, said that just before the fire started, they saw a man outside wearing a goat mask and carrying a lit torch. The duty inspector got in contact to let me know about her theory that it was linked to our case. Whilst she's despatched a number of units, I said we'd attend also."

Matthew rubbed his face in an attempt to wake himself up. "What's happening now?"

"It seems that officers got there quite quickly and are closing in on the perp, who was seen running away. Officers are in pursuit now."

Matthew quickly grabbed his coat and jumped in Louise's car. She sped towards the incident, the blues and twos helping to clear their way. He got on the radio to link with the incident commander.

"This is DCI McCallum. Can you give me a sit rep?"

Inspector Gillian McKie was on the ground, managing the incident. "Of course, sir. The fire service has almost got the fire under control, and I can see some of the people that were inside are being helped out by the fire crews. We have a number of ambulances here to look after them.

There is a small team of officers pursuing the perp on foot and by car. He took off through the woods and I've just asked the helicopter to deploy."

"Thank you, Inspector. We should be there in about three minutes."

They took a bit longer than Matthew had predicted, arriving to a vista of blue flashing lights as vehicles from all three emergency services filled the small car park of the community hall and the road alongside the building. The stench of smoke filled the air, but the worst of the fire was out, and the fire crews were damping down the last remnants of the blaze. Despite their quick response, Matthew could see the building was quite badly damaged.

He found Inspector McKie. She was a little flustered as she saw Matthew but quickly got off her radio. "Evening, sir, the helicopter is deployed and they have him on the infra-red. The team is closing in."

"That's great. What about the people in the hall?"

"All out. The ambulance crews are treating most of them for smoke inhalation, but one lady collapsed and was rushed to hospital. I hope we got here in time."

As she finished speaking there was a crackle from the radio. She gave an apologetic eye roll to Matthew and pushed the call button. "Go ahead."

A voice crackled from the radio. "We've got him, ma'am. Perp is apprehended."

13

Matthew and Louise sat in the interview room opposite the man who had been apprehended after a short but dramatic chase. He appeared to be quite young, well over six feet tall, with scruffy blond hair and clothes to match. He was well built, matching the descriptions given at the two previous crime scenes. More importantly, and at odds with the rest of his ensemble, he was wearing an expensive pair of bright yellow trainers.

They had recovered two items from the man when he was captured. A mobile phone, which was with the tech team, to see if they could get any incriminating evidence from it, and a sophisticated earpiece that allowed discreet two-way communication with someone. A goat mask and long robes were found discarded behind the community hall.

Matthew wasted no time. They had him and the sooner he got this interview done and the case file submitted to the procurator fiscal, the sooner he could get the chief and the super off his back.

"OK. My name is DCI Matthew McCallum, and this is DS Louise Cookson. This interview is being recorded, and I remind you that you are entitled to legal counsel as you have been charged with two counts of murder and several counts of attempted murder. Do you understand what I am saying and your rights as they have been read to you?"

The man stared at them both, not saying a word.

"Can I start with your name. You didn't give one when you were brought into custody."

The man said nothing for a minute.

"Sir, your name?"

His speech was slow and laboured but eventually he spoke. "My name is Joseph."

"Joseph what?"

He shrugged.

"You don't know your last name?"

He shrugged again.

"OK, Joseph. Can I ask again. Do you understand that you have been arrested for murder and are entitled to legal counsel?"

He said nothing.

Matthew looked at Louise. There was something wrong here. He barely seemed cognisant of his surroundings, let alone what he was being asked. Matthew knew it was risky to continue without him having a solicitor present, especially as he seemed... Matthew wasn't sure what the right terminology was these days... mentally ill?

He shook his head at Louise but asked one last question. He picked up the earpiece and tried to get Joseph to focus on it.

"Joseph. Was someone talking to you through this earpiece tonight?"

Joseph's eyes suddenly lit up and a beaming smile came across his face. "Lucifer. He speak to me. In my ear."

*

Matthew decided to put Joseph back in the custody cell while they organised a duty solicitor. If this man had some sort of disability that made it difficult for him to understand what was going on, their case would be bounced out of court within seconds, if they had been seen to be manipulating his interview answers so that he incriminated himself. Matthew couldn't believe it. For a short moment when the radio message came through, he thought he had just wrapped up what was becoming a high-profile case within a few days. A great result in anyone's book. Now he wasn't so sure.

He gathered Louise, Harry and Jed in the incident room and updated them on what happened in the preliminary interview.

"We've got a problem, team. The man in custody seems to have some sort of disability that is potentially preventing him from understanding or answering our questions. I've asked for him to be given a duty solicitor because we can't afford to interview him again without there being legal counsel present. The one key thing we have gleaned is that someone was speaking to him through the earpiece we found on him. More importantly he said the person speaking to him was called Lucifer. Given his apparent mental deficiencies, I've got a horrible feeling that someone is instructing him to do these awful things."

Jed spoke first. "Well, that's a bugger, sir because I have fast-tracked his fingerprints and DNA. He is definitely our man. We have a fingerprint match from the hook at the first scene. We have a DNA match at the second scene and his DNA is all over the mask and robe we recovered tonight."

"Bloody hell. What about you, DC McDonald?"

"Oh aye, the yellow trainers he's wearing are a match for the two descriptions we had at both crime scenes, as is his general build. We also have a potential home address. A lassie phoned in after our appeal saying the description sounded like her neighbour who lives in a wee flat on a street behind the castle. She said his name is Joseph Anderson."

"Is that being checked?"

"Aye, we have officers going to the property as we speak."

Matthew turned to Louise. "Do we have anything from the tech boys yet about the phone?"

"Not yet, sir. I will chase them up."

Matthew shook his head. "I can't believe this. I thought we had a watertight case and now it looks like we are not going to be able to land it."

14

Matthew called the briefing to order. They had decided to leave the next interview until this morning to give time for the solicitor to be organised and see if they could further cement the evidence against Joseph Anderson.

"OK, team, I believe DS Cookson has brought you all up to speed on what happened last night. We are planning to interview our suspect this morning under formal caution, and we hope that we can find a way to conduct the interview whilst respecting this man's apparent disability. I'm sure I don't need to tell you this is a legal minefield, but we have very strong evidence against this man."

There were a number of nods from the floor. A woman put her hand up. Matthew gestured for her to speak.

"Sir, I'm Caroline Fleck from the Behavioural Analysis Unit. You asked me to come in to profile our perp, but I guess it would be helpful if I sat in on the interview to profile him in person."

Matthew didn't recognise her from his previous engagements with her unit. She was smartly dressed in a sky-blue shift dress, covered by a light-coloured jacket. She had light brown hair that was crafted into a smart, bobbed style. She seemed relatively young, but then everyone seemed young to Matthew these days. She peered over rectangular tortoiseshell framed glasses, which reminded Matthew of his old school librarian.

"Oh sorry, yes, Caroline. Welcome. Not quite the profiling work I had envisaged but I agree it would be good for you to give me a live assessment of our suspect. We also have strong evidence to suggest he was communicating with someone last night through an earpiece. I might need you to do some profiling on that scenario."

"Of course, sir."

He looked around the room. "Any other updates?"

DC Morag Williams spoke up. "We've finished the interviews with our devil-worshipping group. Whilst they weren't particularly co-operative, they all seem to have strong alibis for at least one of the dates of our murders. I'm not sure they are in the frame for this."

"OK, but given what we suspect, is it not possible that one of them could be the person communicating with our suspect?"

Morag seemed a bit embarrassed to be called out in this way but tried to ride it out. "Er... well, I guess that's possible if the man we have in custody was the one present at the crime scenes. It does potentially bring into question the validity of their alibis."

Matthew gave Morag a slightly patronising smile. He considered himself to be a good boss but didn't abide sloppiness and was always quick to remind the rank and file of their duties and obligations, especially when it came to something as high profile as this.

As he scanned the room for any other updates, he realised Louise was looking at her phone. Given what had just happened with Morag, he didn't really want to be seen to be questioning another officer's motivations, so he waited until she caught his eye.

"Oh, sorry, sir, we've just had an update from the tech team about his phone."

"Ah good. What have they found?"

"It's really odd, sir. The only thing they found on the phone was an app that allows live streaming to a cloud-based video service. It seems as though the app records and then stores live video. Other than that, there are no contact lists, no email and no record of any phone calls or texts in or out of the phone."

Matthew let the information process for a minute as all eyes were fixed on him. "Hmm, I think this adds weight to our theory. Do you think he was being instructed to do these things through the earpiece and was then told to video it?"

Louise pulled a pained expression. "If that's true, we have a seriously fucked-up individual who is still out there."

As the room of detectives and support staff took in the implications of what they were hearing, Harry put his hand up. Matthew prompted him to speak.

"Shite, sir. I've just got a message to say one of the lassies from last night's incident at the community centre has *carked* it."

15

The duty solicitor introduced himself as Cameron Davis and wasted no time in stating the case for the defence.

"DCI McCallum. I've had a chance to talk to my client and review the charges made against him. I want to state right at the start that I do not believe Joseph here has the mental capacity to understand what he has allegedly done. I would like a formal psychological assessment before any interview is conducted."

Matthew held his hands up. "Look, Mr Davis, I am sympathetic to your position. In the short, preliminary interview that DS Cookson and I did last night, we identified that Joseph had some difficulties in understanding what we were saying, which is why we left this formal interview to this morning, until he was able to have you present."

"So, you agree to my request?"

"No, not entirely. I feel it's important that we state the case against Joseph for the record and attempt to see if he can give us any information about the murders. It will be in his best interest."

Cameron frowned but did not comment further.

Matthew fixed his gaze on Joseph, who stared back with an emotionless face. "OK. For the record. Firstly, can you confirm that your full name is Joseph Anderson?"

Joseph pulled a funny face but didn't answer.

"OK, for the recording, the suspect did not respond. Joseph Anderson, you have been charged with three counts of murder and nine counts of attempted murder that were carried out over the last three consecutive evenings in properties in Musselburgh, Edinburgh city centre and Craigentinny. We have matched your fingerprints to the first crime scene and have DNA matches at the other two. We also have two separate witness statements that place you at the scenes of the first two murders. Do you have anything to say about these charges?"

Joseph smiled. "What's time?"

"Er... it's 9.30am Joseph. What has that got to do with what I just said to you?"

"Have milkshake at 9.30am. Every day. Do you have milkshake?"

Matthew looked at Louise and Caroline. It wasn't going well.

Cameron interjected. "I think this is proving my point, DCI McCallum. He doesn't understand what you are saying."

Louise took over. "Let me try, Mr Davis." She touched Joseph's hand gently to get his attention. "Joseph, if I get you some milkshake, do you think you could answer some questions?"

He smiled. "Yes please."

They buzzed through to get the milkshake and Louise carried on, maintaining the hand contact to keep him focused.

"Joseph, do you remember going to a big house near a golf course, with a cloth and a bottle?"

Cameron protested. "DS Cookson. You are leading my client."

"Please, Mr Davis, we need to try and get Joseph to help us here."

There were no further protests.

"Joseph?"

His expression became more serious, and he cocked his head to one side as he processed the question. "The cloth," he said suddenly.

"Yes, Joseph. Did you have a cloth with you?"

He nodded. "Put cloth on man's mouth. Bad man. Bad man."

"Why was he bad, Joseph?"

"Lucifer tell me."

Louise was on a roll. He seemed to be responding to her questions with a cognisance that hadn't previously been there. She ploughed on.

"Was Lucifer speaking to you in your ear?"

Joseph nodded.

"Did you put a rope around his neck?"

Joseph started to rock. "Bad man. Bad man."

"OK, Joseph, it's fine. You're doing amazing. What about the girl, Joseph? Was she a bad girl?"

His expression changed. A smile formed. "Funny hair."

"Yes, Joseph, she had pigtails."

"Funny hair," he repeated.

Louise looked at Matthew, a subtle nod telling her to carry on.

"Did you have a knife, Joseph?"

Joseph closed his eyes and started to rock again.

"Joseph. Did you use the knife on the girl with the funny hair?"

He opened his eyes, as tears began to escape.

Cameron couldn't hold back any longer. "DS Cookson. DCI McCallum. I must insist that you stop this interview. You are leading my client to incriminate himself by the questions you are asking."

Matthew spoke before Louise could ask anything else. "Mr Davis. We have a cast-iron case against your client. We have fingerprints and DNA that place him at all three crime scenes and witness statements that place him at the first two. I think from the limited amount of information we have just managed to get, he has confirmed his presence at the scenes of these crimes. Now, I can see that Joseph is probably unaware of exactly what happened here, but he seems cognisant enough to have carried out instructions he was given. I do believe there is another person involved, who was instructing him to do these terrible things, but we cannot ignore his part in these awful crimes."

As the speech ended there was a knock at the door, as Joseph's milkshake arrived. Matthew took that as a sign to take a break.

"OK, we'll take a half hour break and reconvene at 10.10am."

As they walked out of the room, leaving a happy Joseph guzzling his milkshake, Matthew turned to Louise and Caroline. "What a fecking mess!"

16

Joshua was glued to the local news. The story was running. His story. Something had gone wrong. He had lost his stooge. The stupid fool had got himself caught. The details of the crimes on the news were still incomplete. He screamed out. People were not hearing his message.

He looked at the smashed picture frame, still lying on the floor. A lurch in his stomach reminding him of the awful moment when he realised his mother was dead. The car on its roof, the result of a side swipe with an HGV that had sent their car into a rolling spin. As they hung upside down, secured by their seatbelts, he'd looked over to his mother. She wasn't moving. He knew then that she was dead. He tried to get himself free, but his body wasn't working. The next thing he remembered was being dragged out of the car by a fire crew and rushed into an ambulance. He couldn't feel his legs. Emergency services rushed around the scene and then he saw it. His mother in a black body bag.

He picked up the photo frame and looked at her picture. He closed his eyes and put his head back. The memories of that horrible night came flooding back.

"So, what's your name?"

"Just get on with it please."

"OK, big boy. I can do quick."

She stripped off her dress revealing red lingerie. As she unclipped her bra, revealing huge breasts, Joshua looked away. He heard her removing her panties but lay with his face staring at the wall. He flinched as she began to stroke his penis, but he couldn't help but respond to the stimulus. She straddled him quickly and began to rock her hips backwards and forwards, fake groans emanating from her raspy throat. It didn't take long for the act to finish. The whole while Joshua didn't look at her. She dismounted from him, saying nothing. He quickly stood up, slightly unsteady from the immediate stress relief that made his legs wobbly. He put on his clothes. He didn't look at her. He didn't speak to her. He just threw the money on the bed and left.

That incident had been the cause of the accident. His mother was not concentrating on the road as she preached to him once again about his sins. How she knew he had been with a prostitute was beyond him. The whole trip was spattered with damnation, preaching about the devil's work and the weakness of sinners. Joshua was sick of it. He was a grown man. He didn't need her.

The tears welled up. He knew he didn't really mean that. She was his world. No one liked him and she filled the gaps created by his loneliness. He poured himself a neat vodka. The burning liquid jumping him out of his malaise.

His attention was drawn back to the news update as it flicked to the burning embers of the Craigentinny community hall. The reporter was giving the latest updates. Joshua put his head back and breathed deeply. "*Finally,*" he muttered to himself. Someone had died. A necessary sacrifice for each step of his journey. He placed the picture frame flat on the desk, averting his mother's disapproving gaze. He'd got past the grief. For now.

He wasn't scared of death and if everything went well, his pain would be gone forever. He had to keep going, to complete the journey to his version of absolute salvation. Without his little helper he was going to have to change his plans. The grand finale was going to have to be different. Bigger and better. He drummed his fingers on the desk. Maybe this was a good thing. Maybe this development was a blessing in disguise. Maybe this was a better way to get him noticed. He looked at the picture of DCI Matthew McCallum that was still pinned to the desk with his letter opener. "Maybe, I'll invite you too, McCallum." His brain went into overdrive. New plans began to form. He smiled.

*

Matthew stood outside the nick with Louise and Caroline as they all took a moment for a nicotine fix. Matthew cursed between drags. "We're never gonna land this case. Are we?"

Louise pulled a sympathetic face. "I don't think so, sir. Any good brief will get him off on diminished responsibility. I'm not even sure if the PF will accept a case file."

Matthew threw his smoked tab down. "Fecking shite. We have one of the most robust cases for a murder charge

I can ever remember and we're not gonna be able to use it. Why is this happening to me?"

Louise and Caroline shot an amused expression at each other. It was unlike Matthew to wallow in self-pity. He picked up on the looks and smiled. "OK, OK, I'll suck it up, but we need a plan. What do you think, Caroline?"

"Well, sir, I think we need to get a bail hearing done ASAP with a recommendation that he is detained in a secure mental health facility to give us time to do a proper psychological evaluation on him. That will allow both an independent assessment, which the defence will want, and an opportunity for me to evaluate him and try to profile this other person we think is involved."

"DS Cookson?"

"I agree. I think the longer we go on questioning him in the way we have been, the more likely we are to expose ourselves to claims of leading the suspect to incriminate himself. He is clearly open to suggestion and I'm not sure whether any of his answers are really framed in reality."

Caroline continued before Matthew could respond. "I agree. I also think there are a ton of key questions about these killings and how Joseph was able to carry them out. He is clearly neurodivergent and from the limited time I've spent with him, I think he has got a complex mental illness and some sort of impinged development. I can just about see how he carried out the killings if someone was talking him through what to do, but how did he get to the crime scenes and why does he seem to have no remorse or recollection of what he's done? We need more time to properly assess him."

Matthew lit another cigarette and pondered for a

moment. "I think you are both right. I'll go back in and inform his solicitor that we won't be conducting any further interviews. I'll try to get a bail hearing organised for the morning and outline our plan to his solicitor. We'll retain him in custody as we still have time under the PACE rules. In the meantime, can you make sure the case file is in order, DS Cookson, and can you start doing your profiling work, Caroline?"

"Of course, sir," they replied.

He took a moment to finish off his cigarette. As he prepared to go back into the station, his phone pinged. It was a text message from his friend Professor Roger Mountfield, reminding him of the formal awards dinner that was being held at the University of Edinburgh that evening. It had been in Matthew's diary for months but with all the commotion of the case, it had completely slipped his mind.

He agonised over what to do. He'd hardly had a second to himself over the last few days and deserved a break, but would his bosses look kindly on him taking some downtime in the middle of a high-profile murder case? He texted back. *I'll be there*. He would get all his ducks in a row and give himself the night off. At least that's what he hoped.

17

Matthew stood in front of his full-length mirror putting the finishes touches to his ensemble. The annual university award ceremony was a big event and demanded formal dress: black tie for gentlemen and evening gowns for the ladies. It was also an opportunity for him to exercise his vocal cords as part of the university's senior choral society.

He kept eyeing his phone, desperately hoping it would not ring and disturb his plans. He had sent Joseph Anderson back into custody with little protest from his solicitor. The bail hearing was scheduled for 10.30am. He had appeared at the agreed press conference where he deflected all the questions about Joseph, merely trotting out the usual line of *a man is in custody and helping us with our inquiries.* The chief super had agreed to release more details of the victims and the manner of their deaths, including the theory that there was some link to devil worship. The statement also mentioned the theory that there was another person involved and the public were implored to tell the police about anything they knew or thought was relevant. Matthew knew that if he couldn't land a case against Joseph Anderson, the pressure would be right back on him.

His mental recall of the afternoon's events was disturbed by the toot of the taxi that had come to pick him up. He took one last look in the mirror and set off for an evening of pomp and ceremony.

After a brief drinks reception in the grand hall, Matthew joined the professor on the stage to open the evening with a number of classical choral numbers, supported by a bank of talented undergraduates in the orchestra. Matthew belted out each one with gusto, happy to ease the stresses of the last few days. They finished to rapturous applause and Matthew felt himself beaming from ear to ear, something that had been sadly missing from his recent working life.

The professor patted him on the back as they left the stage. "You're in good voice tonight, old boy. Time for some good food and wine."

The meal was amazing, and the evening was a triumph. Lots of happy people were being congratulated for a myriad of awards. Matthew sat next to the professor, enjoying catching up on anything and everything since they had last shared a brandy in his university apartment a few weeks ago. Eventually the conversation inevitably turned to work.

"I saw you on the news earlier this evening. Seems like you've got an intriguing case there."

Matthew rolled his eyes. "You're telling me. The randomness of the victims is perplexing."

"Yes, did I hear right that he attacked a group of women at a Weightbusters meeting?"

"That's right. Tried to burn down the community hall they were in. Truly bizarre."

"Do you have any theories?"

"Not really. The first two victims were individuals, not a group like this last lot. One was a personal trainer and the other a nurse. The most intriguing thing is the devil symbolism that has been present at each crime scene."

"Yes, I heard that in your press conference. You said there had been things like goat heads, inverted pentagrams and the number 666 present at the crime scenes."

"Yes, my guvnor thought we should give the public the gruesome details in case it triggered something with someone."

"And has it?"

"I've not had anything reported to me yet."

"So, what about this guy you have in custody. Have you got him... how do you say... bang to rights?"

"I probably shouldn't be discussing this with you but we are fairly sure the lad we have in custody committed the crimes, but we are certain he was being instructed to do these things. You see, he seems to have a neuro deficiency but is capable of following instructions without question."

"What? To kill people!"

"I know it sounds odd but yes, it seems as though he may have been told to do these horrible things without any sense of what he was actually doing. We found a sophisticated earpiece on his person when we caught him. We're pretty certain someone was talking him through what to do at each scene and possibly getting him to video the murders."

"Bloody hell, old boy, that is one unsettling scenario."

"I know. We are getting a full psych assessment done

on him to see if we can confirm this assumption, whilst simultaneously trying to find this second perp."

"Well, if there is anything you think I can help with, please don't hesitate to ask."

"I did wonder with your expertise whether you could see anything in this devil symbolism?"

"The problem is that religious symbology is a massive area, cutting across all sorts of cultures, religions and individual belief systems. The symbolism you reference can be associated with the devil but it's all a bit crude. I'll have a ponder on it, but I can't promise you any answers."

They both drifted off with their own thoughts as the evening began to wind down. Matthew had discreetly checked his phone a number of times and was relieved that he had not been disturbed.

The murders had been carried out on three consecutive nights, so it followed that something was going to happen that evening if the killing spree was to continue. *Or,* Matthew pondered, *had the arrest put a brake on the killing spree? Was this potential other perp, the possible mastermind behind these crimes, put off his schedule by not having his little helper to do his dirty work?*

As he got in the cab to go home, this theory of a second perp was still haunting him. Apart from the earpiece and Joseph's reference to Lucifer speaking to him, they had no evidence that this was even a viable theory. Matthew desperately hoped that this wasn't another wild goose chase.

*

The professor poured himself a brandy as he settled in his favourite armchair by the fire, after an enjoyable but exhausting evening.

He had been a professor of classics at Edinburgh for nearly thirty years and something about what Matthew had said that evening was bothering him. It was the randomness of the victims. There was something that was telling him that the perpetrator of these crimes was very clever. That the selection of the victims was not random. There was some deeper meaning that went beyond the actual people that had been killed.

He took a large gulp of his brandy and closed his eyes. Thinking.

18

It was nearly lunchtime and Matthew was pleased that the bail hearing had gone as planned. Joseph Anderson had been remanded in a secure mental health facility for an independent psychological evaluation. It would also give Caroline an opportunity to complete her evaluation and wider profiling.

Despite there being no further incidents overnight, connected to the case, Matthew was still nervous. He was convinced that, at best, they had only interrupted the killing spree. Anderson could not be the only perp. It just wasn't possible unless he was an outstanding actor.

Louise joined him in the incident room. "Ah. Any updates for me?"

"Not much. The team have been trying to tie up a few loose ends. We spoke to the owner of the second house, and she provided details of who rented it from her, but once again we followed a trail of fake identities and blind alleys. DC Williams is going back over the alibis of the devil-worshipping lot, but they are getting more and more uncooperative and claiming police harassment. We've had a few of the usual nutters phoning up claiming to be the mastermind behind these crimes but none of them are credible. Other than that, the public appeal has been really flat. The only positive thing is that we have a bit more background on Anderson."

"Oh, do tell."

"He was abandoned outside a hospital in Edinburgh when he was born. Despite appeals for his mother to come forward, she was never located. He was brought up in local authority care all his life and the flat he lives in is a supported housing unit. They confirmed he does have a mental disability and his main support officer is going to the secure unit to help the psychological evaluation."

"So, he's not faking it then. He really does have some mental health issues."

"It seems so."

"He can't be doing this alone then."

"No."

*

The kick to the stomach hurt the most as he lay on the floor. "Dirty, dirty weirdo," they shouted as he lay on the hard, grey concrete of the school playground. More kicks, as the metallic taste of blood entered his throat. He flinched as the blows rained down and then...

Joshua jolted awake. He had fallen asleep, sitting in his wheelchair, his laptop screen shut down due to lack of attention. The dreams were not going away. Every one connected to his mother. The beatings in the school playground were a regular occurrence and every time she would drag Joshua back to school to confront the headmaster. There was no such thing as safeguarding in

71

those days. Incidents like the ones that Joshua experienced were put down to the hard knocks of growing up. *Character building* the headmaster would say each time his mother confronted the bullying.

The memories shook him out of his weariness. He was going to show these people. Every bastard who had put him down, abused him, would know what Joshua Billington had become. He was sure that most of these people had achieved nothing in their miserable lives. Well, now he would remind them how miserable their lives really were.

The arrest of Joseph stalled his plans. His journey to salvation was going to take longer than he had planned, but the one thing he had was time. If it took a bit longer to ensure that he achieved his ultimate goal, then so be it.

He grabbed his crutches and gingerly pulled himself up. He winced at the pain as he began to move towards the kitchen. He needed someone to do his dirty work while he was in this state and his relationship with Joseph had been a huge bonus. The poor fool didn't know right from wrong and was the perfect stool pigeon for what Joshua needed him to do. It was just a shame he panicked at the community hall and got himself nabbed by the police. *Oh well, can't be helped. Time for plan B.*

As he stood in his kitchen waiting for the kettle to boil, he started to flex his legs. A rush of adrenalin hit him. They felt better than yesterday. The pain was still there, but there was more feeling, more motion. A good sign. He hobbled back and forth to his desk, first taking the mug of coffee and then following up with a pack of Hobnobs.

As he sipped the coffee and bit hungrily into the first biscuit, sending crumbs across the desk, his fingers danced over the keyboard. Plan B had always been there, to deal with this exact scenario. He just hadn't expected to use it so soon. Joshua had planned every detail of every step, down to the minutest detail. Plan B only meant a few subtle tweaks.

An hour passed and everything was back in place. He allowed himself a brief smile.

19

Another twenty-four hours had passed, and Matthew was relieved that there had been no further incidences on the case. The arrest of Joseph Anderson had stopped the killings, but Matthew's self-doubt still crept in. *Was this because Joseph was acting alone?* He shook his head, responding to his internal monologue. It just didn't seem likely. Despite Joseph's mental limitations, the earpiece and his responses about someone called Lucifer talking to him, seemed to fit with the limited theories they had.

DC Williams seemed liked a dogged detective, but Matthew didn't think the devil worshippers she was pursuing were really in the frame. The thought haunted him. Was there a criminal mastermind sitting out there, plotting his or her next move, and what would they do without Joseph to commit the murders?

Just as he was about to get up to refresh his coffee, Louise and Caroline came through the door. Caroline spoke first. "We have the psych evaluation on Joseph Anderson, and I have managed to do my initial profiling. We've got a lot to talk about."

Matthew looked down at his empty mug. A refill would have to wait.

"Right, Caroline. What have you got?"

"The doctor has assessed him as having a dissociative disorder which means he does not remember large parts of what he does and also does not understand the implications of what he is doing. The condition means that sufferers disassociate from their actions and carry on as though nothing has happened. They act like they are in a trance, almost like they black out for large periods of time. During these episodes they have limited recall of their actions and don't therefore understand that they may have done something wrong. This, coupled with Joseph's mental immaturity, means many of his interactions are like talking to a child, making him the perfect patsy to be manipulated."

"Oh, so the doctor agrees with our theory that Joseph was being guided to do these things by another person."

"Yes, he does. He believes that Joseph's complex mental condition makes him easily open to suggestion, and his childlike mental state will make him compliant."

"So, the doctor is saying that Joseph does not understand that he has killed people?"

"Sort of. The disorder is predominant in its impacts on the sufferer's mental state but is not absolute. You saw when Louise asked him some questions about the acts of killing that he became agitated and a bit emotional. His brain recalls small snippets of these incidents and somewhere in there he does know that what he has done is wrong, but the seriousness of the disorder blanks out the worst aspects of the acts he commits."

"Jeez, this is not good. What else?"

"During the evaluation the doctor did ask him questions about the crimes and although his responses continued to be limited, there was enough there to confirm that Joseph was at each crime scene. He also confirmed that someone spoke to him via the earpiece, which almost certainly confirms this is how he was able to carry out these acts. Someone was telling him what to do."

"Bloody hell. We need to ramp up our investigations about this second person then. If this is all true, we have a psycho out there who's just lost his stool pigeon."

Matthew's face was a mix of stress and concentration, but he eventually cracked on.

"Anything else?"

"One thing. We asked about his trainers, and he said someone bought them for him. He didn't seem to make any connection between the person speaking in his ear and the gift, but Louise and I are running with a theory that they have actually met. Joseph would not necessarily remember this but did seem sure that someone had given them to him as a gift."

Matthew looked at Louise. "What are you doing about this?"

"Some of the team are over at his place now interviewing his neighbours. If someone did visit him, we are hoping that one of them may have seen something."

"OK good. Where does this leave us with any prosecution?"

Louise frowned. "There's no doubt this is going to be a difficult one, sir. I think I need to go and discuss this with someone from the PF to see what they think."

Matthew nodded. "You're right. If the doctor's assessment is taken into account, there is little chance we will get a murder charge. The best we can hope for is manslaughter with diminished responsibility."

Louise pulled a face. "Something on your mind?"

"Well, sir. I don't mean to be disrespectful, but won't some people see Joseph Anderson as another victim?"

Matthew stared off into the distance. The case was a nightmare. They seemingly had their perpetrator bang to rights on one of the most serious cases that Matthew had worked on for a while, but he knew that Louise was right, and any good brief would get Joseph Anderson off in a second.

He stood up, not responding to Louise's challenge. "I need a ciggie. Let's reconvene in half an hour and you can tell me about the profiling of our mystery mastermind."

20

The flat smelled musty. Nothing had really been done in the place since his mother had gone. His limbs were improving but not enough to do any housework. Joshua flung open a few windows, hoping it would freshen everything up. He couldn't bear the thought of having to get an outsider in to clean.

The spring air blowing through the windows was bracing but it perked Joshua up. He had worked obsessively, planning every step towards his salvation. He smiled to himself. It was done. Six more steps and then he could rest. The world would know his name. No longer the insignificant creature that everyone sneered at and bullied. *Oh no.* Some people would thank their lucky stars that they hadn't been chosen for his retribution. There just wasn't time to get revenge on everyone who had hurt him. It couldn't be helped. He was already behind due to Joseph's shortcomings, and he wasn't about to get off track again.

He sat at his desk and drank his coffee, reviewing the extensive notes he had made about each step. He picked up a pen and circled the name of his old headmaster. He was going to enjoy that one.

The doorbell rang, disturbing his concentration. "Coooeee. Joshua, it's Mrs Robertson from next door. I've come to see if you are OK and need anything... are you there?"

Joshua grimaced at the interruption but as he looked around the flat, he knew he had to do something about the mess. *Maybe the old bat could do his cleaning*, he thought to himself.

He quickly hid all his notes in the desk drawer and locked it. Wheeling his way towards the front door, he called out. "Coming, Mrs Robertson."

*

Louise's challenge about how they should treat Joseph Anderson remained unanswered when they reconvened in Matthew's office. The mood was tense.

"OK, Caroline. Tell me about our mystery mastermind."

Caroline glanced at Louise, a subtle look of support that told her she was right, and Matthew was just being pig-headed. It happened. Senior officers had their own mind and challenging performance targets, both of which were a brick wall that junior officers would get used to banging their heads against. She let it go and started her explanation of the profiling.

"OK, sir. The profiling I have done is based on the assumption that we have someone that is masterminding whatever sick game this is supposed to be, using Joseph as a pawn in the execution of his plan."

"*His* plan?"

"Yes, sir, I believe the perp is a man. Having studied Joseph, I think he responds better to the authority of a male. He seems more relaxed with women, evidenced by the way he interacted with Louise at the first interview and the way he engaged with his support officer yesterday. I strongly feel he associates females with a more caring approach and males as authority figures that need to be obeyed. Hence his compliance with the instructions we are sure he was being given by the earpiece."

"OK. I'll buy that."

"This person is highly intelligent, possibly someone who excelled educationally, but I believe they are a loner. They will have very limited personal relationships and probably live alone or with elderly parents. They are demonstrating clear psychopathic behaviour through the manner of the killings and the lack of remorse that is demonstrated by the way they manipulated Joseph. I also believe they must have some prior knowledge of Joseph's condition to use him in this way. It's possible that this person has been part of Joseph's medical care and saw a great opportunity to exploit him. Finally, unlike a sociopath, who despite having the same psychopathic tendencies will blend in easily with other people, I think our perp will stand out. I think his behaviour will unsettle people and they won't want to be near him, increasing the likelihood of him being a loner. I think there is a strong possibility he was bullied unmercifully at school, for being a swot and potentially due to something about his appearance or manner. However, despite all this he will be supremely confident in what he is doing and will not stop until he has completed whatever sick game he is playing."

"Do you think he's after revenge?"

"I think revenge has a part in his actions but I'm not sure that's the full explanation. Psychopaths are inherently unstable, but their actions are generally triggered by something. I think this perp has experienced something traumatic that has triggered this killing spree. He may have been the subject of a recent serious assault or lost one of the few people close to him. The biggest problem is the victimology. It's all over the place. Whilst the nature of some psychopathic serial killers is that they will pick victims at random, I can't help feeling that his selection of the victims is more considered. The devil symbolism means something and may, as I believe Louise previously suggested, have some religious connotations. This is the area that I need to do some more work on."

"That's great work and please keep at it. It will give us some much-needed focus on the investigation."

"Thank you, sir."

"So, DS Cookson, what are you doing with this profiling work in terms of moving our investigations forward?"

"Caroline and I spoke last night and subject to your agreement have come up with a number of investigative tasks for the team, based on the profile."

Matthew nodded.

"Firstly, we are going to look into all the people who have been part of Joseph's care, to see if we can find anyone that matches the profile. Secondly, we are going to review all recent cases of assault to see if there are any possible suspects. Finally, we are going to review all the recent deaths in the area to see if we can find anyone linked to the deceased that could fit the profile. I'm also waiting for the feedback from the interviews with Joseph's neighbours."

"I like it. Lots of good solid detective work in there. You have my authority to proceed."

Louise gave a pained smile, happy to have got something out of the *grumpy old sod*. As they got up to leave, Matthew spoke again.

"Actually, let me know when you are meeting with the PF about Joseph's case. You may be right. Perhaps we should reconsider our position on him."

Out of his gaze, Louise looked at Caroline, a triumphant smirk on her face.

21

Joshua waited a few minutes for her to leave and let out a scream. The flat was sparkling but her presence had pushed him to the edge. Invading his privacy, banging on about his mother and all the inane gossip she had heard down the bingo.

He took a number of deep breaths, trying to calm the stress and rage. If he had been more mobile, he was pretty sure he would have put his hands round her neck and suffocated the life out of her.

He grabbed his notes out of the drawer, trying to hold back the tears that had welled up as he once again thought about his mother. He could hear her preaching to him... *cleanliness is next to godliness.*

He shook himself out of it. The place was clean now and if everything went to plan, he wouldn't be here by the time it needed to be done again.

He eyed the first entry on his list. It couldn't be more perfect for his next step. The annual spring conference for the associates of Brair Investment Bankers. He placed the little surprise in his backpack and called a cab. The event was being held in the civic centre. Open access and lots of people around. His wheelchair made him a little conspicuous, but he was confident he could execute his plan with minimum fuss.

While he waited for the cab, he opened his email. He decided that McCallum could be a worthy adversary. It would help with his journey. Someone who would be wholly engaged, obsessed even, with stopping him. He smiled and typed the email.

*

Matthew was deep in thought as the latest in a never-ending stream of emails pinged into his inbox. The team were beavering away with the new tasks, and he had a frisson of excitement about the focus the profiling work had given the investigation.

He was about to shut his laptop down and get back out there with the troops when he noticed an email from a strange email address. His gut reaction was to ignore it as a piece of spam, but his curiosity got the better of him. As he opened the email, his heart froze at the words on the screen.

Hello DCI McCallum,

I think maybe you are looking for me. Here's something for you to watch. It must be a DEVIL of a job trying to find me...

The message was followed by a string of laughing emojis. Another modern-day obsession that annoyed Matthew.

He knew he probably shouldn't open the video file without getting someone to virus check it, but he couldn't wait. If this email was genuine, the mastermind behind these killings had just raised the stakes. For some reason he was engaging directly with Matthew, like a grandmaster wanting to engage in a remote game of chess. He clicked on the file.

The opening scenes were fuzzy and jerky as the person behind the recording – *Joseph?* – fumbled with the recording device. Eventually the image came sharply into focus and Matthew caught himself in a breath as he watched the pleading eyes and urgent muffled screams of a man, hanging from a hook in the ceiling with a rope around his neck and tape across his mouth. One of his feet was trying to maintain contact with the chair, his movements making the rope move subtly, the creaking an eerie backdrop to the unfolding scene.

Matthew watched transfixed as the camera didn't move, fixed on the terrified face of the victim, his urgings becoming more and more desperate as every second passed.

The horror lasted a few more minutes before there was a sudden crash. The chair fell over and the man dropped. Matthew winced at the sound of the man's neck snapping. The video played out for another thirty seconds as it showed the man swinging gently from side to side. Dead.

Matthew had seen many horrific things in his career, but this had genuinely disturbed him. He grabbed the small bottle of whisky that was squirreled away in his bottom drawer and took a long slug.

Caroline's profile had been right about one thing. They had a psychopathic bastard on their hands.

22

Joshua made himself look as smart as he could, donning the dark grey suit that only a few days ago had been worn at his mother's funeral. He had done the best he could with his lifeless hair and put on a pair of fake glasses to enhance the image of a *knob-head banker*. He finished it off with a trilby hat.

The taxi driver dropped him right outside and helped him get back into his wheelchair. Joshua could see the event was already in full swing and he slowly wheeled his way to the entrance. As he approached the main door, he was met by a tall blonde, in a short dress that left nothing to the imagination. Her fake smile was framed by an excessively made-up face, finished off with bright red lipstick. He ignored her empty welcome and quickly looked away as she leant down to greet him, exposing her ample cleavage. He had already dealt with that other *slut* and just couldn't abide having to deal with another one. He quickly pushed past her and entered the main foyer.

The place was packed with delegates. It looked like there was a table for registration over to the right of the foyer, with the main event stretching out into the large conference area.

Joshua scanned the immediate area. It looked like he needed a delegate's badge as there were a couple of sentries checking credentials before people were allowed to go into the main conference space.

The registration table was busy. A couple of hassled administrators were trying to deal with the large numbers of people that had turned up. Joshua began to wheel himself towards the chaos. He noticed that all the badges were laid out on one of the tables. He waited for the right moment, checking that the two people at the desk were distracted. He grabbed a delegate's badge from the registration table. *Derek Jameson* was going to have a problem getting in. He wheeled himself towards the entrance to the event and was immediately waved through by the security staff.

Joshua moved through the extensive exhibition floor, populated by companies trying to sell the bankers everything from exotic holidays to the latest in electric golf trollies. The sound of overprivileged, overpaid idiots fawning over the products and being fawned over by the people trying to sell them their wares made his stomach churn. They were deserving of his retribution, he mused.

As he moved towards the back of the event, he realised he had found the refreshments area. There were armies of waiters and waitresses bringing trays of food and drinks, leaving them on large round tables for people to graze as they cruised the event.

"*Perfect*," Joshua mumbled. He discreetly pulled out the tins of caviar from his backpack. As he made like he was perusing what nibbles to partake he slipped one of the tins into the middle of the table. He wheeled away and repeated the process in three different places.

He moved away from the food area and waited, discreetly watching the tables from a distance.

As soon as he noticed someone spooning some of the caviar onto their plate, he wheeled himself out, wiping Mr Jameson's badge clean and dumping it in the bin. Job done.

*

Caroline and Louise responded to Matthew's text quickly and were in his office watching the video within thirty minutes of his request. They had their hands over their mouth as they watched the horror unfold.

Caroline responded first. "What a sick bastard! I assume that it's Joseph behind the camera?"

"I think there is no doubt about that, and we can now absolutely confirm that our first victim was murdered. What do you make of his decision to send this to me?" asked Matthew.

"I think it confirms that this is a highly intelligent person. He is exhibiting power and confidence. He wants to engage you in his sick game. Psychopaths crave attention for their actions. I'm sure he has seen you at the press conference and decided that you are someone he wants to engage with. You should probably see it as a compliment. He sees you as someone that is potentially clever enough to understand his actions and he will be motivated by the thrill of the chase. Whether you like it or not, sir, he has decided that you are his nemesis. It's a kill or be killed situation. I would be very careful from now on."

Matthew rubbed his chin but didn't say anything. Louise broke the silence.

"Sir, are you OK?"

Matthew came out of his daze. "Oh, yes, fine. Just thinking. We need to update the team about this development, and I want you to give a full explanation of your profiling to them at the briefing later, Caroline. Also, get one of the tech boys to see if they can trace the origin of this email, DS Cookson."

They nodded in acknowledgement.

"Also, I've changed my mind about the charge for Anderson. I want a murder charge. I don't care what his mental disorders are. How can anyone stand there and watch another person die like that? It's horrendous."

"But, sir, you know the advice from our meeting with the PF was that they were unlikely to support a murder charge."

There was a brief stand-off as Matthew stared at Louise. Nothing was said. The tension rose.

Eventually, Matthew stood up. "Come on. I've made my mind up, so let's get back out there. This psycho has just drawn the battle lines, and I'm not about to hide away from this."

As they began to walk out, Louise was struggling to hide her frustration. She had worked with Matthew for a while now and had got used to his pig-headed attitude and grumpy persona, but some days she just ran out of patience. She was just about to say something to Matthew when her phone beeped. She stopped and clicked on the notification. "Oh, shite, sir. There's been an incident at a bankers' conference that's being held at the civic centre. Several casualties. Possible poisoning."

Matthew looked at Louise. "Bloody hell. Has he struck again?"

*

Joshua sat in a coffee shop across the street from the civic centre, as he watched the growing number of emergency vehicles crowd around the entrance. People were being brought out on stretchers and loaded onto ambulances. Elsewhere, large crowds of delegates were gathering on the large esplanade as the police removed them from the crime scene. Joshua closed his eyes and revelled in the chaos.

He opened his eyes and re-engaged with the scene. *Where was he?* He needed to see McCallum. He hoped he had received his little gift and was ready to engage. A few agonising minutes went by but eventually an unmarked car pulled up. Jumping out of the car was the female copper he had seen on the news and another woman in a smart business suit. He waited with anticipation as the passenger door opened and his opponent appeared.

As he got out of the car, he looked straight over to the café that Joshua was sitting in. Joshua sat upright, like a meerkat sensing danger. *Had he seen him?* There was a tense few seconds as McCallum's gaze hung in his direction but eventually, he looked away. Joshua relaxed and watched some more. A smile rapidly spreading across his face.

23

The civic centre was still in a state of panic as police officers and staff from the centre were ushering the delegates out as paramedics attended to the stricken bodies scattered across the main lobby.

Matthew spotted Jed examining a body. "What have we got, Sherlock?"

Jed looked up, concern etched on his face. "I don't want to jump to conclusions, sir but I'm pretty sure this is a mass poisoning. We have six dead, including this poor laddie, and three more on their way to hospital. My best guess is cyanide poisoning."

"Why?"

"You see the unusual redness of his skin. This happens when the poison forces oxygen to stay in the blood and stops it getting into the cells. Also, there is a faint smell of almonds around his mouth, nose and lips. All classic signs of cyanide poisoning."

A uniformed inspector joined the group. "Sir I'm Inspector Kate Hoolahan. I was with the first responders. We've managed to ascertain that the victims were eating at the time of their collapse. Witnesses say they were dropping like flies."

"Do we know *what* they were eating?"

"No, the witnesses were not conclusive, but the scenes of crime are bagging up all the food for forensic examination."

Matthew turned back to Jed. "Would that strengthen your view?"

"If there is a high enough concentration of the poison in the food they were eating, then yes, it's feasible that was the method used. If the witness statements are right, and people were literally falling over after consuming food, we should find very high concentrations in the stuff we are collecting."

As Matthew surveyed the scene, there was more commotion at the door as the press clamoured for a story or a gory picture. Matthew barked at Louise, "Get those parasites out of here and set up a cordon well away from the entrance."

Louise soon got large protective barriers put up to hide the crime scene from snoopers and photographers' zoom lenses. Matthew watched as bodies were zipped up in body bags and the SOCOs finished securing the food.

He felt a pang of panic. The gruesome video and this case of mass murder was an escalation in the case he was not prepared for but as he tried to calm his stress, he had a sudden thought. He rushed back over to where Jed was just finishing the examination of his victim. "Have you found any devil symbology on any of the victims?"

Jed looked around. "Er, no. I don't think so. I haven't looked at the wider scene though."

Matthew started pacing around, conscious not to compromise the scene but desperate to see if he could find something that could link this to the previous murders. As he moved quickly around the scene, he couldn't find anything. *Was he wrong about this? Was this an unrelated case? Did he have a mass poisoner on his hands as well as a devil-obsessed serial killer?*

As he frantically looked around for something to answer his questions, Louise came back into the hall. "We've got the cordon in place, sir, and all the delegates are out. The crime scene is now secure."

There was a moment when Louise wasn't sure if Matthew had heard her. He shook his head. "Er, oh, great, I'm…"

"Are you OK, sir? You seem a bit distracted?"

"Is this our serial killer? Where's the devil symbology? How do we know it's him? Without Joseph Anderson to do his bidding, he's changed his approach… if this is even his work."

"I dunno, sir, it seems too coincidental not to be him."

"I know, I agree but we need to be sure. I want every piece of evidence examined urgently. We have to know."

"OK, I'll keep an eye on that, but I need to catch up with the other investigation teams who were pursuing the inquiries linked to the profiling."

"Yes, yes of course. We need a briefing later today. Get everyone back to the nick for 5pm. We've a lot to talk about."

*

The professor sat in his study watching the local news as he ate his lunch. The news was dominated by a story of apparent mass poisoning of bankers at the civic centre.

He was transfixed. Why was someone killing bankers? He watched some more. His thoughts turned to Matthew. Could this be connected to his murders with the demonic symbols?

The brain-worm that had been festering ever since they had the brief chat about the case at the awards dinner was still there. Roger couldn't help feeling that there was something deep and hidden in the psychology of the killings. The reporters hadn't mentioned anything about devil symbology, which seemed to suggest the cases weren't linked, but he wasn't convinced this was true.

As he listened to the reporters speculating about the motives, Roger couldn't help feeling that it was the perception of bankers that was at play here. If the reports were to be believed, the poisonings were random and indiscriminate. It didn't sound like individual people had been targeted, more the institution of... he stopped himself in the thought... he was going to say *greedy bankers*. That could be it. The perception of bankers, especially the type at this event, was that they were a brunch of greedy bastards that would kill their own mother to make a financial killing.

He shook his head, disturbed by the thought.

A theory began to form. He had to speak to Matthew.

24

Matthew was restless as he waited for the detective teams to file into the briefing room. He'd received a text from the professor asking to see him. Matthew had put it off to the evening as he had to get the briefing done but, if his old mate had a theory about the case, he wanted to hear it. The professor was one of the most intelligent people that Matthew had ever met and valued his counsel.

As people seemed to be taking an eternity to settle down, Matthew let his irritation get the better of him. "Can we get settled, please. We've a lot to get through tonight and I don't think our murderer is going to give you time to have another cup of coffee."

It worked. A sea of faces suddenly stared at him, quiet and attentive.

"OK, Caroline Fleck, our BAU rep is going to give you an updated profile on our second perp. We have clear evidence, backed up by an email sent to me, that we have another person directing these crimes."

Caroline took the stage and explained the profile and the reasons behind her assumptions. The team listened, frantically scribbling down their own notes as the personality of the serial killer was revealed.

As questions for Caroline tailed off, Matthew moved quickly on to the next part of the briefing. "So, the profile has given us a renewed focus on the case, and I know that some of you have already been following the new lines of investigation. DS Cookson will summarise what we have found so far."

"Thank you, sir. We have been pursuing three lines of inquiry linked to the profile. Firstly, we have looked at people linked to Joseph Anderson's care regime, but I'm afraid we've drawn a blank on that one. No one seems to match the profile. Secondly, we have begun to review cases of serious assault over the last three months and have a number of victims that could match the profile, so we are pursuing those. We are also looking at deaths over the same period to profile the relatives. This is by far the biggest job, but we are cracking on with it."

"Thank you. I know you are all working hard and there is a lot to get through, but this killer seems to be in a hurry. If we assume that today's poisoning was his work, we managed to slow him down for a day or two by arresting Joseph Anderson but, he seems to have found a way to carry out his crimes without additional help. We need to keep up the pace."

Matthew watched the reactions, which were mostly positive. He knew he was stretching the team to breaking point, but he had to keep them focused.

"OK, for my part, I need to tell you that the killer has engaged me directly. I've had an email from him containing a video of the first murder. The file has been put in the casework folder on the network, if you want to view it, but I warn you that it's grim viewing. Caroline believes this act cements her profile in that we have a hyper-intelligent psychopath on our hands. Someone who is supremely confident in their actions and is craving attention. He seems to have appointed me as his *adversaire*. I am fully expecting further contact from him."

DC McDonald piped up. "So, he hasnae contacted you about today's incident?"

"No, and this is troubling me. Whilst we are assuming that this is his work, he has not contacted me to claim responsibility. Without Joseph Anderson at the scene, and no apparent devil symbology, we don't actually have any obvious ties to his previous work."

A low murmur spread across the room as people speculated on what they'd heard. Matthew quickly brought them back.

"OK, quiet please. Sherlock will give you the latest forensic update on today's crime scene. Whether this is our man or not, we still have the caseload of this incident."

Jed stepped to the front. "Thank you, sir. Preliminary analysis suggests that all the victims were killed by cyanide poisoning. Large concentrations of cyanide were found in four tins of caviar that were placed on the food tables in the main exhibition space. This is the only place it was found but it was no surprise that the victims had an instant reaction, as the concentration levels in the caviar were so high. It would have brought on immediate cardiac failure, which we expect will be confirmed by the post-mortems. Other than that, there is little forensic evidence as the scene was compromised by the mass of people in the hall and the chaos that reigned immediately afterwards."

"Thank you." He turned to Louise. "Have we secured the CCTV from the time of the murders?"

"It's being collected as we speak. We should be able to view it this evening."

Matthew nodded. The stress levels were rising but he was satisfied they had a clear focus on the case. Hard work would always deliver a result, but the big question was whether they were moving fast enough to stop further killings.

As the briefing seemed to be drifting off to its natural conclusion, DC Williams entered the room.

"DC Williams. Nice of you to join us."

"Sorry, sir, but I was just finishing up the interviews with Joseph Anderson's neighbours. We've had a development. One of his neighbours said Joseph had a visitor last week."

"OK, anything significant to report?"

"Yes, sir. The person who visited Joseph Anderson was in a wheelchair."

25

No, Mother, please stop it, you're hurting me...

Wicked child, laying with the devil, wicked child...

Ow, please stop, Mother, I'm sorry...

Sorry doesn't cut it, you worthless sinner, pray to God for forgiveness...

Forgive me, Mother, please

Come here, child, hug your mother... there, that's better... that's it, you only need me, don't you, Joshua...

Joshua jolted awake. He tried to focus. The head fog cleared. As he focused on the view out of the window, he realised the last bit of daylight had long since gone out of the spring sky, replaced by a clear, cool starry night.

He had fallen asleep on the sofa, exhausted by the events of the day. The adrenalin rush from executing the perfect crime and then watching McCallum floundering around at the crime scene had left him euphoric, but the vivid dreams had once again disturbed him.

As he sat there, trying to come to, he realised they were more than dreams. They were flashbacks to dark times. Real, desperate traumatic events. His mother's oppressive parenting played out, day after day. The latest flashback had been all too familiar. Like any young man, Joshua needed sex, but every time he paid for the privilege, his mother found out. Full of damnation and hellfire. She just didn't understand.

Joshua started to well up at the memories. She would force him to kneel in front of her, praying for forgiveness, reading line after line of the Bible... and then she would do those things to him... the touching. The caressing. *Why did she do it?*

The anger began to rise. She was a hypocrite, driven by her own warped sense of right and wrong. Joshua shook the memories away and manoeuvred himself off the sofa into his wheelchair. He was hungry. He heated a pizza in the microwave and went back to his office.

*

Matthew sat in the professor's apartment, savouring the rich taste of the brandy as he allowed it to swill around his mouth before it slid smoothly down his throat. "Oh aye, I needed that."

"A long day, my friend?"

"A long few days. So, tell me. What's been keeping you awake?"

The professor leant forward, his forehead furrowed in concentration. "I was watching the news at lunchtime and saw this latest atrocity. Is it the same man?"

"We don't know. It seems likely but as we have his stooge in custody and there was no devil symbology at the scene, we can't be sure."

"The thing is, I've been thinking a lot about the motivation behind these murders, ever since we spoke about it the other night. The devil symbology suggests some religious connections and I kept asking myself why someone was killing bankers and people who are overweight."

Matthew fixed the professor with an expectant stare. "Go on. I can see your massive brain has come up with a theory."

The professor laughed. "Ah yes. I think I have. You see, the last two incidents have focused on groups of people, rather than individuals. The acts are random and indiscriminate. In other words, individual people are not being targeted. So, I asked myself what could be behind the psychology of the killings, and I'm sure the victims have been targeted due to their actions."

Matthew screwed his face up. "Sorry, I'm not following."

"Think about it. Everyone hates bankers. They are perceived as greedy with loose morals. What if our killer is motivated by an extreme interpretation of religious teachings? Could they be targeting people they perceive as sinners and the devil symbology is their way of telling us that the victims are going to hell for their actions?"

"Bloody hell. That's quite a theory. How does this play out with the other victims?"

"Well, I started to think about Christian teachings about sin. Whilst it's not actually mentioned in the Bible, the concept of the seven deadly sins is a central tenet in Christian teaching. It's feasible that our killer is focusing on the seven deadly sins and is killing people they perceive fall into one of the categories."

"Huh. There was a film about that, wasn't there? I think Brad Pitt was in it."

"Oh, I don't know about that, not really my thing, but let's just follow this idea for a minute. The bankers could be greed, the overweight people could be gluttony and the girl could be lust. The only one that I can't quite hook in is the first one."

"What are the other deadly sins?"

"There's sloth, wrath, pride and envy."

Matthew stroked his chin. "The guy was a personal trainer. Could it be about pride... you know obsessed about his appearance, or envy... other people being jealous of how he looked? He was a very fit man."

The professor took a sip of brandy. "I guess it's possible."

They stared into space as they processed the implications of the new theory. Matthew eventually broke the silence.

"If we can just find some devil symbology to link these last murders to the first three incidents, I think your theory has some real legs. I'll brief my profiler about it."

"You realise what this means, if I'm right."

Matthew's brow furrowed. "Yes, he's gonna do this at least three more times."

They refilled their glasses and unwrapped a couple of cigars. Matthew's brain never stopped but he was grateful for the few minutes of physical rest indulging in the quality brandy and Cuban cigars that were always a fixture in the professor's apartment.

As the evening drifted on, Matthew could feel himself fighting the onset of sleep. He perked himself up. "It's no good, if I stay here, I'm gonna fall asleep. I need to be fresh for the morning."

As Matthew began the short walk to his house, his phone beeped. It was Louise. As he went to read the message, he had a pang of guilt. Louise seemed to be working 24/7 and he knew he took her for granted. The fact she was messaging him at this hour just added to his guilt.

He opened the message and clicked on the video link. It was the CCTV footage from the civic centre. He couldn't believe what he was watching.

26

Matthew sat in the incident room with Louise, playing the CCTV footage over and over.

"This is unbelievable."

"Oh aye, sir. Do you think the wee man is deliberately goading us?"

Matthew shook his head. The image they were replaying showed a man in a wheelchair moving slowly through the main expedition space of the civic centre. Whilst it wasn't immediately obvious to the naked eye, Louise had eventually spotted something. She zoomed in on the back of the wheelchair. There, emblazoned on the back of the chair, was a distinctive image of the devil.

As they followed the footage, the man was placing what seemed to be the tins of caviar, on four of the food tables.

"Well, I think we have our link. A man in a wheelchair, with a devil symbol on the back, placing something on the exact food tables where the poisoned caviar was found. I don't think we need much more evidence that this is our man."

Louise flicked up an enlarged image of the man on the screen. The image was grainy, and his face was mostly obscured by the hat. They both studied the image intently.

Matthew drew in a sharp intake of breath. "Who is this? Who is this murdering bastard?"

They got up and refilled their coffee cups. Any benefit Matthew had gleaned from the alcohol had long since passed. Mental and physical exhaustion were now at play as the clock ticked past 1am. Matthew did what he always did in these situations and poured out his stresses on Louise.

"This is a great development, but I can't help feeling we are drowning here. We have so many lines of inquiry ongoing, but this bastard is moving too fast. We need to consolidate everything we have and focus on finding him. I've also got some interesting ideas from my friend the professor. He has a theory about why this guy is doing these things which I need to talk to Caroline about."

"Oh really? Do tell."

Matthew let out a huge yawn. "No. Let's leave this to the morning. It's stupid o'clock and we need to be back for the briefing at 9am. Go and get some rest."

As she began to walk out, Matthew's guilt came back in waves. "DS Cookson... sorry, Louise. You do an amazing job. You do know that, don't you?"

Louise looked around and smiled. "Thank you, sir."

*

The briefing the next morning was frantic. New developments. The wheelchair. The fuzzy CCTV image. The poisoned caviar, placed by the perp. The new theories about the motivations behind the crimes, helping Caroline develop the profile. Detectives poring over recent assaults and deaths, trying to match the profile to someone who had been through a recent trauma. A trauma that could explain why this person had started his killing spree. Despite the exhaustion across the team, the developments seemed to galvanise everyone.

As the detective team left the room to continue with their tasks, Matthew sat down with Louise, Caroline and Jed.

"We're getting close. Aren't we?"

Louise responded first. "Aye, sir. All the pieces are fitting together. I reckon we might have narrowed down the suspect list by the end of the day."

Matthew exhaled. "I really hope so. The super wants an update which means the chief is on his back." He rubbed his face. "Caroline, what do you think about the prof's theories?"

"Well, as I said in the briefing, I think it's got some real possibilities. If nothing else, I think we can be sure we have a significant religious aspect to these crimes, which seems quite extreme. Louise and I have discussed talking to some of the local priests to see if they have anyone in their flock that seems to have a more extreme interpretation of religious teachings."

Matthew nodded. "Yes, I guess it's worth a try. The tighter we throw the net around this nutter, the sooner we can stop his killing spree."

He turned his attentions to Jed.

"What about you?"

"The civic centre scene was chaotic from a forensics

perspective, but we might have got some good prints and even some DNA off the caviar tins. There are no matches to anyone we know, but it's gonna help if we get any suspects. I'll sniff this bastard out if it's the last thing I do."

Matthew smiled. He knew he probably didn't deserve such a dedicated, driven team, but he was going to take anything he could get right now.

*

Joshua sat in a coffee shop, nursing a steaming espresso. The place was busy. Stressed mums with screaming babies trying desperately to get a takeaway coffee before too many more disapproving stares. The suited and booted, running on adrenaline and caffeine, as they did another fourteen-hour day. The ladies who lunched whose pitch went up and down as they regaled stories of their sad upper-class lives. Joshua hated them all, but his focus was across the street.

He had been surprised at how easy it had been to find the instructions and materials needed to create an improvised explosive device. His heart started to race as he waited. The man who had framed so much of the trauma of his school life was about to get his payback. The violence and anger that this man had allowed in the inner-city school that Joshua had been forced to go to, was a sin that could not be forgiven. He watched over and over as his mother ripped into this man about the latest bullying or worse, serious assaults, that he allowed to happen to Joshua during his tenure as Headmaster. An

107

uncaring bully himself, who saw school as a place to learn the hard knocks of life. His mother had tried to protect him, but the mental and physical scars never left him.

He fingered his phone nervously. One push of the send key and... boom. People were beginning to stare at him. His gaze was so fixed, so determined, people started to follow his eyeline. Joshua quickly looked away and took a sip of the bitter coffee, wincing at the sharpness. Faces that had been staring looked away. He risked another glance back at the car sitting outside the mini supermarket. The man had parked up to do some shopping. Joshua had attached the bomb with a magnetic strip underneath the offside wheel arch as soon as he was out of sight.

Where was he? Joshua started to sweat; his hands clammy as he fiddled with the phone. He finished his coffee, which did nothing to cool him down. He got out a hanky and wiped his brow. People were still staring. Oh, how he wished he could blow this place up as well, but it wasn't his time. Not yet, anyway.

Five more agonising minutes passed as he waited for the man to return. Eventually, there he was. The man opened his car door and got in.

Joshua closed his eyes and pressed send.

The reaction was instant. The explosion filled the air, followed by scream after scream as people reacted to what had just happened. The windows of the coffee shop had been hit by falling debris but only cracks appeared on the panes, as they resisted the strength of the explosion. Joshua's calculations of the blast radius had been correct. He was OK.

The coffee shop was a mass of frightened people jostling to get outside, cradling loved ones as they got on their phones to call the emergency services. As the mushroom cloud from the bomb was dispersing, it revealed the blast area, strewn with bits of metal and other debris. And bodies.

Joshua stayed where he was, straining to see through the crowds. *Was he dead? He had to be. No one would survive that. Would they?*

Joshua leant gingerly on his crutches as he began to move outside, jostled by frantic people who didn't know whether to stay inside or leave the apparent safety of the coffee shop. He had to be sure. He eventually got to the door. The air was filled with the stench of the blast. The first sirens could be heard as the mass of dazed people looked on. Some were attending to victims that were away from the heat of the inferno engulfing the devastated car. Joshua was sure he could make out the charred remains of the man sitting in the driver's seat. A gruesome outline framed within the smoke and flames. He let out a deep breath. It was done.

As he watched the inferno, he smiled as he saw his wheelchair that had been upended by the blast, laying on the pavement, burning well. A symbol that he hoped McCallum would by now understand. He had worked tirelessly on his physio and his mobility had improved dramatically over the last few days. It was a lucky break as the wheelchair had to go. He was sure the CCTV in the civic centre would have exposed his actions… as he had planned. Each time giving the police a few more clues, a few more chances to identify him. This is how it had to be.

If his final act was to be celebrated, everyone, including McCallum and his band of merry coppers, needed to know who he was and why he was doing these things. He turned and hobbled away from the scene. A sense of calm washed over him.

27

The briefing with Chief Superintendent Alexander was drawing to a close as their phones beeped simultaneously. There was a split second of quiet as they took in what they were reading. Matthew reacted first.

"Oh shite."

Within a few minutes he was at the cordon with Louise. A busy street in the Saint Leonards district of Edinburgh, full of local independent shops. The air was filled with the stench of the explosion. The emergency services all doing their jobs. Victims being attended to by paramedics, firefighters trying to douse the last flames of the explosion and the police trying to hold back a large crowd, including manic reporters desperate for a story.

Matthew's detective radar was immediately switched on. "Get one of the DCs to start taking photos of the crowd. This has got to be his next act. If Caroline's updated profile is right, this man wants the attention. He wants to see the impact of his crimes. He'll be here somewhere. Maybe in a wheelchair."

Louise quickly grabbed one of the team and tasked that out. As they ducked under the tape and got closer to the main scene, Louise nudged Matthew's arm. "Sir, look."

Matthew closed his eyes and shook his head. About fifty yards away, to the right of the exploded car was a wheelchair, on its side and smouldering from the effects of the firefighter's water. "*Clever*," he muttered. The perp had made sure that the combination of the fire and the water had eradicated any chance of them getting forensic evidence.

Matthew looked around. Was the wheelchair a ruse? Was the man fully mobile or was he using some other method to get around? "He's on foot. If he really is injured, he must be using crutches or a stick to get around. Get the team to recce the crowd. I don't want to miss him."

He knew his tone was curt and stressed but Louise set off without any reaction. He knew she was used to it. Jed Spencer was stood a few yards away surveying the scene. Matthew walked over to him. "What have we got?"

"I'm guessing not a lot. The fire and water will have washed away most forensic clues, but we should be able to get a fix on the type of explosive and any accelerants he used. We'll go over everything else but I'm not that hopeful."

"The wheelchair as well?"

"You think this is the same guy and that's the wheelchair he used at the civic centre?"

"I'll put money on it. Once the fire service releases the scene, see if you can make out whether the chair has a devil symbol on the back and whether there is any forensics you can use. It's too much of a coincidence that the chair is right next to the blast scene. This guy's big on symbology. He's left it as a clue for me, to see if I pick up on his sick messages."

"OK, sir, we'll process it as soon as we can."

Matthew stepped away from the main scene and the long lenses of the reporters and TV cameras. He desperately needed a nicotine fix but thought better of it, given the nature of the scene. He scanned the sea of faces, ghoulishly looking at the carnage. *Where are you?*

The pace of the man's crimes was overwhelming. The team hardly had time to process the latest lines of inquiry before the next crime scene was upon them. Matthew could feel the stress in his stomach as it churned away. The wheelchair bothered him. Was it a prop? Was the man fit and healthy, using the chair to make them think he was disabled? Matthew's mind went back to Joseph. Was the perp using Joseph because he did have mobility issues? Since they had apprehended Joseph, was he forced to get about more or was he just playing them? He got on the radio. "DS Cookson. Any sightings? Over."

She responded immediately. "No, sir. We are walking amongst the crowd now and taking photos. Nothing yet. Over."

"OK, thanks. Over and out."

He paced around, consumed by his own stress and self-pity. He prided himself on his clear-up record and his steady, calm approach to major crimes, so why was this one overwhelming him?

He stood for a few more minutes, his brain filled with a million thoughts. He shook them all off and walked back to the scene. He'd had his moment of self-pity. *It was time to catch this bastard.*

Matthew gave a glib statement to the press, covering the usual platitudes about help from the public and how they were working on the assumption that this was another crime by the 'devil killer' as the press were now calling him.

He left the team to process the scene, instructing Louise to get them back at 5pm for a debrief. He walked back to the station but got railroaded by the sights and smells of his local. He needed a pint.

*

Joshua watched the scene from afar, binoculars trained on the female copper who always seemed to be by McCallum's side. She was weaving in and out of the crowd with her team of detectives. They were taking photos of the crowd.

Interesting. Had they got a decent image from the CCTV and were taking photos for comparison purposes? Joshua was impressed. He could tell McCallum was a hard-working copper, but he had a feeling his sidekick might be the real brains and brawn in his unit. He kept the binoculars trained on her. She was quite pretty but had that slightly worn look from too much work and too little sleep. Her expression was serious and determined. He watched her some more.

Eventually she disappeared back under the cordon. He put the binoculars back in his bag and hobbled away. "We'll meet soon, young lady," he said quietly.

*

The pint, consumed with a plate of pie and chips, had restored Matthew's mojo. It was a little after 2pm, a few hours before his team were due back, probably with another overwhelming list of clues and theories. He agonised over whether they were missing something obvious. Was there a critical clue that would crack this case that was being lost in the volume of investigative tasks and the speed of the crimes?

He mused on the prof's theories and Caroline's endorsement of them. She was sure this guy was a loner, making it harder to find him. If he had limited social interaction, he was not likely to come to many people's attention. The religious aspect was now pretty solid, and he wondered where this guy was fulfilling his spiritual needs. Some of the team were scouring the local churches, hoping that one of the priests would immediately identify their perp. Someone with extreme religious views. Someone that took the teachings of God to a different place than the norm.

He sighed. What was he doing here, eating and drinking while his hard-working team were out there, looking for this bastard? He stood up. He had to get back to the station.

*

Joshua sat across the other side of the pub. He was about to go home when McCallum had inexplicably walked straight past where he had been standing, leaning against a tree, watching the aftermath of his latest handiwork. He was intrigued. He was slow, hobbling along the street behind him, but was surprised when McCallum quickly turned into the doorway of a pub.

He followed him inside and made for the far corner. He ordered some food and a pint of coke. He watched as McCallum wolfed down a plate of food and a pint of bitter. His facial expressions amused Joshua. You could almost see the cogs whirring in his head and the steam coming out of his ears. Trying to work out who Joshua was and what he was going to do next.

28

The briefing started. Matthew could sense a palpable energy in the room. He hoped it was a good sign.

"Right, team, I don't need to tell you that this latest crime has cranked up the pressure on all of us. We now have international scrutiny on this, not helped by the bastard press giving him a nickname of the 'Edinburgh Devil Killer'. The chief constable is fielding enquiries from far and wide, not least from the good citizens of Edinburgh who are now frightened to go out. So, Sherlock, can we start with an update on the forensics around today's scene?"

"Yes, sir. As we expected there were minimal forensic clues due to the fire and water around the incident. We have managed to ascertain that the bomb was a crude improvised explosive device, that was remotely detonated by a mobile phone. Unfortunately, the construction of the device is surprisingly simple and the instructions of how to do this are freely available on the dark web. The wheelchair was mostly burnt out, but there was enough of the seat back left unscathed to confirm that it was the same one that was seen on CCTV at the civic centre incident, with the devil symbol on the back. It seems as though the perp deliberately left it in the blast radius to eradicate any forensic clues. This guy clearly knows his stuff when it comes to forensic countermeasures."

"What about the man in the car?"

"Well, the ME is trying to do an autopsy on what is left of the corpse, but DVLA records have the car registered to a Graham Randolph. He is sixty-three, a retired headteacher from one of the secondary schools in central Edinburgh. We are hoping that, if nothing else, dental records will confirm his identity."

"What about the other victims, DS Cookson?"

"Three women and one man. Formal identification is still taking place, but we are working on the assumption that the victim in the car was the intended target, and these others are just collateral damage."

Matthew turned to Caroline. "Any theories?"

"Well, firstly the wheelchair at the scene seems to be the perp's way of making sure we know it is his work. I agree with Louise that the other victims are collateral damage, which suggests this murder was somehow more personal. I think we need to look into the background of the victim in the car to see if we can make any links. It's going to need some more leg work."

Matthew shook his head, looking around the room. "This is not good. We seem to be grasping at straws here. Please tell me we have something more to go on."

DC Harry McDonald raised his hand. Matthew nodded for him to carry on.

"Sir, I've been leading on the investigations around the original profiling work that Caroline has done. As you know we drew a blank around the people that are part of Joseph Anderson's care team and also found nothing in respect of recent assault victims. Discussions with the clergy from all the local churches has also drawn a blank."

Matthew sighed. "I do hope you telling me all the things you haven't found is leading up to something you have found."

Harry smiled. "Oh aye, sir. We have three good matches to the profile, who are relatives of recently deceased individuals. All three cases could reasonably be described as traumatic."

"Go on."

"Firstly, we have an Alexander McNeil, age thirty-two from East Pilton. He recently lost his wee five-year-old daughter to leukaemia. He's estranged from his wife, living alone in a crappy bedsit. Initial inquiries suggest he rarely saw the young lassie but will undoubtedly have been affected by her death. Critically he's an ex-army veteran who lost one of his legs and uses a wheelchair to get around. Secondly, we have a Joshua Billington, age thirty-five from central Edinburgh. He was involved in a serious road accident out on the A71, late at night a few weeks ago. He was badly injured, but his maw was killed. It seems he lived with her and has limited social interactions, not working and living off benefits. According to hospital records, he was issued with crutches and a wheelchair due to his leg injuries. Lastly, we have a Hamish Dungannon, age thirty-six from Musselburgh. He lost his sixteen-year-old son in a climbing accident. Seems they were avid rock climbers but had an accident when some of their equipment failed. The laddie fell to his death, but the father survived. Again, he has injuries that placed him in a wheelchair. There is also no maw on the scene and no other bairns."

As Harry's update drifted to a conclusion, the team of detectives began to talk about what they were hearing. Matthew stood there for a moment, taking it all in.

"Wow. That's good work. Might we finally have some solid lines of inquiry? What do you think, Caroline?"

"Well, I've been through the three cases with DC McDonald and the circumstances certainly match the profile, but I would need to meet each one to see if they exhibit the traits of our psychopath. Crucially, if my profiling about today's incident is right, we can see if any of these suspects have links with today's victim."

"OK, but do you think it's feasible that each of these traumas could trigger the sort of mass murder that we are seeing?"

"It has to be possible. Someone with inherently psychopathic tendencies is very susceptible to traumatic triggers and could certainly act irrationally as a response to a loss of a loved one. The army vet could very well have PTSD; losing his leg and the death of his only child would be a powerful trigger. The same could be applied to the rock climber if his whole world revolved around his son. As for the guy living with his mother, I could only see this being viable if he had some strong bond with her, making her death the type of traumatic trigger incident we have been talking about."

Matthew shook his head. "I dunno. Whilst I can see that all three of these men have had traumatic episodes, I can't see why it would trigger the kind of mass murder we are seeing here. It seems so out of proportion."

"Well, yes, therein lies the point. To us, these acts seem entirely irrational, but we are sure that we have someone who is mentally unstable, not operating within normal societal boundaries, who could quite possibly interpret their recent trauma as a grave injustice. It's like they are raging against society, seeking revenge for the perceived injustice. The simple truth is that we need to bring each of these men in and profile them further to see if our theories fit."

As the murmuring in the room restarted, Matthew was distracted by a text notification. He clicked on the message. As he looked at the picture, he grabbed the chair he was standing next to, steadying himself against the shock of what he was looking at. *What the hell is this?*

29

Joshua stood gingerly by the wardrobe in his mother's bedroom. His left leg was still painful, and he leant on the crutch to ease his suffering. He could almost hear his mother preaching about his injuries. She would say it was God's way of reminding him about his sins. Necessary reparations to save his soul and seek God's forgiveness.

He opened the wardrobe door and pulled one of her dresses towards him. He put it up to his face and breathed in deeply. He could still smell her. That weird combination of talcum powder and lavender. His journey was going to take him to her. To her place of salvation. A heaven that he didn't really understand or believe in, but the only place he could be now she was gone.

He rifled through the rest of the clothes in her wardrobe, the touch and smell of each one increasing the pain in his heart. He shook his head. He was so confused. She was his world. She loved him beyond all others, had looked after him, patched him up when he was hurt and kept him going. However, the more time he had to reflect on his life, the more he thought about the darkness in her. The religious obsession, the punishments she meted out in the name of her God, the weird touching and caressing.

Somewhere in his confused mind, he knew these things were wrong, but he had no one else. He never knew his father. It had been just her from day one.

He wiped away the tears and moved to the chest of drawers. He opened up the top drawer. It was full of her bras and knickers. A coldness washed over him. Memories of darker times triggered by the sight of her underwear. He leant heavily on the crutch.

As he stood there, trying to shake the dark images now flowing through his mind, the doorbell rang.

*

Matthew sat in the interview room waiting for his team to bring in one of the three suspects. Since he received the text message with the photo of him in the pub, he had been like a bear with a sore head. Louise and Caroline, in particular, had noticed his agitation, but all their enquiries about what was wrong were met with a short, glib response and instructions to get on with their work.

He couldn't help it. He was so embarrassed. To be photographed eating and drinking in the middle of the day while his team were hard at work dealing with the latest atrocity, shamed him more than he cared to admit. That the perp was sitting in the same pub, watching him do it was beyond anything he could process. How could he have been so stupid, so unaware of his surroundings and the people around him. He was a detective, for fuck's sake. Trained to be ever vigilant.

He just couldn't bring himself to tell them. He knew

it would have to come out at some point but for now he needed to wallow in his self-persecution.

The team had been tasked to go to the addresses of the three suspects and bring them in for questioning. He would just have to get over himself and focus on finding this bastard. Maybe, somewhere in this shitstorm he could use the photo to his advantage.

Suddenly the door opened. Caroline and Harry walked in with Alexander McNeil, the army veteran.

*

Joshua slowly opened the door. The woman copper was stood there with a uniformed officer. He had expected this day to come. It was, after all, part of his plan, but he was a little surprised that it had happened so quickly.

Joshua fixed his gaze on the visitors. "Detective Sergeant Louise Cookson and… who might you be?"

He tried to suppress a smile as he looked at Louise's shocked face.

"Er… yes I'm Detective Sergeant Cookson and this is PC Jeffrey Davis,' she stuttered. "I'm curious. How do you know who I am?"

"You're all over the news, DS Cookson. I've been following the 'Edinburgh Devil Killer' story with some interest. You and DCI McCallum seem to be floundering around in your attempts to catch this man."

Joshua could see the involuntarily wince in her expression.

"Can we come in please, Mr Billington?"

"Of course."

"Where's your wheelchair?"

Joshua eyed her curiously. He had been right. She was sharp and intelligent. Like that cat in *Hong Kong Phooey* who always cleared the crimes up for their hapless boss.

"Oh, it's gone back to the hospital. They picked it up a couple of days ago. My recovery has been much better the last few days, and I can cope with just the crutches and my stick."

"The hospital will be able to verify that, will they?"

Joshua smiled. "I rather think that's up to you to find out. Now, can I ask what you want from me? I'm sure you are not here just to track down errant wheelchairs... are you?"

He noticed the flicker of annoyance in Louise's face. She might be a good copper, but he realised already that her involuntary facial expressions gave away what she was thinking. He looked at her expectantly.

"We'd like you to come down to the police station with us, Mr Billington, to answer some questions."

"Oh really? Am I under arrest?"

"Not at this stage, but you are a person of interest in this case."

Joshua let out a booming laugh. "A person of interest. What a quaint way of putting it. I'm guessing you don't have a shred of evidence against me, otherwise you would be arresting me."

"We would appreciate your co-operation."

Joshua stared at her, ramping up the tension in the room. She held a firm expression as he tried to intimidate her with the silence. Eventually he relented. "Will I meet the infamous Detective Chief Inspector Matthew McCallum?"

"Yes, he's waiting to speak to you."
He smiled inwardly and followed her out of the door.

30

Matthew and Caroline had just finished their interview with Alexander McNeil when Louise entered the interview room. She could immediately tell from Matthew's facial expression that he had a lot on his mind.

"How did it go, sir?"

Matthew drew in a sharp breath. "He's not our man. He's had a major trauma in his life with the death of his daughter but everything else about him checks out, including some seemingly cast-iron alibis for two of the murder dates that the team are checking as we speak."

"Oh. Erm..."

"What is it? Spit it out. I'm not in any frame of mind for you to pussy-foot around me today."

Louise tried to hide her shock at the outburst, flashing a surprised look at Caroline, who just rolled her eyes.

"I'm sorry, sir, it's just that we have Joshua Billington in interview room two but a brief from the procreator fiscal has just turned up unannounced. They want to speak you about Joseph Anderson's case."

There was silence. Matthew had his face down. Louise looked at Caroline. Did he hear what she had said? Was he about to blow up? She risked a nudge.

"Sir, are you OK?"

More silence.

Just as Louise was about to speak again, Matthew stood up and walked out of the interview room without another word.

Louise followed his progress open mouthed, turning back to Caroline as he stormed out of the door. "What the hell was that all about?"

"I don't know, but he is particularly grumpy this morning. Something's happened that's got him really stressed, but he won't talk about it. I'm pretty sure he got a text message at the end of the briefing yesterday which has shit him up. He's been weird ever since."

"Bloody hell. What was he like with our first suspect?"

"He was alright. Did the usual, but you could tell he was preoccupied about something."

Louise shook her head. "What the hell am I supposed to do now? I've got our second suspect ready to interview and a bloody jobsworth from the PF insisting they speak to him."

"You know where he goes when he needs to de-stress."

Louise nodded. "Oh aye. I'd better go and see if I can find him."

Louise ran down the stairs to the back door of the station that led into the yard. As she went outside and turned the corner, he was there. Smoking a cigar. He glanced up at her. "I'm sorry. It's all rather getting to me at the moment."

"Is there something I can do, sir?"

Matthew let out a pitying laugh. "No. This is one I can't lean on you to sort out."

Louise pulled a quizzical expression, which Matthew chose to ignore.

He stubbed out the cigar tab under his foot. "Come on. Let's nip in to see our Mr Billington and apologise for the delay in seeing him. Then, let's get rid of the PF as quickly as we can."

*

Joshua sat in the interview room, his breathing shallow and relaxed. His plan was working but he could feel the nervous tension as he waited expectantly for McCallum. This next conversation was going to be key. He had to see if McCallum was worthy of his time. He needed a worthy adversary, someone that understood his story and his ultimate destination. He knew his life had little meaning without his mother, but he had to exit this world with someone taking notice. The murders were only part of it, necessary steps to complete his journey, but it would be worthless if he couldn't get the attention he deserved. He had to be big news, a legend, a name that people referred to with frightened reverence. He closed his eyes and breathed deeply. *Why am I sitting here waiting?*

A few minutes later the door opened and the face which was on a piece of paper on his desk with a letter opener between his eyes, greeted him with a curt, stressed expression.

"Mr Billington, I'm DCI McCallum. I'm really sorry but I wonder if I could just ask you to wait a bit longer. An urgent issue has arisen that I just need to deal with. I'll be as quick as I can."

Without a second to respond, Joshua sat, staring at the door to the interview room. His rage began to build.

*

Matthew hardly had time to sit down before the brief from the PF launched in.

"I don't appreciate being kept waiting, DCI McCallum."

Matthew bit his tongue. Melanie Chambers was a notoriously difficult individual to deal with at the PF's office and he knew it would do him no favours in all future interactions if he blew up now.

"What can I do for you, Ms Chambers?"

"This case file your team has submitted."

"What about it?"

"Do you really think the PF is going to support a murder charge, given the tragic circumstances surrounding this young man?"

Matthew shot a glance at Louise, who remained stony faced.

"Joseph Anderson killed three people and could have killed many more at the community centre if the fire service had not done such a good job. His crimes were violent, with no mercy."

"That's as may be, but I understand you think he was instructed to do these crimes by another person, via an earpiece you found on his person."

"That's right, and we have a suspect in the building as we speak, who we believe could be the mastermind behind these crimes."

Melanie flicked through the file. "The consultant psychiatrist report states that Joseph has a dissociative disorder that means he does not understand his actions and is vulnerable to suggestion."

"I believe so."

Melanie looked straight at Matthew and shook her head. "Are you deluded, DCI McCallum? If I allowed this file to go to prosecution, you would be laughed out of court within a few minutes. No jury in the land is going to convict this man of murder under these circumstances."

With that Melanie stood up. "Your case file is rejected. I would advise you to put together a file that seeks the retention of Joseph Anderson in a secure mental health facility on an indefinite basis because, trust me, that is the only thing you will get against this poor boy."

Matthew said no more as he watched Melanie storm out of the room. He closed his eyes for a second before suddenly standing up, the noise of the chair scraping on the floor making Louise jump.

"Come on. Let's nail this bastard."

They walked along the corridor, back towards interview room two. Matthew was trying to calm his mood, hoping that this suspect would be the big break he was looking for. As he opened the door, his day just got a bit worse.

Joshua Billington had gone.

31

"Where did he go? Why did you let him out?"

The station duty officer stopped what she was doing and looked around to find the source of the bellowing that had come from behind her. Everyone in the reception area of the station hushed at the interruption and were all looking at the same thing: a red-faced copper who was obviously upset about something.

She looked back to the person she had been dealing with and gave a quiet apology, before turning to face the rage. Gemma Atkins was used to dealing with all sorts of people from stroppy, sometimes violent, members of the public at her front counter to self-important senior cops who thought the world revolved around them. As she approached Matthew, his face seemed to redden further.

"I would appreciate it if you did not barge in here shouting your mouth off and embarrassing yourself in front of the general public."

He lowered the volume, but the anger still spilled out in a gritted-teeth barrage. "How dare you speak to me like that? Do you have any idea what you may have done? You've potentially let out the man that has been masterminding all these murders and now we have no idea where he might be."

Gemma withstood the barrage, unflinching and stony faced. "Was he under arrest?"

She tried to hide her triumphant smile as she saw the cracks appear in Matthew's raging persona. He stuttered over his words. "Well... er... no he wasn't but... er... we were just about to establish his guilt and you've taken that opportunity away."

"He came back to the front desk and said you had been keeping him waiting too long. Said he had things to do. As he wasn't under arrest, I had no option but to let him go."

Just as it seemed Matthew was about to explode into another rant, the door to the duty office opened.

"DCI McCallum. Can I see you upstairs? Now!"

Everyone turned to look at the new person who had entered the room, including all the members of the public who were now watching this spectacle, like some live fly-on-the-wall documentary.

Gemma looked on, glad that the interruption had stopped this going any further and mildly amused as Matthew immediately strode out of the office without another word.

*

"What the hell was that?"

Detective Chief Superintendent James Alexander stood in his office, fixing Matthew with an intimidating stare.

Matthew tried to defend himself. "The front counter let one of our main suspects just walk out of the door. She didn't speak to me or any of my team before she did that. He may be the bloody killer we're after and she's just let him go. Now we are going to have to try and find him again."

"You hadn't placed him under arrest."

"I hadn't had the bloody chance to. That cow, Melanie Chambers from the PF's office, insisted on speaking to me about Joseph Anderson's case file, meaning I was delayed in speaking to him."

James took in a deep breath. "Do you really think your behaviour now and at the front counter is becoming of a senior police officer? I don't care what the circumstances are. You do not go shouting your mouth off in front of the general public and abusing a colleague who is only doing her job. If your bloody rant has been recorded by one of the people in reception and put on YouTube, I'll kick your arse out of this station and off this case, quicker than you can say Heart of Midlothian. Do I make myself clear?"

Matthew bowed his head. "Yes, sir. Of course, sir. I will go and apologise to her immediately and get my team back on the case. Please accept my apologies that you felt the need to do this, sir."

*

Matthew stood outside the super's office for a minute. Crestfallen. The rage had subsided, replaced with a deep sense of shame and an uncharacteristic feeling of panic. He had never known a case to consume him like this. He wasn't sure whether it was the speed this perp was working at, meaning his team were struggling to keep up with the multiple lines of inquiry, or the sense that this man had some hold over him. The surveillance in the pub unnerved him. How long had this man been watching him?

He began to walk slowly back to the front counter, not looking forward to having to apologise to Gemma.

In the end, she took his apology with good grace and Matthew felt humbled at her ability to forgive and forget. As he walked back to the incident room, he got a text message from Louise.

Sir, DC Williams has just brought in Hamish Dungannon. He's in interview room 1.

*

Images flashed in and out of his mind. *Why are you doing that, Mother… it's not right… I can't stop it, Mother, I'm…* He bolted awake, a chill consuming his body. His mother's love had been unconditional, but she had forced him to do those things that didn't seem right. It confused him. She was all fire and damnation whenever he tried to satisfy his sexual desires, but when she had the need… he shivered again.

Joshua was annoyed with himself. He'd fallen asleep in the hotel room he had hastily arranged after leaving the police station. He was surprised at how quick McCallum's team had got onto him, but now the game was afoot, he needed to keep up the pace. He'd grabbed all he needed from his home. It was time to set up the next step in his journey.

He was disappointed in McCallum. Making him wait in that dingy interview room showed a lack of respect. He wanted to spar with him, see how clever he was, but the waiting was intolerable. That moment would have to wait. Joshua had to complete this next step.

As he began to arrange the tools he needed on the bed, the key question remained. Was McCallum worthy of his attention? Would he find him in time? Because it was time for Joshua's destiny to be tested and McCallum was the one who was going to shape it.

32

It was gone 6pm as Matthew sat in his office, mentally exhausted by the events of the day. The interview with Hamish Dungannon had followed the same pattern as the one with Alexander McNeil. A traumatised father, grieving for the loss of a child but not their psychopath. He shook his head at the memory of his bust-up at the front counter. He regretted his behaviour, but his sentiments had been right. It was now clear that Joshua Billington was their prime suspect and he had been allowed to limp out of the station with hardly a whimper.

As he pondered what to do next, Louise and Caroline arrived at his door. He gestured them in.

"What have we got?"

Louise took the lead. "We've got two good bits of progress, sir."

Matthew raised his eyebrows expectantly. "Go on."

"DC McDonald has profiled the victim in the car with Caroline's help."

"The headteacher?"

"Yes, that's right. It seems he was the head of St Barnabas senior school in Edinburgh for nearly twenty-five years and had a fearsome reputation for running his school with an iron fist. There are numerous complaints on file at the local authority about bullying and abuse of students, but he was never charged with anything. Critically, St Barnabas was the school that Joshua Billington attended."

Matthew leant forward, his attention piqued. He looked at Caroline. "What do you make of this?"

"I think this cements my profiling work. It's perfectly feasible that Joshua was one of this man's victims, and it would follow that this man would be high on the list of people that he wanted to seek revenge against. You could also argue that the physical act of blowing his victim up adds more credence to the religious aspects of this case. Fire is very symbolic of the devil's work."

Matthew rubbed his face. "He's got to be our man. This Joshua Billington. Have we found him yet, DS Cookson?"

Louise allowed herself a brief smile. "That's the other hopeful development. Some of the team went over to his flat. He's not there, but the door's open. I told the team not to enter as I imagined you would want to be the one to search his flat."

Matthew stood up. "Too bloody right. Let's go."

*

It didn't take long for Matthew, Caroline and Louise to get to Joshua's place in Cowgate, a small ground-floor flat bordering a park. Harry McDonald was guarding the front door with a uniformed officer.

"Evening, sir."

"What have we got?"

"I arrived about three-quarters of an hour ago. As I went to knock on the door, it pushed inwards. I opened the door fully and called out for Mr Billington, but nae reply. I spoke to one of his neighbours, a Mrs Robertson. She said he popped back earlier but went out with a large rucksack on, within fifteen minutes of arriving. She hasnae seen him since."

"And we can rely on her statement?"

"Oh aye, sir, the old lassie seems like the neighbourhood busybody. She had us clocked the minute we arrived. Peering out of her kitchen window like some elderly guard dog."

"Some respect for our elders please, DC McDonald."

Matthew pushed the door open and called out, not really expecting an answer but keen to follow clear protocols before entering the property. He looked at DS Cookson. "OK, based on the evidence that you have all brought me in the last few hours and Mr Billington's apparent disappearance, I believe we have probable cause to enter and search this property. Do you agree?"

They all nodded and proceeded to enter the property straight into the main living space, with the open-plan kitchenette to the left. Their first impressions were of a clean, ordered house. Nothing seemed to be out of place; there were no empty unwashed plates in the sink, no rubbish strewn around the house. A ridiculously normal setting for someone they suspected was a psychopath. Matthew stopped in the middle of the living room and turned to Caroline. "What do you make of this?"

She frowned. "It does seem an incredibly normal space for someone we suspect has some serious mental issues. Maybe he has a cleaner."

They all scanned the immediate space. Matthew gave the orders. "OK, DC McDonald, can you search the bedrooms, and we will concentrate on this area and what looks like a small study space in the room to the right."

The team dispersed across the small flat as Matthew leafed through a pile of recent post that had been neatly stacked on the coffee table, next to a small leather sofa. There was nothing of interest. As he placed the pile back down, Louise called him from the study space. "Sir, I think you'd better come in here."

Matthew moved quickly to the study and looked at Louise expectantly. She moved to the side to reveal a picture of Matthew staked to the desk with a letter opener. Sellotaped to the handle of the letter opener was a note. Matthew walked over to the 'exhibit' and looked at the note. His heart sank.

33

The takeaway pizza Joshua had ordered was now a distant memory as he sat on the lovely soft double bed in his small but adequate hotel room. Everything was set for his next step. Whilst everything was in place for all the final steps of his journey, this next step was risky. He was relying on McCallum's intelligence and guile to find him in time. If he didn't, Joshua would be dead and his chance to tell his story would be gone.

He kept an eye on his laptop. Waiting, hoping that they would find his message. Within a few minutes he got his wish. The small surveillance cameras he had placed across the flat were now recording the 'home invasion'. DCI McCallum, DS Cookson, the other woman he'd seen outside the civic centre and a rough-looking detective, were entering his flat. He watched as they stood in the middle of the living room, scanning the immediate area. Joshua licked his lips. *Come on McCallum, go to the study*.

As it was, the *Hong Kong Phooey* cat was at it again. DS Cookson sniffing out the clues like she always did. She'd found it and called him in. Joshua leant forward as he switched to the camera that was attached to the lamp in his study, waiting for the moment McCallum read his note. He began to laugh, louder and louder as McCallum looked at the note and frowned. Every word he read making him more and more distressed. Beautiful.

*

Matthew ripped the note off the handle of the letter opener and began to read the words of a psychopath.

Hello DCI McCallum,

If you are reading this, I'm guessing you are now certain that I'm your so-called criminal mastermind. The 'Edinburgh Devil Killer' as the press have so nicely labelled me. My story is important, Matthew. It needs to be heard, and every bit of press coverage helps me to complete my journey to salvation. The journey to be with the only person that ever loved me. My mother. The person who was cruelly taken away from me before her time, which means the sinners have to die. If her God thought it was right that I should be left alone, lonelier and more devoid of positive human contact than I've ever been, then people have to pay.

You see, I am a lover of classic poetry, and there is one poem that has always engaged me. When Mother died, I realised why. It was shaping my destiny. It was telling me what to do in these circumstances, a map to reach my ultimate goal. To be with Mother in her heaven. The journey is hard, Matthew. There are many circles to navigate, each one full of sinners that need to be punished. I'm guessing you haven't worked it out yet. The Devil's Code.

The thing is, you need to prove to me that you are a worthy adversary. I've studied you for a long time and you seem like a cultured, educated man. Not like many of those other bumbling coppers around you, although I think your DS Cookson may be as sharp a cookie as you.

So, I'm going to give you a clue. My mother expected me to love her God, to worship her God, to live a Christian life, but I just can't, Matthew. I reject everything about her God. They call me a heretic, which means I am on step six in my journey. It's time for my punishment.

You have to find me by midnight, or I will die, and you will have failed your part in my journey. To allow me to tell you the full story. I will be lit up like a beacon in a place where the devil has been. A hill that watches over us all. Please don't let me down, Matthew.

Joshua Billington

P.S. If you are struggling, why don't you ask your friend, the professor.

Matthew sat down on the desk chair, his hand over his mouth, every word haunting him. He passed it to Louise as Caroline joined them.

"What is it, sir?"

"You'd better read that after DS Cookson, Caroline. We need to act fast."

They read it.

Caroline reacted first. "My God… oh sorry, probably not the best use of words at this stage but… bloody hell, this guy has some front."

Matthew stood up. "Look, we need to move fast. He's playing a game with us, but I have to take his threat

143

seriously. If he plans to kill himself at midnight, we will lose everything. I'm not going to let this bastard win this stupid game. We need a plan, so give me your immediate thoughts."

Caroline continued to take the lead and poured out her thoughts. "I'm not sure there's much else to say about the note. He's laid it all out. The trigger of his mother's death, the loneliness and sadness I profiled, the religious aspects and his apparent rejection of his mother's beliefs, and the need for someone to finally take notice of him before he dies. That last bit is worrying because he seems to accept death as the ultimate goal of this game he is playing, meaning he will have no natural survival instinct. I don't know what he means about a classic poem, circles or why killing sinners seems to be part of the journey to his death, but if nothing else it shows a very disturbed young man who has no compunction to want to live. The important thing, sir, is that he desperately wants you to hear and be part of his story. The change to using your first name is a deliberate step to a greater level of intimacy. Whether you like it or not, he sees you as a vital cog in his final days."

Matthew listened as Caroline blurted out everything on her mind, hardly taking a breath between sentences. When she finished, he said nothing, shifting his gaze to Louise. She picked up on the non-verbal request to give her opinion.

"I dunno what to say, sir. How are we supposed to find in him less than five hours? The only clue is a hill in Edinburgh. I mean for feck's sake, there are hills all over Edinburgh. We just don't have the manpower to go blindly searching every goddam hill, especially in the dark."

Matthew rubbed his face again. "What about the helicopter?"

"I can try, sir, but as you know they cover a wide area, and we may struggle if they are deployed to other jobs."

"Make the call, and tell them that it's their top priority. Get every resource you can and start deploying them in 4x4s to as many of the high points near Edinburgh centre as you can. If he plans to set fire to something, or even himself, maybe we will get lucky, and it will guide us to him. I want you to silver command this while I go and see the professor. I don't know what he's got to do with this, but I can't leave any stone unturned. Keep me up to date on the radio please."

Louise jumped into action, leaving Caroline and Matthew staring at the note. "Come with me. If the professor has some insight into this situation, I'd like you to hear it as well."

"Of course, sir."

As they left the study, Harry McDonald re-emerged from the bedrooms. "DC McDonald. I want you to bag up anything useful you can find. Get his laptop, the note, some DNA samples from his and the mother's belongings and anything else you think might be useful. Get Sherlock over here ASAP to pick this stuff up and then go and join DS Cookson."

Matthew's adrenalin was flowing. The panic had been replaced by a sense of focus. He was ready to meet this psychopath.

34

Joshua watched and listened in with absolute glee. The race was on. The helicopter was an interesting development, and he would have to think about how to avoid detection, at least until he was ready. It was just past 7pm and the light was fading outside. He shut down his laptop, snuggled down in his bed and closed his eyes. He only needed an hour to set up his little performance, which meant he had around four hours to rest. He smiled as he thought about DS Cookson and her merry band of coppers searching the hills of Edinburgh while he was safely tucked up in bed. He let out a deep breath and fell asleep.

*

Matthew and Caroline raced on foot towards the University of Edinburgh, which was mercifully close to where they had just been. As they reached the porter's lodge, Matthew took a minute to catch his breath. The porter looked on with mild amusement as he waited for this strange, sweaty man to get enough breath to say something.

Matthew pulled out his badge. "I'm DCI McCallum. I need to see Professor Roger Mountfield urgently."

The porter picked up the phone and dialled his apartment. No answer. "I'm sorry, sir, he isn't in his accommodation, but I can definitely confirm that he is on campus, as he hasn't signed out with me."

"Can I go and search for him? It's urgent."

The porter nodded and let them through the gate. They rushed towards the far corner of the quad and up two flights of stairs to the professor's apartment. They rapped on his door several times. The porter was right. He wasn't inside. Matthew's brain went into overdrive. He looked at his watch. "The dining hall. He's probably having supper."

They ran back down the stairs and turned right towards the large ornate building that housed the dining hall. Matthew had been inside many times, but today he only had one objective. To find the professor.

They burst through the door, garnering a number of disapproving looks from the numerous academics who were milling around. They slowed down and walked purposefully towards the entrance to the dining hall. Matthew stood in the doorway and scanned the room. The professors generally ate on the higher tables, but as he looked along the line, the professor wasn't there. He spun round, taking a left towards the bar, Caroline trying to keep up with the manic pace of Matthew's search. He wasn't in the bar. Matthew picked up his phone and dialled his mobile. Voicemail. He drew a hand through his hair. "Shite. Where is he?"

*

Louise managed to procure three 4x4s. The detective team and a few uniformed officers she had begged and borrowed off the duty inspector were now bundling into the vehicles. She was in one, Harry McDonald in another and Morag Williams in the last. Louise dished out the orders.

"Right, keep comms on the open frequency and report anything you see to me immediately. Morag, can your team search around the castle, Calton Hill and the Royal Terrace. Harry, can your team do the southern edge of the Crags and Holyrood and I'll do the northern side. I'm just about to speak to NPAS about the helicopter so will let you know as soon as they are in our area to help."

The vehicles dispersed to their designated search areas as Louise got on the phone to the National Police Air Service. After a tense conversation with their control room, she got a deployment, but it was going to be at least an hour and a half before they could be in the area. She radioed the information out as the searching began.

*

Matthew was walking aimlessly around the university campus, trying to think where else the professor could be, when he heard Louise's update.

"Crap, it's gonna be past 9pm by the time the helicopter can be here, and if I can't locate the professor to find out what he knows about this, we're knackered."

Without Louise doing her usual calm sidekick role, Caroline knew she had to step up. "Look, sir, if the helicopter arrives at that time, it still gives them nearly three hours to search. It sounds like Louise and the team are deployed and the professor can't have gone far. Let's go back to the porter's lodge and see if he has any idea where else he might be."

Despite the growing coolness of the night, Matthew was still sweating from his exertions. He took a lungful of the crisp evening air and closed his eyes for a moment. "You're right. We have to keep going. We're gonna find this bastard if it's the last thing we do."

*

Louise scanned the area with powerful torches as they drove along Queens Drive and then up through Holyrood Park. As they reached a higher point they parked up and started to search in a grid pattern, regularly stumbling over uneven ground. When she tripped for the umpteenth time, she cursed under her breath. *Shite, this is ridiculous. We're never gonna find him like this.* She radioed her team to get back to the 4x4 so they could move on to the next spot. She checked in with Morag and Harry. Nothing and no one had been spotted.

*

Matthew was growing more impatient as he waited for the porter to make a series of phone calls around the university, trying to locate the professor. Just as he was about to lose all patience, a familiar voice came from behind him.

"Matthew, my dear boy. What are you doing here?"

Matthew turned. The professor. "Where have you been? We've been looking all over for you for nearly an hour."

The professor looked confused. "Really? What's up? I've just been out for my evening constitutional. Such a lovely, crisp evening."

Before Matthew could say anything else, the porter interjected. "Professor, you really need to make sure you sign out with me at the lodge if you are leaving the campus. If there was a fire, we would have thought you were still on site and could have spent hours trying to find you."

The professor waved a dismissive hand. "Oh, Trevor, I'm sorry about that, but you know how absent-minded I can be sometimes."

Matthew couldn't believe what he was seeing. He was a few hours away from disaster and these two were having a debate about bloody fire procedures. "Look, I'm sorry to cut across this guys, but I need to speak to you urgently. We don't have much time."

The professor grunted a few conciliatory tones at the porter and started to walk into the grounds with Matthew and Caroline. "OK, what's got you all stirred up?"

"What do you know about a Joshua Billington?"

The professor immediately stopped walking. His breathing suddenly became heavy, and he leant on the railing that skirted the path. Matthew and Caroline crowded round him. "Prof, are you OK?"

They waited, letting the professor control his breathing. Eventually, he recovered his composure and looked at them both, fear on his face. "I never in all my days thought I would hear that name again."

35

Another fifteen minutes had passed by the time Matthew and Caroline had helped the professor up the stairs to his apartment and sat him down in his favourite armchair with a stiff brandy.

"Look, I didn't mean to upset you, but we are pretty sure that Joshua Billington is the person responsible for all these killings, and we need to find him by midnight or we think he is going to kill himself. I have to stop him doing that. I'm not going to let him take the easy way out of this horror show."

The professor took a couple of sips of the brandy before speaking. "I can't say I'm really surprised. That boy is seriously disturbed, and his mother is just as bad. We had so many run-ins with her about Joshua's behaviour on campus. He kept acting really oddly, wrote the most disturbing essays and generally made people uneasy around him. Every time we warned him about his behaviour, his mother would be on our doorstep berating us for not understanding how special her son was."

"Was he one of your students?"

"Yes, he was a classics undergraduate. Academically he was exceptional. Came to us as a straight A student

151

from one of the local state schools. The university snapped him up with grades like that. The problem was that he has some serious mental health issues and had a disturbing way of bringing his madness into his writing. The final straw was his dissertation. It was the most disturbing thing I think I have ever read. He was expelled from the university as a result."

"What was it about?"

"Dante's Inferno. You know, the first part of the 'Divine Comedy'? I mean it was…" the professor stopped and gasped. "…oh my, how could I be so stupid? How did I not see it when you asked me about your case and all the devil symbology? …Oh Lord, Joshua's playing out his interpretation of Dante's Inferno for real."

"What?"

"Don't you see? I was wrong about the seven deadly sins. There are some similarities but the killings he's been committing match the circles in the Inferno. The first circle is limbo, which must be your fitness man, the second is lust, which is the girl and the third is gluttony, which is the people at that slimming club."

"OK, but what about the bankers and this recent explosion?"

"As I originally said, the bankers are the manifestation of greed, the fourth circle in the poem. As for the explosion, it must somehow represent anger, the fifth circle."

Caroline had been quiet all this time, fascinated by the exchange, but as she listened to the professor's theories, the reason for the fifth batch of killings struck her. "It's the headmaster. I think Joshua was punishing him for the anger that he displayed as Head and the culture of bullying and abuse he allowed to fester in the school. Joshua was a victim of this."

They both looked at her, the prof downing the last of his brandy and nodding sagely. "I think you are right, young lady. His mind would definitely work that way."

Matthew carried on. "Tell me more about his dissertation. It might help us to better understand his madness."

"Well, Dante's Inferno is quite rightly seen as a classic. It is a very complex piece which leads to a wide range of interpretations about the core meaning of the poem."

"But not the one Joshua gave?"

"No indeed. The basics are that the poem describes Dante's journey through the nine circles of hell, which he has to navigate to meet his dead love Beatrice in heaven. Beatrice sends a character called Virgil to guide him through the circles and keep him safe. Dante meets sinners in each circle, that are characterised by the actions we have already talked about, like lust and greed. By the time he finishes the journey he has a far greater appreciation of hell as a spiritual realm. The key point is that Dante feels great pity for the people trapped in hell. There isn't any suggestion that Dante feels the need to kill the sinners. In fact, many people see this as a poem about true love, as he travels towards a reunion with Beatrice."

"So, Joshua's interpretation was the antithesis of this?"

"Correct. The writing was dark and disturbing. He believed that the poem was a mantra that all sinners should be killed. It felt to me like an extreme religious interpretation of the poem, no doubt fuelled by his

153

mother, who was what some might call a religious nutcase."

"Well, his mother's dead. Killed in a car accident. We think this may be the trigger for his actions."

The professor's hand began to shake. "No doubt. Their relationship was... well, odd."

Matthew and Caroline were transfixed and urged the professor to carry on, refilling his glass as encouragement, trying to settle his nerves.

"Joshua described his interpretation of each step in graphic detail, as it related to the murder of sinners. I remember him talking about watching sinners hang, his interpretation of limbo, which now makes sense as to why he killed your fitness man in this way. He wrote about raping and murdering women, burning people, revelling in the joy of watching their flesh melting and... my word, it was all so horrible."

"Do you still have the dissertation? It might help Caroline's work if she could read it all."

The professor's mind was racing. "I don't know. It was about fifteen years ago. I don't know whether we would have kept..."

The professor once again put his hand to his mouth. "Oh, my word. Do you know how old Joshua is?"

Matthew looked at Caroline. "He's thirty-five. Is that relevant?" she said.

The professor's hand began to shake again as he tried to refill his brandy glass. He gave up and put the bottle down, shutting his eyes and pushing his head back into the chair. Matthew and Caroline looked at each other, not knowing what to do. Matthew looked at his watch.

It was fast approaching 9pm, and they were running out of time.

Eventually, the professor opened his eyes and looked back at them both. "I'm sorry. This is all a bit overwhelming. I can't believe that this disturbed man is actually playing this out in real life."

Matthew asked the obvious question. "What's his age got to do with it? Why has that upset you so much?"

"Dante was thirty-five years old when he undertook his journey. In all his mental turmoil, I can imagine that Joshua saw this as the ultimate vindication of his actions. To be the same age as Dante when this happened in his life must have been such a powerful trigger for him."

Matthew had resisted the urge to show the professor the note. He wanted to get as much out of the professor before he gave it to him, not wanting the rantings of a madman to cloud his judgement. But, now, he knew it was time.

"What about this? He left it for me."

The professor refilled his glass and read the note, a look of resignation spreading across his face as he took in each line. "*The Devil's Code*. Is that what he's calling this madness?"

He took a sip of brandy. "His love for his mother is not in doubt and I can confirm that in all my interactions with them both, there was an unsettling bond between them. Funnily enough, it actually reminded me a bit of Hitchcock's *Psycho*, because of the way he and his mother seemed like one symbiotic entity. As I said, I knew she was religious, regularly quoting the Bible at me when she felt we had wronged her son. His rejection of her beliefs is a surprise, but it does at least fit with the sixth circle... heresy, as he states here."

"OK, yes I can see that," said Matthew.

"The big problem I see with this note and his apparent intention to kill himself, if you don't find him in time, is that there are still three steps in the poem. Three circles still to navigate. Violence, fraud and treachery. If he kills himself tonight, he hasn't finished the journey. Whilst he is a disturbed young man, he seems dedicated to using this poem as a guide to his version of salvation, which must end with him meeting his mother in heaven. If he kills himself tonight, that won't happen. It just doesn't make sense."

Matthew reached for a spare glass and poured a brandy, gesturing for Caroline to follow suit. She politely refused.

"This is so messed up, but we have to find him. Can you shed any light on the clues as to where he is?"

"No, I'm afraid not. As far as I know, there are no hills in Edinburgh associated with the devil."

As Matthew savoured the calming effect of the brandy and Caroline frantically scribbled notes on everything that the professor was saying, the silence was broken by Matthew's phone ringing.

"McCallum."

As he listened to the voice on the end of his phone, his expression grew darker, and he shook his head as the implications of what he was hearing sunk in. He disconnected.

Caroline reacted first. "What is it, sir?"

"That was Sherlock. He's at Joshua's house, helping to process the scene. He said they have found surveillance cameras all across the house. Joshua was watching and listening to us when we searched the house. Sherlock is certain that he will have heard all of our operational plans. He knows exactly what we are planning to do to find him."

36

Louise and the rest of the team had been searching for over an hour but had found nothing. It was gone 9.30pm when the helicopter team radioed to say they were in the area. She contacted Matthew to update him. He called them all back to the station, leaving the helicopter to search alone.

It was nearly 10pm by the time they were all back in the incident room at Edinburgh Police Station. Matthew wasted no time in updating the team.

"Right, Caroline and I have just spoken to Professor Roger Mountfield, a classics professor at the university. He's confirmed that Joshua Billington was a student of his, who was expelled from the university for his behaviour. Most disturbingly he wrote graphic, disturbing essays about murder and killing sinners. He is obsessed with Dante's Inferno which describes a journey through the nine circles of hell. Hence the devil symbology he has left at each scene. It seems he has an extreme interpretation of what this poem's message is, which he outlined in his dissertation. The professor is certain that Joshua is using this as a sick and perverted guide to some sort of salvation, that ends with Joshua's death. The most concerning and confusing bit is that he is threatening to kill himself tonight, but this will only complete six of the nine steps. We know this man has serious mental issues, but his actions tonight don't make any sense."

The team listened intently, their expressions growing grimmer as Matthew's update carried on.

"The bottom line is that we need to find him and stop him killing himself. We may not understand the mind of this psycho, but I'm damned if I am going to let him exit this world before we get a chance to interrogate the bastard and hold him to account for his actions."

Matthew's passionate speech was met with a sea of determined faces. He turned to Louise.

"What's the update on the search?"

"We've been out for over an hour in three teams. Morag's team searched the castle, Calton Hill and Royal Terrace areas, Harry's team did the southern edge of the Crags and Holyrood, and my team did the northern edge. We found nothing."

Matthew glanced at his watch. It was just gone 10.15pm. "How long has the helicopter been searching?"

"About forty minutes. I'm in constant contact with them but they haven't spotted anything yet."

Matthew scanned the room. "Does anyone know what this madman is referring to when he says a hill in Edinburgh where the devil has been?" He wasn't pleased by the blank faces staring back at him.

*

Joshua stirred from a relaxing sleep. His journey was nearing the end and a calmness he had rarely experienced in his troubled life was washing over him. He glanced at his watch. It was just past 10.30pm. It was time to move. He put on his thick coat, gloves and woollen hat. He checked he had everything, slinging the full pack onto his back. He went into the bathroom of his hotel room and grabbed the two large bath towels, soaking them in cold water. He put them in a separate bag and walked back into the main part of his hotel room. The weather was holding. It was a dry and crisp evening, the stars bright and powerful as he gazed out of the window. He could hear the sound of a helicopter somewhere in the distance. He smiled and left the room.

He started walking towards his destination, following Queens Lane until he reached the eastern edge of Holyrood Park. Progress was slow as the pain in his legs reminded him of where this had all started. His mobility had improved massively but he still leant on his walking stick to ease some of the residual pain. He glanced up at the hill he needed to climb. It was not going to make the pain any better, but it had to be done.

He passed a few people as he walked, not at all conspicuous to the police helicopter that he had spotted buzzing around. However, as he found the footpath he had been looking for, the one that would take him to the top of Whinny Hill, he knew he would have to start trying to avoid detection. If the helicopter picked up his body heat on the hills, this late in the evening, he knew the game would be up. He got the wet towels out of the bag and draped them over his head and around his shoulders. The coldness hit him immediately and his teeth began to chatter. He steeled himself against the discomfort. He started to walk up the footpath, gritting his teeth against the pain in his legs. He had a weak torchlight navigating his way, as the light from Queens Lane rapidly faded.

The exertion of climbing the hill at least warmed him up against the painful coldness that was now seeping into his skin from the wet towels. The temperature was close to freezing, which was making it much worse. Despite the discomfort, Joshua's inner calm remained. He was suffering for his sins. His mother would approve.

It took half an hour to navigate to the top of Whinny Hill, not helped by the regular slips and stumbles. As he took off his pack, a relief to get the weight off his back, he heard the helicopter approaching. He crouched into a ball and pulled the wet towels over him. The noise of the rotors got closer. He closed his eyes and kept his breathing shallow. The noise intensified. They must be right above him. Had they seen him? Had the wet towels not worked? He stayed still. Eventually the helicopter started to move away. He breathed heavily and removed the towels. It was 11.20pm. It was time to set up his spectacle. Would McCallum find him in time?

*

Matthew sat in the control room, waiting for something to happen. Louise had been in constant contact with the helicopter crew, but nothing had been sighted. He looked at his watch. It was 11.30pm.

He stood up, angry. He grabbed his coat and barked orders at the team. "Right, we can't sit around here doing nothing. Get back out in the 4x4s and start searching again. DS Cookson will tell us the minute the helicopter gets a hit. This madman wants to be found and I'm sure he is going to give us a clue soon. Be alert and be ready. He is not going to win."

The teams leapt into action and bundled outside, jumping into their respective 4x4s. Matthew was with Louise. She checked in with the helicopter but shook her head resignedly at Matthew as the crew once again gave no update.

37

Joshua arranged the wood he had lugged up in his backpack in a circle. He got out a small bottle of petrol and soaked each one. He took out a white sheet, on which he had drawn the image of an inverted pentagram, placing it on one edge of the circle of wood. He placed a small rug in the centre of the wood and sat down cross-legged. He was exposed now. If the helicopter flew over, he would be seen. That was fine. He looked at his watch. Twenty minutes until his fate was decided. Would his journey end today or would McCallum be worthy and help him finish his journey in the way he had intended? He waited five more minutes before setting the wood alight. It lit with a powerful whoosh and Joshua had to shield his eyes from the sudden inferno. The ring of fire was raging around him, but for now he was unharmed. He poured the remainder of the petrol over his coat and waited.

*

Matthew and Louise scanned the darkness, as the powerful searchlight, complemented by the headlights of the 4x4, searched up the northern side of Holyrood Park. There were twelve minutes to go and as Matthew began to curse his luck, two things happened simultaneously.

Firstly, his phone rang. It was the professor. He started speaking as soon as Matthew connected the call, his voice panicked and breathless. "Matthew, Matthew, I've remembered something. The hill in Edinburgh. It's Whinny Hill. They found some artefacts connected to the devil up their last year. It must be where he is referring to."

As Matthew thanked the professor, Louise grabbed his arm urgently as she listened to a message from the helicopter. "Sir, the helicopter has spotted something. A fire has been lit on one of the hills and there seems to be someone sitting in the middle of it."

Matthew's adrenalin response gave him a rush. "Is it on Whinny Hill?"

"Yes, sir. How did you know?"

*

The fire was burning well in a circle around him. The chills he'd experienced, wrapped in the cold wet towels, had gone and small beads of sweat appeared on his forehead as he waited for his fate to be determined. The smell of the petrol on his clothes reminded him that one spark from the fire could ignite him at any second. He looked at his watch.

11.54pm. McCallum was cutting it fine. He turned the lighter over and over in his hand.

As he sat waiting, the police helicopter continued to hover right above him, their powerful searchlight illuminating him like some bolt from the heaven. He snorted at the irony. His mother would no doubt approve.

Joshua looked out beyond the circle of light created by the helicopter. *McCallum must be on his way.* The helicopter must have radioed his position to him. Now it was a case of whether McCallum could reach him in time.

11.58pm. Still no sign. Just the helicopter hovering above. He gripped the lighter a bit tighter. For a moment, Joshua's resolve escaped him. He wanted McCallum to find him. He wanted McCallum to hear his story. He needed McCallum to save him so he could finish his journey in the way he intended.

11.59pm. Joshua watched the second hand on his watch tick round the dial. Fifteen seconds. He sighed. McCallum was not worthy. He had made a mistake in thinking he was a decent adversary. The second hand hit the twelve.

Midnight. He flicked open the lighter.

*

Lactic acid was overwhelming every muscle in his body as Matthew clambered up Whinny Hill beside Louise. The 4x4 had only got them so far. The last section had to be covered on foot. They tried to lead the way with their torches but the effort to climb meant the illumination was sporadic. They stumbled at regular intervals. As they reached the pinnacle, Matthew glanced at his watch. 11.59pm. He could see the light from the helicopter. He was close.

His lungs were burning with the effort, and he stopped for a second, trying to catch his breath as Louise joined him. "Come on, sir. Nearly there," she said. They ran over the pinnacle. A macabre scene greeted them. A man was sitting in the middle of a ring of fire, illuminated by the helicopter searchlight. Matthew suddenly got a second wind as he ran ahead of Louise towards the scene.

As he got within twenty feet, he reeled back as they realised the man had set himself alight. Matthew shielded his eyes against the flames but in a split second he acted.

"No, you don't, you bastard!" he shouted as he ran as fast as he could through the ring of fire, grabbing the man and bundling him out of the other side with a crunching rugby tackle. Matthew tore off his jacket and started to smother the flames that had engulfed the man's petrol-soaked clothing.

Louise joined them, wide-eyed with fear. "What the hell did you do that for?" she shouted at Matthew as they both beat at the flames.

As the flames subsided, the man they could now confirm was Joshua Billington was limp and unconscious. Matthew lay down on the ground. Exhausted. "Get the air ambulance here urgently." With that his eyes closed, and he passed out.

38

His eyes blinked open. A number of concerned faces looked down at him. Doctors and nurses. He shook his head to refocus his vision. Over the left shoulder of one of the medical staff, the reliable face of DS Cookson stared back at him, concern etched into every line in her face. He tried to talk but his mouth was dry and painful. The nurse offered him a sip of water. He swilled it around his mouth as sensations began to return to various parts of his body. As they did so, Matthew realised he had pain running down his right side. The doctor picked up on his pained expression.

"Mr McCallum. Please try to lay still. You have first-degree burns on many parts of your right side. On your face, down your arm and on the upper part of your leg. We have been treating them, but you need to remain as still as you can so as not to agitate the burns."

After a few minutes of checks, the doctors and nurses left the room, leaving Louise staring down at Matthew.

"You stupid, stupid bastard. What the hell were you thinking? You could have got yourself killed."

Matthew tried to smile at Louise but the burns on his face made it hard. He grabbed her hand. "I'm sorry but I wasn't gonna let that psycho take the easy way out. Please tell me he's alive."

Louise nodded. "Yes, sir. He's in a pretty bad way, second- and third-degree burns, but they have managed to treat him and think he will survive. They have him in an induced coma to aid the healing. It's going to be a while before we can speak to him."

Matthew nodded and closed his eyes.

*

"Is he OK?"

Louise jumped at the interruption. She had been staring at her boss's prone figure for... she wasn't sure how long... all the while confused by her reaction. When she saw him entering the inferno engulfing Joshua Billington, she had a fear reaction like none she had ever had. It wasn't a reaction about a colleague. It was a reaction you would have about a family member. Someone you... she hesitated at the thought... someone you loved. Matthew was old enough to be her father and she had never had any romantic stirrings when she was around him. But, as she played the words over in her head, she realised what it was. A father. Hers had abandoned her when she was three. She never knew what happened to him and after a while didn't really care. Her mother and sister had been all she needed growing up and her burgeoning police career kept her busy in her adult life. Despite his grumpy moods and constantly taking her for granted, Louise realised that Matthew was her surrogate father.

"DS Cookson?"

She turned to see the chief superintendent.

"Oh, sorry, sir, I was miles away. This has all come as a bit of a shock."

He smiled sympathetically. "I know. I'm sorry about that. You and the team need to take a few days off. It seems our perp isn't going anywhere for a while and you all need time to process what happened and recharge your batteries. It'll also give this one a chance to get back on his feet."

She gave a weak smile. "Thank you, sir. It has been a while since anyone has had a day off. I'll let everyone know."

*

It was dark as Matthew stirred from a deep sleep. There was a bit of light creeping under the crack in the door to the private room he had been given on the burns unit of Royal Edinburgh Hospital. He had no sense of time, but the darkness told him it must be the middle of the night. He moved slightly but flinched as the pain shot down his right side. He let the pain subside before he tried again. After much effort and gritting his teeth against the pain, he managed to sit up. He had to see him. He had to see the man who had turned his life upside down in such a short time.

He gingerly pulled the covers off and swung his legs so they dangled off the edge of the bed. A pair of plain blue slippers and a paisley dressing gown he didn't recognise were by his bed. *DS Cookson*, he thought to himself. Exactly the sort of practical thinking that had got her where she was today. His legs were unsteady from too much time lying down, but he managed to guide his feet into the slippers and pulled the dressing gown over the thin hospital gown he was wearing. He stood for a minute, letting the blood in his body reacquaint itself with his limbs. He took off the pulse monitor and shuffled towards the door.

He peered out. The nurses' station was down the other end of the ward, helping him to avoid detection on his midnight mission. He looked around. There were other rooms and open ward bays both left and right. He went left, further away from the nurses' station. As he reached the end of the corridor, it bent round to the left. As he adjusted his view, he knew he had found Joshua Billington's room. A police officer was sat outside.

He cursed to himself but was glad that standard protocols were in place to guard the prisoner. He began to walk slowly towards the room. He was about twenty yards away when the officer suddenly noticed his presence and stood up, immediately confronting the strange figure that was limping towards him.

"You can't be down here, sir. It's a restricted area. Can I get one of the nurses to help you to where you need to be?"

Matthew continued to shuffle slowly towards the officer, getting within a few yards before he raised his face up to the officer. "Don't you know who I am?"

The officer's face was etched with confusion. "Er… no, sir. I'm afraid I don't but you can't…"

"I'm Detective Chief Inspector Matthew McCallum and this is my prisoner. I look like this because I had to

170

jump into a fire to stop this psycho from killing himself. Now please move out of my way. I wish to see the man in that room."

The officer had a split second to decide. He hadn't been briefed that a DCI was on the ward and couldn't work out whether this guy was kosher or just some crazy old man who'd got out of his bed. Matthew was relieved when he went for discretion over valour and stepped aside.

Matthew walked in. There was limited light in the room, mostly illuminated by the numerous machines that were humming and beeping, keeping Joshua Billington alive. He moved towards the bed and stared at the face of the man who had made his life a living hell.

He wasn't sure what he was hoping to achieve by watching the gentle rise and fall of Joshua's breathing as he lay in an induced state of unconsciousness. Maybe it was validation that his crazy decision to jump into the fire had been worth it. That the man he had bundled out of the raging inferno was still alive. Joshua had dressings all over his body, trying to heal and protect burns that were far worse than anything Matthew was suffering. He watched for a while but eventually tiredness and the ever-present pain down his right side reminded him that his midnight mission probably wasn't the best idea he'd had.

He left the room. "Thank you, Officer. Please stay alert. This man is responsible for killing lots of people. I don't want anything happening to him until I'm well enough to bring him to justice."

39

TWO DAYS LATER

It was 3am as Dunnie and his boys snorted cocaine off the mirrors strewn across the tables of the pub. The landlord was always ready to accommodate the gang for another lock-in, a combination of protection, the huge amounts of money they spent as a result of their drug dealing and the free coke they threw his way.

The mood was buoyant. The drugs and alcohol removed all inhibitions as the banter played out. Everything from how shit Hearts had played that weekend to how many times they had shagged some tart the previous evening. Mostly bullshit but a camaraderie that Dunnie was fiercely protective of.

Dunnie got his name because he was from Dunfermline, an outsider who had become a big name in Edinburgh from his ruthless approach to anyone who crossed him. He was the king of the drug distribution market in the Leith area of Edinburgh, one of the most deprived areas in the city, ripe for his sort of business. He had moved to Edinburgh to join his cousin who had been the main man for many years. Dunnie took over when his cousin had been taken out by a rival gang. His retribution was swift and decisive, helping him to slip into the main role unopposed. For three years now, he had ruled the roost, taking out every 'have a go Charlie' that tried to muscle in on his business. The police never touched him because he always made sure nothing led back to him. There was always a foot soldier to act as police fodder when the need arose.

Dunnie took a swig of whisky and scanned the room. His six lieutenants sat around him, laughing and joking.

"Oi, oi, oi."

The noise abated. They all looked at Dunnie like spaced-out meerkats.

"Maco, Biff. Woz this I hears about those fucking *faighens* from Newhaven, messing on our patch."

The two most trusted lieutenants stiffened up, trying to shake off the relaxing effects of the drugs and alcohol. Biff spoke first. "Er... I ain't heard nothing, Dunnie. The boys in my area have been dealing well." He looked at Maco, who stuttered a similarly unconvincing response.

He slammed his hand on the nearest table, making them all jump. "Now yoose all listen carefully. I'm hearing that the Newhaven crew has a new top man, and I ain't having him finking he can piss on my patch."

The gang's happy mood had instantly changed with Dunnie's sudden outburst, and they stared wide-eyed, waiting for his commands. His face was full of rage as he left them in no doubt what he wanted.

"Yoose all better get oot there and watch your patches. If there's any suggestion that those boys are trying to

173

muscle in on my business I will deal with this wee problem, quickly and efficiently. Do yoose understand?"

"Yes, Dunnie," they chorused.

They sat, unmoving. "Well go on, then – fucking get out there."

They began to move towards the door of the pub. A second later a huge explosion ripped the door off its hinges. Filing through the door were ten men, tooled up with guns, which were now pointing at Dunnie and his crew.

*

Louise stirred from another solid sleep. The two days she'd had off were a welcome boost to both her physical and mental health. She had not realised how much the case had consumed her and the rest had been just what she needed. Lots of sleep, staying in her pyjamas for long parts of the day, catching up on the TV she normally had no time to watch and ordering in takeaways, had been like a mini holiday.

But now, as she glanced at the time on her phone... 6.30am... the reality of her next scheduled shift loomed large. There was a briefing at the nick at 10am, though she wasn't too sure what she could task out the team to do, given that they had the perp lying unconscious in a hospital bed.

As she ate her toast and caffeined up, she realised that Matthew would be telling them to get all their ducks in a row, making sure every piece of evidence against Joshua Billington was watertight so that the PF didn't knock the case file back.

She washed her breakfast things and got ready. Time to get back in the game.

*

The room of detectives seemed bright and enthusiastic. Everyone had benefitted from the unexpected break. Louise took command, by default. Before she could bring the room to order, Harry McDonald piped up. "How's the gaffer?"

Louise realised that she hadn't even rung the hospital on her two days off, let alone go and see him, immediately feeling guilty for her selfishness. She rode it out. "Oh, fine. He's getting a bit restless, but the doctors say he should be fine. Just needs to rest for a few more days."

The general murmuring at her response soon subsided and the team looked at her expectantly.

"OK, as you know Mr Billington is currently in an induced coma, to aid his recovery from significant burns. If DCI McCallum had not saved him from the fire, our case would be as dead as he would have been. We owe our boss a huge debt of gratitude for leaving us a case we can still prosecute."

Despite Louise feeling like her speech was fawning over Matthew, it was met with appreciative and supportive nods.

"OK, so while we wait for our perp to be ready for questioning, make sure you have all your evidence logged and documented in the case file. Triple check everything. I don't want any reason for a brief to get this bastard off."

Louise's flow was broken by Jed Spencer putting his hand up. She nodded for him to speak. "Ma'am, when will I be able to get DNA and fingerprint samples from our perp? I need to cross reference them with all the samples we picked up at the house."

Louise frowned. "The doctors are not letting us at him until he is awake and coherent. Now, whilst that is frustrating, once again we must do everything by the book."

As Louise was speaking, she could see Jed seemed unusually agitated. "Is that OK, Sherlock?"

"Oh, er… yes, ma'am, it's just that I have processed the DNA at the house and it's leading me to some interesting places, but I'd rather get the confirmation samples before I bring it to you."

Louise looked at him curiously. "OK, mystery man, I'll talk to the doctors when I go and see DCI McCallum later."

She looked around the room. "Anything else?"

Morag put her hand up. "Yes, DC Williams."

"Ma'am, I don't know whether you've seen the major incident logs this morning, but there was a mass shooting in Leith last night. Seems it was part of a dispute about drug distribution. A new crew from Newhaven had been encroaching onto the Leith patch and last night decided to take out the competition. The top man in Leith, Mark Chambers, aka Dunnie, was shot along with six of his gang."

"Why is that of interest in this case?"

"Well, ma'am, the pub that these guys were shot in was their HQ of sorts. It's one of the most notorious and violent places in Leith."

"And?"

"The pub's called The Devil's Hole."

40

Louise decided to walk to the hospital from the station. Despite the lovely rest, a few hours back in the station had brought the stress right back and she was grateful for the fresh spring air. She was joined by Caroline.

"What did you make of that update from Morag?" said Caroline.

"I dunno. We need to be careful not to twitch at every devil connection we see."

"I know, but it's a bit strange."

"It's got to be a coincidence. I mean, our perp is unconscious and being guarded in a hospital bed. He has a cast-iron alibi. Us!"

"Uh huh, but don't forget the first three steps in this sick game he is playing were committed by someone else. What's to say he didn't initiate this before his little November the fifth moment?"

"I don't see it. How is it connected?"

"Well, I remember the professor being confused by his recent actions because he said he still had three steps to go in his journey if he was following this Dante's Inferno thing. The point is, the next circle in the poem is violence."

Louise stopped walking and looked at Caroline. "Oh shite. The pub is one of the most violent places in Edinburgh... jeez, I can't believe it's part of this."

They started to walk again. "OK, but if you want my professional opinion, I think we need to look into it."

They walked the rest of the way in silence. Eventually they arrived at the burns unit and went straight to see whether Joshua Billington was awake. The officer guarding the room immediately stood to attention as Louise and Caroline approached. "The doctor's in there, ma'am."

Louise didn't stand on ceremony and opened the door, earning a disapproving look from the physician as she did so. "What's the update?"

He ignored her for a few seconds, finishing off what he was doing, before turning around, the disapproving look still apparent. "Mr Billington's wounds are healing well but he is still severely burned, and it will be my recommendation that we keep him sedated for a few more days yet."

Louise's patience was running thin, and she barked at the doctor, "This man is responsible for the deaths of nearly twenty people. The sooner you can patch him up and get him ready for our interrogation, the better."

The doctor held firm. "My priority, Detective Sergeant, is to keep this man alive. I'm sorry if that is an inconvenience to you, but that is how it is." With that he pushed past her and walked out of the room.

Louise raised her eyebrows at Caroline. "Someone got out of the wrong side of the bed this morning."

They moved on to Matthew's room and were pleased

to find him drinking a cup of tea and reading the paper. "Ah. Great to see you both."

Louise spoke first. "And you, sir. How are you?"

"Still a bit sore, but the burns were pretty superficial and have healed well. I'll be out tomorrow."

"Really? Is that wise?"

Matthew grunted. "I've never in my life laid about in bed like this and I'm not about to bloody well waste any more time. It's time to nail this bastard."

"He's still sedated, sir."

"What! Why?"

"His burns are much more severe than yours and the doctors are saying they need to keep him under sedation to aid the healing."

"Oh, for God's sake. Get his doctor in here. I'll speak to him."

Caroline interjected. "The doctor was quite rude to Louise when she asked him about it, sir. They don't seem like they care what we need."

Matthew shook his head. "We need that bastard awake. I don't want to waste a minute before we get him formally cautioned and in front of a bloody jury."

"Yeah, it's a pain, sir, especially as Sherlock can't finish his forensic work until he can get confirmation samples from Joshua."

"Oh, sod this. Get that bloody doctor in here now."

Louise didn't immediately move. Matthew frowned. "Is there something else?"

Louise wasn't sure whether to tell him about the shooting, but Caroline nodded in encouragement.

"Erm... well, the thing is, sir, there was a drug-related

mass shooting last night in Leith. Caroline… well both of us actually, are a bit concerned that it's the work of our perp."

"Really? Why?"

"The pub was The Devil's Hole, and the seventh circle in this poem he's so obsessed with is violence."

Matthew's frown returned. "That's a bit of a leap, seeing as how he was in here at the time."

"I know, sir, but Caroline did make the point that he had others doing his dirty work before. It's possible he set this up before he set himself on fire."

Matthew shook his head. "Holy shit."

41

ONE WEEK LATER

In the end, the doctor paid no heed to Matthew or Louise's requests for immediate access to Joshua. A week had passed before there was any chance of him being awake to face their interrogation. The doctors had done an amazing job treating Joshua's wounds, skin grafts dealing with the most severe ones, leaving him permanently disfigured but alive.

Matthew was sitting at home, eating toast and drinking coffee as he prepared for his first day back. Despite his determination to get back to work, the doctor's decision had hindered progress in the case and allowed Matthew more recovery time. As he drained the last of his coffee, he had a little adrenalin surge which made him shiver. Today was the day. The doctor had promised that Joshua Billington would be woken up.

As he got ready, he went through all the things he wanted to say and the procedures they needed to follow. The latest case of the pub shooting came into his mind.

Could that really be part of his game and if so, how did he get it done when he was unconscious in bed? Despite this guy's psychopathic traits, Matthew had to remember what Caroline had said in her profiling. He was a clever man.

His deliberations were disturbed by the sound of Louise's car crunching on his gravel driveway. It was time.

*

Joshua's head was pounding. Noises and lights were coming back into his conscious mind. *What had happened to him? Where was he?*

The noises and the lights got more vivid as his vision began to kick in. A few blurred faces, lots of chatter, beeping from machinery.

The noise died down, but the light intensified. His vision cleared. A face he knew.

He tried a smile, but his face felt tight and painful. His speech was raspy and quiet, but he managed to speak. "Is this hell, McCallum?"

The copper said nothing, just stared at him.

"Maybe it's heaven," he said, as nothing was forthcoming from the grizzled and scarred face that was staring at him. He tried a smirk. Now he remembered. "You pulled me out of the fire. That was very brave. Maybe you are worthy."

Without responding to anything he said, the copper started to speak. *I am arresting you... blah, blah, blah... anything you say... blah, blah, blah... entitled to legal representation... blah, blah, blah.*

Joshua closed his eyes, not wanting or listen to the crap that was coming out of his mouth. It was time to tell his story, but he couldn't abide all this police procedure. If McCallum was the worthy adversary he had hoped for, then all he wanted was to sit down and talk. To talk about his pain. To talk about his journey and most importantly how it would end.

*

Matthew finished reading Joshua Billington his rights, frustrated that he had seemingly gone back to sleep. It didn't matter. They had done the important bit. He had been formally cautioned. Now they had to get him out of this place and back to the nick to begin the process of questioning him about all his crimes.

They spoke to the consultant who they'd had so much trouble with. His smug, arrogant attitude told them he felt he had somehow won this battle as he signed off the discharge papers to get Joshua moved to a secure medical unit.

As the paperwork was finalised, Jed came into the ward. "Ahh, good..." said Matthew through gritted teeth, "...perhaps the good doctor will now let us get on with our job."

Joshua was woken again, the DNA and fingerprint samples taken quickly and efficiently.

"Right, Mr Billington. The doctor has signed your discharge papers and you will be moved to a secure medical ward before we start the formal interviews tomorrow morning at 9am. I suggest you organise yourself some legal representation but if you don't have a solicitor, we can appoint one for you."

Joshua fixed an unsettling gaze on Matthew. "Ooh, I'm looking forward to it. I really am."

*

It was getting late. Matthew and Louise had spent several hours in his house, poring over the case file, making sure they had a plan and strategy for the interview with Joshua. As they came close to wrapping up, Matthew's phone rang. He put the caller on speakerphone.

"Yes, Sherlock, what can I do for you? DS Cookson is here with me."

"Well, sir, ma'am. I mentioned to DS Cookson a while back that I had found some interesting things when I processed the DNA samples from Mr Billington's house, but I needed the confirmation samples to verify my findings."

"And what have you found?"

"Well, you may not believe this, but Joshua Billington is the father of Joseph Anderson."

"What? Really? Are you sure?"

"Yes. One hundred per cent sure. But it gets better. You'll never guess who the mother is."

42

This was it. Matthew, Louise and Caroline gathered in the interview room, started the recording and dealt with the procedures that were necessary to commence the interview with Joshua Billington, under formal caution. He sat opposite them, looking calm and relaxed. His hands were handcuffed, but otherwise he was free to move around. The disfigurements on his face, due to the severe burns, reminded McCallum of Freddy Krueger. The unsettling stare that had been evident at the end of their talk in the hospital was back. Matthew tried to ignore it and started the interview.

"Mr Billington. For the recording, please can you confirm that you have refused legal representation for this interview."

There was a brief pause. Joshua looked at them one at a time. Unsettling and creepy.

"Where I'm going, DCI McCallum, I don't need a money-grabbing brief."

"And where are you going?"

Joshua leant forward. "Oh, come now, you're not going to start asking stupid questions, are you? I might just run out of patience if you do."

"Answer the question."

Joshua frowned. "I'm going to be with Mother."

"She's dead."

"You think I don't know that. I'm going to meet her in that heaven she banged on about all the time."

"So, you are going to die."

Joshua laughed. A mocking laugh. "Of course. This is how my journey has to end."

Matthew shot a glance at Louise and Caroline. They nodded, encouraging him to carry on and not be blown off track.

Matthew changed tack. "Tell me. How did you initiate the pub shootings in Leith?"

Joshua pulled a face. "An interesting change in approach. Did they teach you that at detective school? Try and unsettle the perpetrator by suddenly changing tack. Dear me."

"You deny any involvement in these shootings?"

Joshua drummed his fingers on his chin. "OK, I'll play your game. What makes you think it was me?"

"Your sick game is being driven by your obsession with *Dante's Inferno*."

Joshua's eyes widened and a broad smile came over his face. "Well, well. I am impressed. Maybe I underestimated you. How did you work that out?"

Matthew said nothing as Joshua's unsettling stare returned, searching Matthew's face for clues. After a few seconds Joshua sat back in his chair and sighed. "It wasn't you that worked it out, was it?" Joshua looked at Caroline and Louise in turn. "Hmm... as much as I admire your spunk, DS Cookson, I don't think it was you either, or this psycho quack who thinks she can profile me. No... I know exactly who helped you with this. Poetic actually."

Matthew couldn't hide his annoyance at Joshua's superior attitude. "What's that supposed to mean?"

Joshua smirked, pleased he had got a reaction from Matthew. "You'll see. I can't give away all my secrets too early now, can I?"

Matthew stood up suddenly, a move that made everyone in the room jump. "Interview suspended at 9.08am." With that he walked out of the room, closely followed by Caroline and Louise.

They followed him outside to the yard as he lit a cigarette. Louise spoke first. "What was that all about, sir? We've only been in there five minutes."

Matthew took a long drag and looked at them. "I wanted to break his flow. He's acting like he's in charge in there and I'm not having it. You are right, Caroline. He's brash and confident, desperately wanting to put on a show to demonstrate how superior he is."

"You're right, sir, but you need to be careful not to alienate him. I have a feeling his co-operation will be dependent upon us playing his game," replied Caroline.

They all let that hang in the air. He stubbed his cigarette out on the ground. "Come on then. Let's play his game."

They walked back in the room, Matthew starting the recording again. All the while Joshua watched him with an amused expression on his face. "Enjoy your ciggie, DCI McCallum?"

"Your involvement in the Leith pub shootings is the seventh circle in your so-called journey to redemption. It represents sinners that are violent. You clearly initiated something to trigger this atrocity before your little bonfire trick the other night."

Joshua nodded. "Well done. You're right. One phone call to the top man in Newhaven. A little story about the Leith gang planning to take over their patch coupled with a yarn about one of their crew raping his sister, was all that was needed."

"So, you are admitting to being the trigger for these killings?"

"I think I just told you that."

"Why?"

"*Why?* I would have thought that was obvious. The sinners have to die."

"As I understand it, that's not the conventional interpretation of Dante's poem."

Joshua dipped his head and started to laugh. "Oh my. *Conventional.* What a cute way of putting it. I'd have hoped by now that you'd have worked out that I'm anything but conventional."

"The poem is about Dante gaining a greater appreciation of hell as a spiritual realm. The sinners he meets help him to understand this, as he completes his journey to meet his lost love. Where in that does it say anything about killing the sinners?"

Joshua squealed with excitement. "Ooh, look at us. Talking about the classics, like a couple of old pals." Joshua looked over to Caroline and Louise, his expression changing to a look of contempt. "Which makes me wonder why you two bitches are still here. Why don't you piss off and let me and DCI McCallum have our private chat? I'm sure you don't have the first clue what we are talking about."

"They're not going anywhere." Joshua looked back at Matthew and shrugged. "OK, I'll indulge you. Let's work backwards. I assume your little towering inferno stunt was designed to represent the sixth circle. Heresy. You see yourself as someone who has rejected normal beliefs. Maybe you are embarrassed that you didn't agree or understand with your mother's absolute faith in God."

He leant forward again, his voice changing to a whisper, as if he was trying to tell Matthew something without the others hearing. "Do you have any idea what it was like living with a woman like that, preaching on every day about her God? I loved her, with every fibre of my body, but when it came to religion, she was a crazy bitch."

"But you almost died. How would you have completed your journey if I hadn't found you?"

Joshua sat back and frowned. "I'm disappointed in you. Didn't you realise that was your test? I had to see if you were worthy of my time, worthy to hear my story. I was ready to die but I hoped you would work out the clues to where I was and enable us to be here today. And you did. Just." With that Joshua put his handcuffed hands up to his face, stroking the red patches on his face that were still healing. He fixed his eyes on Matthew, a half-smile etched on his face.

Matthew tried not to be unnerved by Joshua's stare and glanced at Caroline and Louise. They had discussed sharing the questioning between the three of them, but they also knew that Joshua may want to run this his own way and it was now clear that he saw Matthew as the man he wanted to share his story with. They gestured for Matthew to carry on.

"The car bomb. I assume the fifth circle. Anger. Your old headmaster was the intended target?"

Joshua took a sharp breath, face twitching in anger. "That man. He made my school life a living hell. Letting those kids beat me up all the time, calling me names and nicking my lunch. My mother was in his face all the time, but the bastard did nothing. He was one of the worst. I enjoyed watching him die."

Matthew tried to ride the lurches in his stomach as he listened to the psychopathic rantings of this disturbed man. A developing confession that should make his job easy when it came to prosecution... but there it was... the ever-present doubt in Matthew's mind as to why Joshua was being so accommodating. Something wasn't right about this, but he knew he had to get through it to give them time to work out what was going to happen next. He pushed on.

"I'm guessing the bankers were your interpretation of greed? The fourth circle."

Joshua's anger subsided. "Yes, that's right."

"The big question though, Mr Billington, is why you got your son to commit the first three murders?"

The mention of his son had the desired impact. Matthew was delighted to see the anger returning to Joshua's face. The pinched mouth, the lines on his forehead more prominent and the unsettling stare. Simmering.

"Of course, I guess he's also your brother in a sick sort of way. Did your mother sexually abuse you to make this happen?"

The explosion was instant. He lurched forward, swinging his handcuffed arms at Matthew, knocking the seat away and banging his legs against the desk between them. The officer who was standing outside rushed in and restrained Joshua before he could do anything else.

Matthew got up close and personal. "Touched a nerve, did I?"

43

Matthew, Caroline and Louise sat in the canteen, drinking coffee and eating bacon sandwiches. They had left Joshua to stew after dropping the bombshell. Jed had been unequivocal in his findings. Despite the horrific conclusion, there was no doubt that the parents of Joseph Anderson were Joshua Billington and his mother.

Matthew spoke to Caroline first. "How do you think it's going?"

"Well, he's very much playing up to the typical profile of someone with severe psychological problems. However, his reaction to you telling him that you knew about Joseph's parentage was interesting. It suggests it was a piece of information he was not going to reveal to us as part of his open confession to his crimes. This hits at the heart of why he acts the way he does. There is no doubt that his absolute dependency on his mother throughout his life has been key to his behaviour patterns, but whatever the circumstances behind them having sexual intercourse to conceive a child, it is part of a deep-seated trauma."

Matthew nodded and turned to Louise. "What about you?"

Louise grabbed a napkin and wiped her mouth. "I dunno, sir. I'm having problems even looking at this psycho. We need to lock him up and throw away the key."

Matthew took a sip of coffee, his mind racing. "Putting aside his reaction to our revelation, I'm really concerned at how accommodating he is being with the confession. He wants us to know what he has done and prove he can still carry out his evil intentions, even when he's unconscious and being guarded by us!"

Caroline responded first. "I agree it's worrying, sir. He has a plan, which he states ends with his death. There seems no doubt that a full confession from him will get him banged up for life, so I have no idea how he thinks this will happen."

"People die in prison all the time," interjected Louise.

"I know and I guess that might be his plan. To goad another inmate into murdering him."

Matthew cut across their conversation. "Look, one step at a time. We have to remember that there are still two steps left in this so-called journey he is taking. I fear he has already initiated these steps and we need to see if we can get anything out of him to help us stop any more atrocities."

Caroline shrugged. "Well, OK, but I think we are going to have to treat him as a high-risk prisoner. Apart from anything else, I would suggest putting him on suicide watch straight away."

Matthew drained the last of his coffee. "OK, I guess that's a reasonable step to take, but I can't help feeling that everything he wants to happen has already been set in motion. We need to get inside his head. Try to work out how he is going to complete these last two steps. We need to be proactive."

Louise re-engaged in the conversation. "Actually, sir, I was thinking about this last night. The next circle is fraud. If we look at his victimology, he is picking random targets, except for his old headmaster. This suggests that he is simply finding people that fit the profile of the sinners in each of his circles and he doesn't mind how many people he hurts. He did it with the Weightbusters, the bankers and the drug gangs. I reckon we should get our team to work with the fraud teams to look at current or recent cases. See if we can get ahead of whatever sick thing he is planning next and try and work out who he might be targeting."

"Yes, yes, a good idea, but what about his laptops. Can't they help us?"

"The tech boys are still working on it. The one we found in the flat had nothing on it bar the links to that cloud-based video site where he stored the recordings of the first three scenes. The one he had with him was burnt quite badly and the team are trying to recover anything they can from the fried hard disk. We reckon that is where his recent activity will be recorded, but there's a good chance the disk is too damaged for us to get anything from it. I will speak to them again but I'm not that hopeful."

"OK, get the team to do what they can and join us back in the interview room in half an hour."

Louise left them to it, energised by having something to do other than listen to the psychopathic rantings of Joshua Billington.

"She's really good, you know."

Matthew looked at Caroline, confused. "Er... I know she is. Why would you say that?"

"I think you take her for granted sometimes."

Matthew was surprised by the sudden change in focus but knew she was right. "Has she said something to you? Is she unhappy?"

"Not really but I can tell she gets annoyed by you sometimes. However, don't underestimate how loyal she is to you. She was distraught when she thought you were going to die after jumping in that fire."

Matthew made some conciliatory noises, trying to hide the embarrassment at being called out in this way. He quickly changed the focus back to Joshua.

"Right, we need to push through on these first three cases and get him to confess that he instructed Joseph to commit the acts."

Caroline screwed up her face. "The problem is, sir, he may be less co-operative now you have broken his rules. He wants to be in control. He wants the interview to reflect what he had planned to say. You've gone off track by riling him up."

"You think I made a mistake, confronting him like that?"

"No, not at all. It had to come out. I'm just warning you that the next part of this interview might be tricky. You might want to strike a more conciliatory tone, leave some long gaps to see if he's itching to fill the silence. I have a feeling he will want to get back in control of the conversation."

It was now late morning as they gathered outside the

interview room, ready for part two. They walked back in, sat down and restarted the recording.

The tension in the room rose as Matthew and Joshua stared at each other. Nothing was said.

Just as Matthew was about to break the silence, Joshua spoke.

"If you disrespect me and my mother one more time, McCallum, you can kiss your confession goodnight."

Matthew continued to stare at Joshua, not saying anything. He had cracked first, and Matthew was interested to see whether Caroline's assertion that he wanted to be in control of the conversation would lead him to say more, so he stayed silent. It worked.

"My mother loved me. With every piece of her heart. She protected me from the bullies; she patched me up when I was hurt; and she filled my loneliness. My father was... well, actually I don't know what he was... I never met the bastard. On her own for thirty-five years. She is... was... a remarkable woman. The baby was a mistake. She just needed to be comforted sometimes and I... well, knew it was wrong. But, when the baby came, we delivered it on the bathroom floor, wrapped it in a blanket and left it outside the hospital."

Matthew heeded the warning and went for a sympathetic tone. "I'm sorry that happened to you. That can't have been easy to deal with."

Joshua looked up at Matthew, the hint of a smile on his face. Matthew took it as a sign that he had navigated his way past the confrontation.

"Can I ask how you came to find Joseph and get him involved?"

"Do you know, at the time she told me to forget about him. Never to speak about it ever again, and we didn't. So, you can imagine my hurt when I found a box under her bed with all the press cuttings. She'd kept them all. The appeals for the mother to come forward, witnesses claiming they'd seen all sorts of things, the nurses naming him Joseph. I don't know why she did it. It floored me for a couple of days. The anger boiled inside me. I could have ended it there and then, but something stopped me."

"What?"

"I needed to be relevant. If I took my own life, I would have been just another statistic. Maybe a paragraph in the local paper. I realised I couldn't bear that and despite her dishonesty, I knew I had to forgive her. To make sure I could be here today. Sitting in front of you, telling my story."

"What happened then? With Joseph?"

"It wasn't difficult. I obviously knew where we had left him, so just tracked birth registrations made at the hospital around that time. When I found him and learned about his condition, I realised he was the perfect foil for my plans, especially as I was still stuck in a wheelchair at the time. I visited him out of the blue. He was such a simpleton. All I needed to do was to give him those garish trainers and he was putty in my hands. I'd read up extensively on his condition and realised I could get him to do my dirty work. He seemed content to follow orders without question. I showed him how the earpiece and phone worked, and he was like a kid at Christmas. I knew it was a risk using him, but it worked… for a while."

Matthew nodded, happy that Joshua's confession was now back on track. He changed tack.

"Tell me about the accident that killed your mother."

The reaction was instant. Like turning a light switch on. Joshua began to rock rapidly.

"I can't do that. I can't do that. I can't do that."

Matthew shot a glance at Caroline. They had lost him again.

44

They sat there, hoping that whatever trauma had beset Joshua would pass. He continued to rock, muttering barely audible words, his eyes disconnecting from the world, staring at the wall. Matthew glanced at Caroline, who gestured for him to wait. They were gambling that this was all part of the process and Joshua would come back from wherever his brain was currently taking him.

A few minutes passed and, without warning, Caroline spoke. "Joshua. Joshua. Are you OK?"

Matthew threw a confused look at her, but she widened her eyes to encourage him to trust her.

"Tell me about the accident. It will help you get past the grief. I promise."

Joshua didn't respond. The rocking and the fixed state continued.

Caroline reached out and gently touched his arm. He screamed at the touch. Everyone in the room jumped at the unexpected sound. As the shock died down, they noticed a tear running down Joshua's cheek. Caroline tried again.

"Joshua. Speak to me. Please."

Joshua slowly reconnected with the room. He shook his head, his eyes closed and he stopped rocking.

"Joshua."

He opened his eyes and stared at Caroline. A fierce, angry stare. "I thought I made it clear that I wasn't gonna talk to you bitches."

"You use that word a lot, even when describing your mother. Do you have a problem with all women?"

Joshua sighed heavily. "Apart from Mother, I never met a woman who didn't make fun of me for the way I looked. They always called me greasy, spotty, sleazy, horrible names like that. Mother used to preach to me about their sinful ways. Their immoral thoughts, their lust for carnal pleasures. The forbidden fruit."

Caroline pushed on. "Did you ever have sexual intercourse with a woman, you know, other than when your mother…?"

There was something about the non-verbal indicators that Joshua was throwing out that made Caroline think she was getting to the truth. This time he hadn't blown up, he hadn't started rocking, but there was something in his manner that told her she had hit another nerve.

"Were you arguing in the car? Was it about sex?"

The tension returned. Joshua was not speaking, but the questions were hitting home. His breathing was getting more laboured. He wrapped his arms around himself, and more tears began to flow.

Caroline glanced at Matthew. He gave her a nod to carry on.

"Joshua. We need to know this stuff. Surely you want us to know the whole story. Don't you?"

Joshua looked up at Caroline. He wiped away the tears. "Stop analysing me, you fucking quack."

Matthew was about to say something, but Caroline interrupted his urge to speak. "Hmm... your mother really did a piece on you. What was it? Did she say those things to you, so you would hate all women, leaving her to use you as her little fuck buddy?"

Matthew let it ride. Caroline had gone way off script, but they left her to it.

Joshua fixed the unsettling stare on Caroline. "I should have killed you instead of that pigtailed slut."

"So, you admit to being involved in her killing?"

Joshua shook his head, changing his focus to Matthew. "Are you gonna let this quack take over our private conversation?"

Matthew decided to let it run. "Answer her question, Mr Billington."

"Of course, I was involved in her killing. Why are you asking questions you know the answers to? I got that freaking nutcase to do my dirty work while I was incapacitated, as I've already told you."

"Are you saying, if it wasn't for the accident, you would have done it yourself?"

"The accident. The accident. Stop talking about the accident. She died. OK. She died in that accident. Everything that happened is because of that accident."

"Do you blame yourself? Was she preaching to you about sex?"

Caroline had hit a home run. Joshua stood up again, the rage showing in his eyes as he spat the words at Caroline.

"Yes, it was my fault. I'd paid a prostitute for sex, and she found out. Banging on about lust and sin, over and over. I'd had enough. I... I... hit her. It made the car swerve out of control. The truck..." He slumped back down on the chair. "...It was all my fault."

45

They had done all they could for one day. Everyone was exhausted by the exchanges, including, it seemed, Joshua himself. Just before they retired for the night, Matthew called Caroline and Louise into his office.

"A hell of a day. What do you make of him, Caroline?"

She shook her head. "He's a very disturbed young man. With a mother like that and no father, it's no surprise he's turned out this way. The poor kid never stood a chance."

Matthew responded. "It doesn't excuse his actions."

"No, of course not, but it goes some way to explaining his psychopathic tendencies."

"I was surprised how he blew so hot and cold. I thought this was all part of his game. To be in control. To lord his power over us."

"I agree. He started off as I expected he would. Brash, confident and superior, but when we took him places he didn't want to go, like talking about the accident, he showed some vulnerability. It shows that somewhere in that confused mind of his, he does recognise that he has done some bad things."

Louise had been quiet but couldn't contain her rage.

"My God, Caroline. Don't make excuses for this psycho. He needs to be locked up and never let out."

Caroline grimaced. "I'm sorry, Louise. I'm not trying to defend him. He needs to pay for all the awful things he's done, but I'm just saying I can empathise with why he's turned out this way."

"Well, I can't. That man is pure evil."

Matthew could sense the stress of a long day was beginning to tell. "OK, let's not fall out over this. We'll reconvene tomorrow. We still have a lot to get through, including trying to work out how he is going to complete his final two steps. Go home and get some rest."

Caroline and Louise left without further comments as Matthew checked his messages. He had one from the professor. They'd found Joshua's dissertation.

*

Matthew was struggling to keep his eyes open as he sat in a wing-back chair in the professor's lodgings, sipping his excellent brandy. The professor did his best to keep him alert.

"Here it is, my boy. Joshua's dissertation. I took a cursory glance at it and much of it reads like a manifesto for the killings he's done. He talks about hanging non-believers as a way of interpreting limbo, the first circle. The murdering of prostitutes, fat people and greedy bankers is all there, linked to the second to fourth circles. He doesn't specifically mention his old headmaster in circle five but does talk about punishing the sinners who oversee bullying and oppression in our education system.

Critically he starts to fantasise about burning down schools and maiming random people by blowing them up. The section on heresy is non-specific but he certainly goes on about those who preach about sin being the worst kind of hypocrites. In the violence section, he talks about the collapse of society, citing drugs and alcohol as the fuels of sin."

"Wow, thanks for finding this. It really does frame his madness. The key question is what does it say about the last two circles? We need to get ahead of this madman and stop whatever he is planning or whatever he has already got in motion."

"Unfortunately, I am afraid this is where his dissertation becomes more rambling. When he talks about the eighth circle, fraud, he rants on about how society is corrupt to its core. He talks about punishing benefit fraudsters, people who prey on old people, the scourge of faceless people committing online fraud and the corporate vultures that prey on the little people, as he puts it. There's too much there to form any sort of opinion as to who he might target."

Matthew took a sip of brandy. "That's maddening. We need a break on this case. We have most of his confession on tape, so there's no doubt he is going down for a long time, but I can't help feeling we are still on the back foot. He isn't finished, Prof."

"I'm sorry to say, old boy, but I agree with you."

Matthew speed-read the sections that referred to the eighth and ninth circles. The professor was right that the range of people he referenced linked to fraud was far too wide to form an educated guess as to what he might do.

The problem was that the section about the ninth circle, treachery, wasn't much better. Joshua ranted about how people had let him down all his life. His father, people in the education system, women, the bullies. Same old. Same old. Matthew threw the document down on the coffee table.

"This is bloody ridiculous. As a piece of evidence, this will cement the main case against him, but it gets us no nearer to working out what he's going to do next."

The professor refilled Matthew's glass as they listened to some classical music. The conversation moved on to more cerebral matters. The professor talked about the upcoming charity events and recent successes of the university alumni, some of whom Matthew had met at various events. For a while it took Matthew to a better place, a place where he wasn't trying to get into the mind of a psychopath.

After a while the effects of the alcohol took effect and both fell asleep. The problem was that Matthew's subconscious wouldn't rest.

He bolted awake. There was something... he grabbed the dissertation and flicked to the last section on treachery. As he read the words over and over, he looked at his friend gently snoozing in his chair and suddenly had a very bad feeling about what Joshua Billington might be planning.

46

Joshua wasn't sure what time it was exactly, but the lights were still out and the secure hospital ward he was in was generally quiet, bar the rhythmic humming of the machines that were keeping the 'inmates' alive. He was in a side room, but the door was open, giving him a clear view into the rest of the ward. He couldn't move. Handcuffed to the bed, making sleeping difficult. He clanked the cuffs against the metal bar for something to do. No one took any notice. He glared at the CCTV cameras, just in case someone was watching.

He lay there, staring at the ceiling. His mind was in turmoil. The previous day had not gone as he hoped. The quack had got to him, taken him off track and exposed his emotional vulnerability about the accident. *Bitch*. His mind turned to McCallum and Cookson. How had they found out about Joseph? He shook his head. *Of course*. The idiot had left his DNA all over the first three crime scenes. He sighed. It was a mistake to use him, but he had been impatient. The moment he saw his mother's coffin enter the fire, he realised what he had to do. The problem was that at the time he was still reliant on his wheelchair, and he was never going to pull off the style of murder he wanted when he was stuck in that thing. He closed his eyes for a moment. It couldn't be helped. It was done now.

He took in some deep breaths to slow his heartbeat down. He was not going to get wound up by this bunch of merry coppers. He was in control and every step of his journey had been executed with perfection, even if the plodding coppers had found out some things sooner than he might have wanted. He opened his eyes and smiled. Today he would make sure he was back in control. He would make sure he kept them entertained while his work continued.

He started to laugh, a big booming laugh, staring straight at the CCTV camera.

*

They reconvened in the same interview room. The same seating arrangements. Joshua looked cool and calm. Matthew decided to go for a businesslike approach.

"Mr Billington. Yesterday, we touched on the first three crimes that we know were committed by Joseph Anderson. We found the links to the videos he recorded for you on your laptop. For the record, I assume you are not going to deny that you were the instigator of these crimes, given Joseph's limited mental capacity."

Joshua sighed. "It was regrettable that I had to involve him, but I had to start my journey, and I wasn't in any fit state to carry out what I needed to happen. He was a liability really, particularly his sloppiness with leaving his DNA all over the crime scenes. But at least the simple fool did everything he was asked to. In that respect his disorder was a…" he snorted at the irony of what he was about to say, "…godsend."

Matthew fixed Joshua with an unflinching expression. "We thank you for your openness in answering our questions, which leaves me no choice but to confirm the charges against you. You will be charged with the murder of eight people across two incidents. Firstly, the poisoning of four people at the civic centre in Edinburgh. Secondly, the murder by explosive device of four people in the main shopping street in the Saint Leonards district of Edinburgh. You will also be charged with conspiracy to commit murder of a further nine people, linked to incidents at a house in Musselburgh, a house in central Edinburgh, the village hall in Craigentinny and the Devil's Hole pub in Leith. Do you understand these charges as they have been read out to you?"

"Of course. That's quite a rap sheet."

They took a short break to refresh their coffee cups and steel themselves for the next section of the interview. They needed to try to find out what he planned to do next. The update Louise had managed to gain overnight from the team about fraud cases didn't fill them with much hope. There were thirty active cases. None of which had any obvious connection to Joshua Billington or indeed had his trademark devil symbology somehow connected to them. They would have to rely on their wits.

Joshua continued to look calm and relaxed as they re-entered. Matthew continued.

"Having established your guilt for these multiple atrocities, the question remains… why?"

"Why? I told you. The sinners had to die."

"No. That's not what I mean. Why do you feel the need to revel in everything you have done? Why do you feel the need to confess so readily to these crimes?"

Joshua eyed him curiously for a few seconds before answering. "I'm a little disappointed in you. I thought you understood me."

Matthew shook his head. "I will never understand a psychopath like you."

"Ooh, name calling now, are we?"

Matthew stared him down.

Joshua sighed. "OK, I can see I am going to have to lay this out for you. Did you know that I was the only one at my mother's funeral? The only one. No one cared if she lived or died. No one cared that she was leaving this world. Do you know how that made me feel on top of everything else I've had to put up with in my life? When I saw her coffin entering those flames, I started to understand what I had to do. I had to join her, but I was not going to be like her, leaving this world with barely a whimper, an insignificant speck in the world that no one cared about. Oh no, I decided that I was going to go out with a bang. People are going to know who I am. Who I was. So, I decided. My path to redemption had to be strewn with the bodies of as many sinners as possible, so I could be back with the one person I truly loved. I realised this was what Dante's Inferno had been guiding me to do, all my life. If some of them were people that had blighted my life... so much the better. I selected you as the person who would hear my story, but I'm beginning to think I made a mistake in choosing you."

Matthew was struggling not to react. Caroline had warned him that Joshua's attitude would seem detached from reality. A clear sign of a severe psychopathic illness. But it didn't make it any easier to listen to. Matthew knew that Louise shared his disgust and could sense her rage as she sat next to him.

"I'm sure the judge and the jury will look forward to hearing your story and I'm sure the gutter press will revel in your evilness."

Joshua raised his eyebrows. "You really aren't listening, are you? I won't be going in front of a judge and a jury. I will be dead long before that happens."

"And how do you propose that's going to happen when we have you locked up?"

Joshua smiled. "Two more steps. Two more steps. Tick tock."

The simmering tension erupted, and Louise lurched forward, grabbing Joshua's top and pulling him towards her. "Tell us what you are planning next, you psycho bastard."

Matthew leapt up and grabbed Louise's arms, whispering quietly to let Joshua go. At first, she didn't look at Matthew, her rage all-consuming as she stared him down.

Joshua began to laugh as Louise eventually relented and sat back down.

"You would do well to show some respect, Mr Billington. Now answer my sergeant's question. If you are so keen for us to hear your story, tell us what you have planned next."

Joshua cocked his head to one side. "What time is it?"

"It's nearly 10am. Why?"

Joshua smiled and started to move his index finger from side to side like a clock pendulum. "Tick tock, tick tock... *boom*!"

47

Boom. That one word sent shockwaves through the room. This time it was Matthew's turn to lose it as he stood up and grabbed Joshua by the throat.

"I'm done with you and your stupid games. You will not get any more airtime from us. You're going to jail and can rot there for the rest of your life. We will stop you completing your journey... and that's a promise."

As they bundled out of the room to find out what he had done, they were left with the words of a madman ringing in their ears. "Good luck with that."

They raced up the stairs to the control room, straight to the duty inspector's office. Luckily it was one of the inspectors Matthew knew. "Ah, Inspector. Have we had a major incident called in? An explosion?"

Amy McMahon was used to these sudden interruptions. Matthew had a habit of doing this, always keen to see what was going on with live incidents. She scanned the information on the large dual screens. Logged incidents were listed on the left-hand screen and live information about officer, vehicle and incident locations were on the map on the right-hand screen.

"Er, no. I can't see anything. Quite a slow morning so far."

Matthew, Louise and Caroline scanned the screens. He spoke first. "I don't understand it. It's past 10am. Is this just another one of his tricks?"

Caroline responded. "I don't know, sir. He seemed quite excited when he asked you for the time. He didn't seem like he was playing us."

Matthew turned around, cursing under his breath, just in time to see Louise storming out. He went to follow her, but Caroline put an arm out to stop him. "Leave her be. She just needs some time to calm down."

They thanked Amy and went out to the yard for a smoke. Louise was nowhere to be seen.

"That's it. I'm not speaking to him again. We have enough of his confession on tape, backed up by the forensics and the videos of the first three crime scenes, to get a file to the PF. I'm gonna starve him of the oxygen he craves. He will have no more airtime with me."

Caroline nodded. "I've no doubt that will hurt him, but we know he's not finished. We might be forced to speak to him again to try to stop him completing the last two steps."

"That's not happening. We'll work it out."

They finished their cigarettes without further discussion. As Matthew stubbed his out on the floor, he gave a snort of derision. "If I can find Louise, at least I can tell her one bit of good news."

"What's that?"

"Now we have Joshua's confession about Joseph Anderson, I think it's time we withdrew the prosecution file against Joseph and leave him alone to be looked after properly."

Caroline smiled as they walked back towards the station door. Just as Matthew was about to reach for the handle, his phone rang. His eyes widened as he saw who it was.

"McCallum. What is it, Inspector?"

Caroline could tell it wasn't good. His face hardened with every word. When he finished the call, he banged his hand on the door. "Come on. It's happened."

They rushed back upstairs, calling Louise on the way. As they rushed into the inspector's office, she was standing up, headset on, barking out instructions to control room despatchers and officers on the scene. The incident log was being updated live... *explosion at the benefits office in Commercial Street... first responders on scene... reports of mass casualties...*

The mapping screen showed multiple police resources moving towards the scene. Matthew put his hand over his mouth, paralysed by anger and frustration. A second later, Louise came in.

Matthew shook his head. "Come on, DS Cookson. We have work to do."

*

It took them barely five minutes to get to the scene. The front of the benefits office had been blown out, glass and debris strewn across the street. Casualties were being attended to by ambulance crews as the fire service dealt with the flames. A large group of people had gathered at the edge of the cordon, including the TV cameras recording every movement.

Matthew tried to ignore the scrutiny as he and Louise approached the incident commander from the fire service. "Morning, sir, I'm DCI McCallum, and this is DS Cookson. We'll be taking the lead on the criminal investigation once you've made the place safe. What's the status?"

"The fire is pretty much under control. My guys are just going to put up some struts to deal with any structural damage to the front of the building, but otherwise the scene is safe. We have a number of casualties, which the ambulance service is dealing with."

"Any idea of the source of the blast?"

"Yes, looks like a home-made device but packed with enough explosive to do this. Crude but effective."

"The same MO as the Saint Leonards fire."

"Yes, if I understand correctly, you think this is the work of your devil serial killer?"

"We do."

"Actually, that's the thing. There is something strange here. We found a stuffed crow."

Matthew and Louise stepped away from the scene, whilst it was made safe, moving away from the prying eyes of the press and TV cameras.

"What the hell do you make of this?"

Louise was scrolling through articles on her phone. "Hmm, seems like a black crow does have a number of religious connotations. It seems that in some religions, they are connected to death and in others they are considered messengers of the gods. I don't think we really needed confirmation that this is the work of that psycho, but once again he's playing his stupid symbology game."

Matthew went to pull out his cigarettes but thought better of it. "So, are we to assume his link to this damn poem is about punishing people he sees as benefit fraudsters?"

Louise sighed. "I dunno. I guess so. Which means the work we did on current fraud cases was a complete waste of time."

Matthew was concerned about Louise. She was letting the case get to her, more than any other he could remember. He knew she wouldn't abide his sympathy, so he kept it businesslike.

"Now we know for definite that he has someone working on the outside, we need to get the team looking at this angle. Get them to look at CCTV in the building and in all the surrounding area. It must have caught someone carrying and planting the device. Also get a warrant for his bank records. He must be paying someone to do this, unless there are some other family members that we don't know about."

"Of course, sir. I'll also get back onto the tech guys to see if they've managed to restore anything from his burned laptop."

"Good idea."

The look of determination on Louise's face told Matthew that he didn't have much to be concerned about.

"Right, the last thing is that we are going to have to try to work out what his final act might be. He's been one step ahead of us throughout this case. We have to start working to pre-empt what he might be doing for his finale. It'll be all about the final circle. Treachery."

"Do you have any ideas, sir?"

"Unfortunately, yes. I've got a horrible feeling I know what he might be planning."

48

Joshua was back in the secure ward, having his burns treated and redressed. The close proximity of the female nurse was making him uncomfortable. Her smell reminded him of darker times and the small amount of cleavage that she kept showing did not help. He closed his eyes, trying to fight back the nausea and the temptation to wring her bloody neck. The clank of the handcuffs reminded him that his desire to carry out that act was fruitless. He sighed. Frustrated and angry. More than anything he needed to know that his latest act had been executed.

He opened his eyes. She had finished dressing his wounds and was stood at the end of his bed, updating the charts. "Oi, missy. Has anything big happened in Edinburgh today? You know, like an explosion or something?"

She looked up briefly but said nothing. A few seconds later she turned and walked out of the ward.

"Oi. I was talking to you. Tell me what's happened. Tell me... NOW!"

*

Matthew and Louise were back in his office. They'd left half the detective team to deal with the scene, collect witness statements and process the forensics but, in reality, they didn't need any of this to know this was Joshua's work. His bizarre interpretation of Dante's eighth circle, punishing sinners that committed fraud. The other half of the team had been tasked with finding Joshua's accomplice, which left them to concentrate on working out what he was planning next.

It was lunchtime, so they'd grabbed a sandwich from the deli next to the station and were tucking into them, while they pondered the possibilities of what Joshua Billington was going to do to finish his journey.

"So, come on, sir. You said you've got a theory about his last act."

Matthew licked his fingers and wiped them on the barely adequate serviette that had been supplied with his sandwich. He grabbed something out of his bag and put it on the desk between him and Louise.

"What's this?"

"It's a copy of his dissertation. The prof managed to find it in their archives and gave me a copy. I've got Caroline going through it with a fine-tooth comb but read the section on the last circle."

Louise continued to eat her sandwich as she began to read the section on treachery. Her expression changed as she read each word, more disturbed with every line.

"Well, what can I say? It's all there. His ranting on about everyone that has betrayed him, hurt him, abused him. The need for sinners to be punished for their crimes. It's like a fifteen-year-old confession. I mean, why the hell didn't the university flag this to us all those years ago?"

"I know. I haven't had the heart to ask the prof that question. I can only assume that by permanently excluding him from the university they thought they'd dealt with it."

"OK, so apart from this whole thing pretty much framing recent events, I'm not seeing anything specific in this last section that will really tell us what he's planning."

Matthew pulled the dissertation back towards him and tapped a paragraph. "It's this. Look."

He turned the paper around for Louise to read it. She still looked confused. Matthew explained his theory.

"You see, think about this sentence... *I reserve my greatest contempt for those who think they know better than me. Those people who think they are more intelligent with an intellect more finely tuned than mine. Those people who use their power to put me down. Isolate me from doing what I am destined to do. Dante has made me understand that this is the worst kind of treachery. They are the most heinous sinners and will be dealt with....*"

"Er, OK. Surely that could describe a host of people."

"Yes, but the bit about intelligence and intellect. The bit about power and destiny. He's talking about people who have challenged him intellectually, taken away his power and are stopping him achieving what he's destined to do."

Louise's eyes lit up. "Oh, you mean he's referring to you?"

Matthew looked confused. "What? No."

"But it makes sense to me now. Why he seems to have fixated on you. Everyone who knows you will say you are

221

a cultured and intelligent man. He admitted that he tested you to see if you were a worthy adversary. Surely, he's threatening you, if you stop him completing his journey."

Matthew's mind was in turmoil. "No, no, that's not what I meant, but I guess I can see logic in your interpretation. There's someone else I was thinking of. Someone else who meets the criteria."

"Who?"

"The professor."

49

Matthew and Louise walked the short distance from the station to the university campus. They had to speak to the professor about their theory. If they were right, he was in danger and needed to start taking some precautions. As they reached the porter's lodge, Matthew's stomach was churning. A small part of his brain was worrying that they may be too late. Joshua had been one step ahead of them this whole time. He showed his warrant card and asked after the professor. He let out a huge breath when the porter confirmed that he was in a lecture but should be back in his quarters shortly.

They made their way to his apartment and waited outside. Five minutes later the portly figure of the professor appeared round the corner. "Ahh, Matthew, my dear boy. What a pleasure to see you..." he looked at Louise with an appreciative nod, "...and you must be his very able sergeant that he talks so much about." Matthew caught a glance from Louise and smirked.

"Come in, come in. I guess we'd better have coffee. Probably a bit early for a brandy."

The professor caught Matthew's stressed expression as he started to pour from the jug of coffee that had been percolating while he had been in his lecture. "Or should I be offering you one, Matthew? I know that look. You've got something on your mind."

Matthew and Louise sat down opposite the professor, glad of the caffeine hit. "I don't know whether you've seen the news, but he's struck again. Bombed the benefits office in Commercial Street."

The professor sipped his coffee tentatively. "The benefits office?"

"Yes, we think it's another one of his twisted interpretations of the Dante poem. Punishing benefit fraudsters linked to the eighth circle."

The professor frowned. "Dear oh dear. That poor boy is sicker than I could ever have imagined."

Matthew was just about to respond when he was railroaded by Louise. "Why didn't you flag up your concerns about his dissertation to the police at the time, Professor?"

The professor leant forward, his face serious. He briefly glanced at Matthew before fixing his gaze back on Louise. "You are right, Matthew. She is a little terrier."

Louise opened her mouth to respond but the professor raised his hand in mock surrender, a mischievous smile on his face.

"I'm sorry, Sergeant. Your question is very valid. At the time, I took the disturbing document to the dean and the rest of the senior faculty. We were all horrified that something so evil, so unsettling could come out of one person's mind. As I mentioned before, we had had previous run-ins with his mother about all sorts of things and no one had the backbone to deal with her again over something so disturbing. We decided that the easiest thing to do was exclude him. She obviously tried to speak to me and the dean on several occasions after that but we held firm. Eventually they gave up and we heaved a sigh of relief that he was gone. I'm so sorry if our actions were misguided and could have stopped these awful tragedies."

Matthew interjected. "Look, I don't think anyone could have predicted that he would turn these disturbing words into actual actions. There was a fifteen-year gap between the two events. All the dissertation has done is give us more evidence to nail this bastard. It's like a retro confession."

The professor grimaced, grateful for the platitudes but still uncomfortable with his role in the horror show that was Joshua Billington's life. He looked at them in turn. "That's not the whole story, is it? I can tell by your faces that there's still something you need to tell me."

Matthew shuffled in his chair, while Louise sipped her coffee, letting Matthew carry on with no further interruptions.

"The thing is, he still has one circle to go, if he is to complete his so-called path to redemption and join his mother in *her heaven* as he puts it. The problem is he managed to engineer this morning's bombing while we had him in police custody. We fear he has already put in motion everything he wants to happen."

"What's that got to do with me?"

"We've been analysing his dissertation, particularly the bit about the ninth circle. DS Cookson and I are concerned about a particular sentence in this section and my profiler has just messaged me to say she shares our concerns. Here. Read it."

The professor took the dissertation and sipped at his coffee as he read the words. He nodded. "You think he may be referring to me?"

"I do. The thing is that when he wrote it, he wouldn't have known you were going to exclude him, but I can imagine your subsequent actions at the time resonated with those words. He has fifteen years of pent-up resentment against you and this university, ready to explode. He is using that damned poem as an excuse to take out his frustrations on everything bad that has happened in his life, but I fear they have all just been steps towards his ultimate goal. To avenge the *treachery* he perceives you have committed against him."

The professor put down his coffee cup, clasped his hands together and stroked his chin. "Well, well. We do have a bit of a muddle here. What do you suggest I do about it?"

"You need to start taking some precautions. Let the dean and the senior team know about the potential threats and start briefing your security team. Get the porter's lodge to be extra vigilant with who they let on site and start getting your team that handle the post to be more alert for larger packets that might contain explosives. I wouldn't walk around on your own outside of the campus, if you can at all help it."

"Oh, that seems like an overreaction."

"I can't let anything happen to you. I would never forgive myself. Please consider doing the things I said. I can come and talk to the dean directly if you think that would help, and I'm happy to supply an officer to be on site round the clock, until we can stop this lunatic hurting anyone else."

The professor got up and poured three glasses of brandy.

"I think maybe it's not too early for these." He took a good mouthful and looked at Matthew. "OK, old boy. I'll do as you say."

50

The following morning Matthew called an operational briefing meeting. He had the bit between his teeth and was determined to get ahead of the game. He called the team together.

"Right, team. You all know the objective: to stop this lunatic finishing his journey and hurting anyone else. I want progress updates from yesterday and any operational plans you have for the next few days. Sherlock, you're first."

"Not much to report. The explosion was from a home-made device that had been placed in a small box. There was enough plastic explosive in there to make the sort of hole in the building that we witnessed. It was detonated by a mobile phone. The problem is the fireball destroyed any sort of forensics we might have otherwise obtained."

"I'm not sure that really matters at this stage, as we know who was behind it. What about the accomplice? Who was looking into that?"

Harry piped up. "I got the warrant for the bank records and checked back in with the tech boys about his lappie. DC Williams did the on-scene stuff."

"OK, tell me about your bit first."

"The bank records didnae show any electronic transactions out of the account. There are a series of cash withdrawals over quite a long period. We reckon he might have paid someone off with a large bundle of cash."

"How much?"

"Well, over a three-month period, he withdrew nearly three grand in cash. He also has nearly thirty grand left in the account."

"What? Where the hell has he got that sort of money from? Does he work?"

"Nah, the only money coming into the bank account was for benefits, so nay idea where he got that sort of money from."

Matthew rubbed his forehead. "My, my. How interesting. So, he blew up a benefits office but was taking benefits himself. Somewhat of a paradox."

Caroline interjected. "Actually, sir, I think he may see himself as someone who deserves the benefits. A valid case, if you know what I mean. I reckon he targeted the benefits office because he perceived that there were too many people claiming benefits who didn't deserve them."

Matthew huffed at the suggestion. "Jesus. Like we need any more evidence of how messed up this *bawbag* is."

"What else, DC McDonald?"

"I'm afraid nowt much. The tech laddies have pretty much given up trying to restore the hard drive from his lappie. It was too damaged in the fire."

"DC Williams?"

"A bit more positive, sir. We have a CCTV image from the benefits office of a man walking in with a medium-sized rucksack. He walks over to the right-hand side of the foyer where there are chairs and desks for people who need to fill in forms. He takes a form from the rack and pretends to fill it in. After a minute or so, he reaches into the rucksack and takes out the box we think has the explosives in it and shoves it under the table. He then takes out something wrapped in a cloth and does the same. We think that was the stuffed crow. The fire service has confirmed this was the epicentre of the blast."

"Do we know who this man is?"

"Not yet, but we've got a good frame of his face, and I've sent it to the facial recognition lab to see if we get a hit on someone that is known to us."

"Good. Anything from the witness statements?"

"Not really. It was a busy morning with people going in and out. No one could really ID this guy, so we may have to rely on the CCTV to nab him."

"DS Cookson?"

"We now have six confirmed dead. As DC Williams and Sherlock said, the fire service has completed its investigation and confirmed the device used and the location of where it exploded."

"OK, apart from the facial match, it doesn't sound like we have much to go on, so we need to concentrate on working out his next steps and protecting the professor."

Louise took the lead. "As a start, I've spoken to the university security team about the threat, and they are enhancing their checks on people entering the grounds and have stepped up their patrols around the campus. We have given them our guidance on suspect mail and how to deal with it, including providing them with a bomb bin.

DC Williams and DC McDonald are organising a round-the-clock presence on campus to assist the security team."

"That's good. It's a start. I want you and Caroline to stay behind after this briefing so we can work out what else we need to do."

"OK, sir."

Matthew dismissed the rest and refilled his coffee cup. When they reconvened in his office, the stress of the situation was evident in his face and general body language. He offloaded.

"How did it come to this? The professor is my dearest friend, and I can't have anything happen to him. We need to do more. We need to stop this bastard."

Caroline responded first. "Look, sir, as you said, we've made a start by putting some extra protection around the professor. However, we ought to consider other possibilities."

Matthew frowned. "I thought you agreed with our assessment about the professor being at risk?"

"I do, but I also think you need to be careful. He's appointed you as his self-styled adversary. I've no doubt the professor is at risk, but I think you are too."

Matthew dismissed the comment and refocused on Louise, ignoring the look of exasperation on Caroline's face as he did so. "We need to use our informant network. He is obviously getting outside help and I'm betting he's paying off some of our criminal fraternity to do his dirty work."

"Yes, sir, I'll get onto that."

There was a brief uncomfortable pause as Matthew's stress continued to throw a dark veil over proceedings.

Caroline rode her annoyance and re-engaged. "There is one other thing, sir."

"What?"

"I've been into the surveillance room on the hospital ward. Joshua's behaviour towards the staff is getting worse. He's getting agitated and keeps asking them to tell him about the explosion. He also keeps shouting things at the CCTV cameras. He wants to know that this latest act was a success, and he also keeps asking to speak to you."

Matthew sat for a moment, expressionless. He rocked slightly in his chair.

"Good, let the bastard stew. I'm not giving him any more of my time."

Caroline sighed. "I'm not sure that's wise, sir."

Matthew stood up. "I've made my decision. Now just leave it. Let him stew."

With that he stormed out of the office. Caroline looked at Louise, shaking her head. "He's being stupid. If he carries on like this, he's going to get himself killed."

Louise looked at Caroline wide-eyed. "I know."

51

Matthew just kept walking. He'd left the station and just walked aimlessly around, his heart pounding, adrenaline keeping him wired. Joshua Billington was outsmarting him and there was nothing he could do about it.

The spring day was cool but sweat formed on his brow and inside his shirt. He ignored it and kept up the pace. He entered the Princes Street Gardens, briefly glancing up at the imposing façade of the castle. The beautiful flower beds were awash with bright yellow daffodils and other early spring flowering plants. Parents and their children ran around, laughing with the joy of it all. As he strode on, the normality of it all made him shiver. At any moment, this madman could disrupt their lives forever. Matthew knew that Caroline was probably right. This final act was personal, and it made sense that he and the professor were his primary targets. It didn't matter though. He could barely bring himself to look at anyone. Ashamed that at any moment, his incompetence might destroy their lives.

He turned left out of the gardens and continued onwards. No plan, just walking off his stress and hoping that something might come to him that would give him an edge in the case. Ten minutes later he realised he was outside the university. He had to see the professor. He had to see if he was OK.

As he went to dial the professor's number, he realised he had three voicemail messages on his phone from Louise, Morag and Harry. In his agitated state he had not felt the phone vibrate in his pocket. He stared at the phone. They were probably ringing him to update something on the case, but he just couldn't concentrate until he saw his friend. He dialled the professor's number. The others would have to wait.

*

Louise paced around the incident room. *Where was he?* She'd left him a message to call her. She was worried. She knew he was probably just walking off his stress or sinking a pint in a pub somewhere, but he was not coping well with this case. He was usually so calm in these sorts of situations, but Joshua Billington was getting to him. Caroline had also left to blow off steam, the latest victim of his bad mood.

As she pondered what to do, Morag and Harry came in the room. Morag spoke first. "Where's the guvnor, ma'am?"

Louise took in a deep breath. "Er... he's not here at the moment... he's um... dealing with some stuff."

They looked at her. The hesitation in Louise's voice was unusual. She was normally a confident and self-assured individual. Unflappable, but they could tell something was up. Harry probed further. "Is everything OK, ma'am? Is there anything we can do?"

"No, no. It's fine. It'll sort itself out. Now what's up?"

Harry glanced at Morag, unconvinced by Louise's stonewalling, but carried on. "I've had a red flag on Joshua Billington's bank account. A large transaction is being processed as we speak. A payment of twenty grand is being transferred out. I'm trying to get a warrant to get the bank to give me more details, but it suggests something is going down."

Louise's face fell. She held her hand up to ask him to pause as she dialled Matthew's number again. The stress was growing, etched on her face. The phone rang and rang. "Shite!" The call had gone to voicemail.

"OK, Harry. Keep onto the judge. We need that warrant. What about you, Morag?"

"We've had a hit on the facial recognition. A criminal lowlife called Jason Connoly. The team have picked him up at his house and are bringing him in now."

Louise dialled again. Voicemail.

*

Twenty minutes later, Louise, Harry and Morag were in an interview room facing Jason Connoly. Louise ran through the formalities and started the recording.

"Mr Connoly. Do you know why you are here?"

"You're stitching me up for summat."

"You understand that you have been formally cautioned for conspiracy to murder at the benefits office on Commercial Street, related to a bombing incident yesterday morning."

"I weren't there."

Louise produced the CCTV image. "This suggests otherwise."

He stared at the picture. Leant back in his chair and said nothing.

"I should remind you that you are being interviewed under caution. I understand that you have refused legal representation. Now that I have shown you this picture, do you wish to change your mind?"

He continued to sit, cross-armed, saying nothing.

"OK, Mr Connoly, I will take your silence as agreement for us to carry on this interview without any legal counsel present."

He shrugged.

Louise leant forward. "Let me be clear. We know who is masterminding these atrocities and we know he hired you to plant the bomb. It will help your defence if you tell us everything you know. You're a small fish. Don't make this worse than it needs to be."

They stayed silent as he stared back at them. They could tell his mind was processing all the options. Eventually he leant forward.

"He paid me three grand to put a box under the table in the handout place 'gether with some stuffed bird. That's all. I didn't know what was in it. Once I was outside, he told me to send a message on the moby. I didn't know it was gunna set off a bomb. Honest."

Louise made a point of scanning his paper record that was printed out in front of them. "Honest. That's an interesting word to use given the eclectic criminal record you have here. I don't believe a word of what you are saying."

"It's true. I had'er go to a post office box and pick up a package. The 'structions and moby were with them. I just did what it said."

"How did he contact you?"

"Word of mouth. A mate of mine mentioned that this dude was offering three grand to do a simple delivery job. He didn't want it, so I took it on. I never met the dude."

Louise studied him intently. Watching the nuances of his facial expressions, watching his body language. For someone that was a career criminal, he wasn't exhibiting the sort of jerky, agitated actions or expressions that were typical of people like him. Born liars. Which led Louise to one conclusion. He was telling the truth.

"OK, let's assume for a minute that I believe you. This is your one chance to help us out. What have you been paid twenty grand to do?"

He screwed up his face. "Eh… what you talkin' aboot. I ain't doin' nothing else for this dude. It was a one-time fing."

Once again, she studied his face. Her heart sank. She was fairly certain he was telling the truth.

52

Morag took Jason Connoly away, leaving Louise and Harry in the interview room. "Where is he, Harry? I know he can be a bit odd sometimes, but this is feeling wrong somehow. He would never ignore our messages for this long."

"How long has he been away?"

Louise looked at her watch. "Must be getting on for three hours now."

"Och, I wouldnae worry about him. He's probably in a pub somewhere drowning his sorrows or sat in his hoose listening to that weird classical rubbish he likes so much."

Louise wrung her hands. "I don't know. We've all left him messages. Whatever stress he's under he would not have wanted to miss the opportunity to interrogate that lowlife we've just had in here. That was potentially a major breakthrough in the case. He just wouldn't…"

As the sentence trailed off, Harry got on the radio. After a quick exchange of messages, he turned back to Louise. "We've had a copper on site for the last couple of hours. He's just finished doing a recce with the security team and met the professor about an hour and a half ago. He hasnae seen the guvnor though."

Louise was fighting back tears. News of the professor being safe was something but she was still paranoid that something bad had happened to Matthew. She turned away from Harry to hide her emotions. "Get onto the control room and ask them to let every officer know that DCI McCallum needs to be found, urgently. Get your officer in the university to do an extensive check of the grounds and make sure he's not with the professor. For my part, I need to go and see the chief super and tell him that the boss is missing."

Harry walked out, leaving Louise on her own. The tears began to flow.

*

Joshua lay in bed, looking out onto the ward. He clanged the handcuffs against the bed frame one more time, just for the hell of it. All his ranting at the staff and constant shouting at the CCTV cameras had not gotten him what he wanted. Confirmation that the place where the money-grabbing scum of this city went to plead their pathetic cases had been blown up.

He was frustrated that neither McCallum nor any of his merry band of coppers had been to see him or dragged him back to the soulless interview room for more of their verbal sparring. If the bombing had happened, they would have to formally caution him for the crime, and he was ready to add to his confession. It was all part of the plan.

As he tried to calm his frustration, he suddenly realised something. He shouted to a passing nurse. "What day is it?"

The nurse stopped and peered in. "Why do you need to know that, Mr Billington?"

After all his ranting, he knew he'd better go for a kinder tone. "Oh, nothing really. It's just hard to keep a sense of time in here."

The nurse frowned but answered his question. "It's Wednesday. The 13th of April."

Joshua almost let out a yelp of excitement. It was difficult when there were no external reference points for the day or the date. His burns were healing well, but the doctors wanted him confined to his bed as much as possible, which didn't help. But, today was the day, McCallum would really see how serious Joshua was about completing his journey.

*

Louise took some time to sort herself out but ended up outside the chief super's office within half an hour. Frustratingly she had to wait for him to finish a meeting but took solace in the strong black coffee that his officious PA had made her. After fifteen minutes his door opened and he invited her in, once the previous guests had departed.

"DS Cookson. I understand you are concerned for the welfare of our DCI?"

"Yes, sir. He left the station over four hours ago in quite a stressed state. You'll know that this case is testing all of us, but he is taking it especially hard and making it very personal. We've left numerous voicemail messages, but he hasn't responded to any of them, which is very strange."

"What about his friend, the professor?"

Louise was surprised how up to speed Chief Superintendent Alexander was with the case. "Oh, we have an officer on site at the university, helping the security team keep things safe there. He saw the professor a few hours ago, though I did ask for another check to be done."

"I understand you have asked the control room inspector to put a general alert out for our missing DCI?"

Again, Louise was taken aback at how up to speed he was with instructions she had only issued in the last hour. "Er, yes, that's right."

The chief super sat there for a moment, not saying anything. Louise started to get nervous. Was he expecting more from her? Eventually he spoke, standing up in the process.

"You've done all the right things, Sergeant. I'll brief the chief and check in with the control room about their progress. In the meantime, I suggest you catch up with your team at the university and make sure the professor is still OK."

Louise realised the act of him standing was a sign the meeting was over. She made a hasty exit and got straight on the phone to Harry. There was no answer.

As she cursed the constant lack of response to her phone calls, she decided to grab the bull by the horns and set off for the university.

She was there within fifteen minutes and soon located the police officer that was on site. The minute she saw his face she knew something was wrong. Louise's knees almost buckled as he spoke the words.

"Ma'am. I'm so sorry."

53

Matthew pulled his coat around him, the fresh spring air biting at his face and cooling his body. The adrenalin had long since dissipated and his body temperature was normalising after the exertion of the stress walking he had been doing for nearly four hours. He was mentally and physically exhausted. He cupped the warm sides of the coffee that he'd bought from the street vendor just outside the nature reserve, revelling in the heat and the caffeine hit.

After speaking to the professor on the phone, he'd turned everything off. His phone. His radio. His brain. He sat on a pine bench overlooking Duddingston Loch. The light wind agitated the water as a combination of seabirds and waders bobbed in and out, fishing, flying, fighting the breeze. Not a care in the world. *Oh, to be a bird.* Matthew was once again stunned by the juxtaposition of the scene. It was beautiful. Calm, serene. Nature at its very best, whilst all the while a madman chained to a hospital bed was plotting his final act of revenge.

He continued to sip his coffee slowly as the sun made a brief appearance. He closed his eyes, arching his neck up to the sky as he allowed the weak heat of the sun to warm his face. He began to relax as the haunting sounds of the gulls filled the air, backdropped by the occasional bark of a dog and the crunch of people walking on the footpaths that circled the loch.

After a few minutes he was aware of someone sat down next to him on the bench. He opened his eyes and looked over.

"Everyone's looking for you."

He sighed and looked at Caroline. "How did you find me?"

"I remember you said this was one of your favourite places to come. Where you de-stress and unwind. I took a calculated gamble to see if you were here."

"That's very impressive."

"It's what you pay me for, sir. To analyse people. To remember the finer details about everyone."

Matthew winced. "I'm sorry. I didn't mean to kick off at you earlier. This case…"

Caroline filled the void left by his unfinished sentence. "It's not a problem, sir. You wouldn't be human if you didn't get stressed by the sort of horrific things this bastard is doing. Give yourself a break. I'm a big girl. I can handle it."

Matthew looked embarrassed and muttered a quiet 'thank you'.

"Do you want to talk about it? I'm a good listener."

Matthew looked at Caroline. "Why am I letting this case get to me? In all my career, I've prided myself on my calm, assured approach to solving crime, whatever the circumstances. But this one is taking me places I don't wanna go."

Caroline nodded. "Maybe this one's a bit more personal."

"How do you mean?"

"You are part of Joshua's story now. Maybe you see things in Joshua's life that remind you of your own situation."

"Like what?"

"I get the feeling you're quite lonely. You live alone. You don't talk about your parents, so I assume they are both gone. The professor seems to be your only real friend and you spend most of your life working."

Matthew didn't respond. He stared out over the loch, breathing in the fresh air, processing what Caroline had said. Eventually he snapped out of his trance and looked at her. "Do you think DS Cookson... er, Louise... would ever..."

Caroline smiled. "Would ever... what?"

"You know. See me as someone she might... er, hang out with outside work."

Caroline stifled a laugh at his bumbling attempts to talk about love. "Well, you're old enough to be her father but... why don't you take a chance? She is a gorgeous human being. Certainly my type."

Caroline waited for the words to process, smirking at Matthew's changing facial expression as he realised what she'd said.

"Oh, so you're..."

"Gay. Yes, sir. Does that surprise you?"

"Oh, er... I dunno. Can't say I ever..."

Caroline roared with laughter. "Oh, sir. Your gaydar is clearly not very well tuned."

He looked confused. "What the hell's a gaydar?"

Caroline laughed some more. "Oh, sir, I think maybe you'd better solve this case before you get entangled in a love match. Sounds like you've been out of the game for too long."

After a few moments riding his embarrassment, Matthew patted Caroline's hands. "Thank you for this. It's just what I needed."

Caroline smiled. "Good. So, what's your plan?"

Matthew looked at her, confusion on his face.

"If you really care about Louise, you need to get back in the game. She is having a meltdown worrying about you. She's been to the chief super about your disappearance and got every copper in the force keeping an eye out for you. If you ever turn your phone back on, I suspect there'll be a hundred messages on there."

He pulled his phone out of his pocket and stared at it with trepidation. Once he turned it on, the horrible world of Joshua Billington and his *Devil's Code* would all be too real again. He looked at Caroline. She nodded encouragement.

He pressed the on switch. The screen burst into life. Within seconds the phone went crazy with beeps and alerts. He looked at the phone, resignedly.

"Thirteen voicemail messages," he said with a hint of shame.

He stood up and put the phone to his ear, listening to each one in turn. Louise asking where he was. Harry updating on some progress with Joshua's bank account. Morag getting a hit on the facial recognition. Five more calls from Louise with no messages, all he guessed in the hope he was going to pick up. A message from the chief super asking him to call. Another three no message calls from Louise. The final one was from Louise. She'd left a message.

As he listened to it, tears welled up. He disconnected. "No, no, no," he screamed.

Caroline looked on concerned. "What is it, sir?"

He sat down again in a resigned slump and put his hand over his face. "It's the professor. He's missing."

54

Steptoe, as he was known in the criminal fraternity, sat in the little cottage on the outskirts of Edinburgh. He was only forty-five but his scrawny body, pronounced hair-covered chin and wild, messy hair had cemented the nickname with his peers some time ago and now, anyone who knew him, didn't call him anything else. He sometimes worried about the fact that people thought he was twenty years older than he was, but he liked his drink and fags too much to really care about it. Most importantly he was good at this type of work. Damn good. Regardless of what he looked like.

He walked around the cottage. It was a nice place, away from prying eyes. The guy who had rented this place knew what he was doing. In fact, as Steptoe read through the extensive notes that had been mailed to him by this guy, he was astonished at the level of detailed planning that had gone into this job.

He checked his bank account, and the twenty grand was there. The abduction of the fat dude from the university had gone like clockwork. Every detail of the abduction had been laid out by this guy and all Steptoe had to do was follow the instructions. The plan had been faultless. He had mapped where every CCTV camera was on the route, making sure they avoided any detection. Going in as a laundry truck, catching the dude as he took his morning walk, subduing him quickly with chloroform, driving out of the back gates with no one stopping them. It was brilliant.

The old guy was locked in one of the bedrooms. All Steptoe had to do was keep him alive and wait for further instructions.

He read some more of the plan. A list of different scenarios was mapped out. It seemed this guy didn't want to leave anything to chance. If one thing went wrong, he was to execute a plan B, or C, or D. It was incredible. Each new step brought more cash. He rubbed his hands and laughed.

As he sank a beer from the well-stocked fridge, he thanked his lucky stars he'd got to this job first. Big jobs like this were managed by The General. The Mr Big in Edinburgh who ran the show. No one knew who he was. These days everything was done on the dark web. The General put the jobs up on the secure site and people like him bid for them. The General took ten per cent, but the rest was all yours. Steptoe had a reputation for jobs like this and The General offered him the gig without hesitation.

He heard groaning come from the bedroom. The old dude must have woken up. He got up and approached the door. More groaning. He unlocked it and went in.

"What's up?"

The old guy still had his eyes shut but was stirring from his sedation. He didn't respond to Steptoe's question. Steptoe went back into the kitchen and got the pre-packed sandwiches out of the fridge, together with a coke. He went back into the bedroom and placed them on the bedside cabinet. The room had an ensuite bathroom, so he wasn't going to be disturbed by the old fart wanting a piss.

He left the room and relocked the door, a satisfied smile on his face. This was going to be one of the easiest jobs he'd ever had.

He grabbed the half-drunk bottle of beer and turned on the TV to watch the football. Waiting for instructions.

55

As Matthew walked into the incident room, the reaction was instant. Louise, manic and wide-eyed, tore into him. "Where the hell have you been? I thought you were…" She turned away, shielding him from her tears. Matthew reached out to touch her shoulder but stopped himself.

"I'm sorry. I know it was unprofessional, but I just needed a break. I needed to sort my head out."

There was an awkward few seconds before Louise sniffed back the tears and turned around. "I'll get the others over here now. Something is going down and we need to act quickly if we are going to find the professor."

Matthew was a bit taken aback by her sudden change in emotions, but he knew she was right. They had to get back to the business of stopping this madman. Emotional baggage would have to wait.

Within ten minutes the core team was sat round the meeting table in the incident room. Matthew took command.

"Right, firstly let me apologise for my impromptu absence and any stress that may have caused. However, I'm back now and we need to be all over the disappearance of the professor. DS Cookson, can you give me the most up-to-date situation?"

Louise was back to her calm, professional persona. "Yes, sir. The professor was last seen on campus around 11am. The porter's lodge has no record of him signing out at the front gate and he had no lectures scheduled for the rest of the day, so no one missed him. We are checking the few CCTV cameras on campus and any in the streets around the university, but at the moment, we've drawn a blank."

"DC McDonald. What about this warrant?"

"Still waiting for the judge, sir, but the bank has confirmed that a twenty grand payment has gone out of Joshua Billington's account today. It has to be a payment linked to the professor's disappearance."

"DC Williams. What about this Connoly guy? Have you done some more checks on him?"

"Yes, sir. The three of us interviewed him about the benefits office bomb and we are satisfied that he was just paid to do that job. He's too small-time to be involved in anything more elaborate."

Matthew drew in a sharp breath and looked at Caroline. "What do you think?"

"I think this is all part of his plan, sir. He's somehow managed to get someone to kidnap the professor from under our noses and left no clues as to where to start looking for him. Which leads me to one conclusion."

"What's that?"

"Despite your reluctance to give him any more airtime, I think he is forcing you to speak to him again. I have a feeling we won't get anywhere with finding the professor unless we continue to play the game by his rules."

After much soul-searching, Matthew resigned himself to doing what Caroline suggested. The team spent the rest of the day following up leads, working with the university security team to search the site and reviewing what little CCTV was available. The main thing they found was a number of areas of vulnerability within the security of the campus, leading Matthew to the conclusion that someone could have got the professor off the site with little fuss. Once again, they had been too late.

*

Joshua lay in bed, getting more agitated by the lack of external stimulus. The constant checks of his vital signs plus the periodic redressing of his wounds were about all he was getting in terms of human contact. The light was fading outside, which meant another day had passed without contact from McCallum.

He let out a deep breath to ease his stress. If his plans had been executed correctly, the benefits office should have had a nice explosive surprise and the professor should be under his control. He pondered the possibilities. Had both these things happened and McCallum was playing it cool? Or, had the people he'd paid let him down? The latter thought made his stomach flip. The whole plan was premised on him organising everything prior to his incarceration. He had no way of communicating with the outside world now he was in the lion's den.

As his mind wrestled with the possibilities, he got his answer. One of the security team came into his room. "Mr Billington. You will be required for a further interview tomorrow morning at 9am with DCI McCallum and DS Cookson. You are reminded that this interview will be under caution, and you are still entitled to legal counsel."

Joshua shut his eyes, smirking. Everything was clearly still on track.

*

Matthew had spent the previous evening alone, listening to music and refuelling after a stressful day. He slept poorly, the plight of the professor constantly on his mind. He couldn't bear the thought that his incompetence and self-indulgence may have cost him his life. When he spoke to him on the phone the previous morning, he had been upbeat and unfazed by the threats. Matthew wondered whether the professor's naivety about the seriousness of the situation had contributed to him being abducted so easily. The only thing that made him feel slightly less agitated was the thought that Joshua Billington was using the professor as some sort of collateral to get at him. It was a few minutes before 9am and he was about to find out.

Matthew sipped at his second coffee of the day as he waited for Louise and Joshua to arrive. A few minutes later, they walked in. More than anything, Matthew wanted to launch himself at this scumbag and beat the location of the professor out of him but... he knew that wasn't going to work. He tried to ignore the smug, self-satisfied expression on Joshua's face as he walked in and sat down. Matthew glanced at Louise, and she gave a subtle, encouraging nod.

"OK, Mr Billington. Firstly, for the record, we are adding a further conspiracy to murder charge to your case file related to a bombing of the benefits office on

Commercial Street. We have your accomplice, so we assume you are not going to deny this was your work?"

Joshua leant forward, a sign that he was in control. "It's very nice to see you again, DCI McCallum. I was beginning to think you'd given up on me."

"Answer the question."

"Oh yes. That was my work. How many scummy fraudsters did I get?"

Matthew gritted his teeth at the comment. "You will be charged with conspiring to murder six more people. And, just so you know, not all of the victims were in the benefits office. Your indiscriminate approach to making your point killed two innocent people on the pavement outside, hit by the debris of your explosive device."

Joshua pulled a face. "Ah well. Collateral damage. It can't be helped."

Matthew was struggling to hold it together.

"Did you find my little calling card… though I guess we're past needing to solve *The Devil's Code*?"

"If you are referring to that stuffed bird you got your lacky to leave behind… then yes. A pointless indulgence on your part."

Joshua smiled and stared at Matthew.

"Now. Let's get to the real reason we are here. Where is the professor?"

Joshua sat back in his chair, a look of self-satisfaction on his face. He drummed his fingers on his chin, like some faux act of considering the question.

"Hmm, there's only one way you'll find him."

"And what's that?"

"You are going to have to let me out."

56

Matthew sat in the chief super's office. He'd been torn off a strip about his impromptu disappearance and the effect it had on the team but, in reality, he'd hardly heard the words. All he wanted was the chief super's approval to allow Joshua Billington out. Once the boss had finished venting, Matthew took his opportunity to update on the latest situation. It didn't go down well.

"Are you mad? What on earth made you think this was a good idea?"

"We've drawn a blank, sir, as far as identifying any leads about the professor's disappearance. I fear his life is in danger the longer we leave it."

The chief super stood up, never a good sign, and looked out of the window. An uncomfortable silence hung in the room. Eventually he turned around.

"What's your plan?"

"I don't know, sir…"

"You don't know!"

"I mean, we haven't developed a plan yet. I wanted to sound you out first."

The chief super's face was turning red with rage. "Has that little sabbatical turned your brain to mush? Did you really think I would entertain such an outlandish idea, especially when you seem to have feck all idea as to how to protect yourselves and bring this situation to a positive conclusion?"

Matthew decided a tactical retreat was necessary and walked out of the chief super's office without another word, giving him no time to react to his insubordination. He could imagine the look on his face. He called the team back together.

"Team, we have a problem. You are aware that Billington is insisting that the only way we will find the professor, is if we let him out. Not surprisingly, the chief super didn't like the idea."

The faces staring back at him were fixed in concentration. A loyal team that Matthew felt he hardly deserved. He decided to go for broke, formalities out the window.

"Louise, Caroline, Morag, Harry. What I'm about to ask you is… well, I think you can guess, is somewhat off script. I don't have time to play politics. I'm inclined to do what Joshua Billington is asking."

Their faces were a mixture of surprise and shock. Matthew didn't give them a chance to speak.

"I fully understand if you don't want any part of this and you can leave the room now. No hard feelings. No recriminations."

Now he waited for them to say something. He could tell they were all trying to process the craziness that had just come out of his mouth. Harry spoke first.

"Oh aye. Feck it. I wasnae gonna make Sergeant anyway. I'm in."

The others looked at each other. Caroline responded next. "I'm in."

Morag stood up. "I'm sorry, sir. I can't do it, but I won't say anything. I'm still going to follow up any leads we can find." She walked out, which just left Louise.

They all stared at her. Stress lines were forming on her brow and her breathing became heavy. "You're prepared to throw your career away for this?"

Matthew reached across and grabbed Louise's hands. "I am. The professor is my dearest friend, and I won't allow my incompetence to cost him his life. I don't have much of my career left anyway. It's the only way."

She shook her head, fighting back tears. "But you're prepared to take us all down with you?"

"I won't let that happen. Once this is over, I will make sure the inevitable investigation into my conduct knows that it was all my fault, that you were only following orders."

Louise closed her eyes and put her head back. She let out a long sigh. "OK, I'm in. What's your plan?"

Matthew's heart leapt. They had shown a level of loyalty he barely deserved.

"Right. Let's get Billington back in the interview room. I don't think we can form any plan until we know what he wants."

They reconvened after lunch and Matthew was relieved that the chief super hadn't hunted him down for another dressing down. He knew he had probably burnt his bridges there and the consequences would be coming but, for now, he only had one thing on his mind. To save his friend. To do a deal with the devil. Ironic.

As he, Louise and Caroline once again sat opposite Joshua Billington, the urge to beat a confession out of him was competing for space in Matthew's mind with the more sensible, calm approach. He went for the latter.

"Let's suppose for one second that I'm inclined to acquiesce to your request. How might this work?"

The smug smirk was back on Joshua's face. He clearly thought he was winning the battle of mind games. He said nothing for a minute, ramping up the tension. He put his handcuffed hands up to his face and rubbed his eyes.

"What time is it?"

"Why?"

"What time is it?"

Matthew was already losing patience. "It's 1.20pm."

Joshua looked up to the ceiling and moved his head from side to side like he was working something out. "Hmm… yes, I think we still have time… unless the poor codger's had a heart attack with all the stress."

Matthew twitched, ready to launch a fist, but Louise grabbed his arm to stop him.

Joshua fixed Matthew with a dark, evil stare. "Goooood. That's what I need from you. Anger. Frustration. A sense of being out of control. It will sharpen your focus if you want to save your friend."

Matthew looked away from everyone, containing his anger. A few seconds later he looked back at Joshua.

"What do you want?"

"I want you to let me out and we'll drive to the location of the professor. In a normal car, with just you. No phones, no earpieces. Nothing that can track where we're going. I want a mobile phone. Nobody is to attempt to follow us, or I will phone my compatriot, who is holding the professor, and give the kill order. If you do these basic things within the next few hours, there is a chance your friend will still be alive."

"Why should I believe a word you say? You've already admitted you've got a death wish."

"It's true. This journey will end with my death. To allow me to join Mother in her heaven. My journey through the nine circles of hell will be complete, and the sinners will have been punished. True salvation."

The words sent shivers down Matthew's spine. He didn't like the implications of what he was hearing. "You're going to kill us both. Aren't you?"

Joshua smiled. "Well, that rather depends on you. Doesn't it."

Matthew glanced over at Louise and Caroline. Their faces were imploring him not to do it. He ignored them.

"OK. I agree. We'll make the arrangements and have you out of here within the hour."

As soon as they walked out, Louise bundled Matthew into the adjoining room. "Are you mad? You are signing your death warrant."

Caroline also spoke up. "Louise is right, sir. You are heading into a trap. You can't possibly believe he is going to let you and the professor live."

Matthew smiled. "I'm banking on it. I need him to think he has the upper hand. That we are totally devoid of any chance to hit back. But I have a plan. Firstly, get me one of those small GPS tracking devices and a sticking plaster. Secondly..." he allowed himself a conspiratorial smile, "...I've worked out the one way to stop him killing anybody, just as long as you can track where we've gone."

Caroline and Louise pulled confused expressions.

"Come on. Get Harry back in the incident room. It's time to end this thing."

57

The plan was set. None of the team liked Matthew's plan, but they had agreed to help him and they weren't going to back out now.

The first part of the plan had been executed. Harry had persuaded the custody sergeant that he was happy to take Joshua back to the secure hospital in his car, instead of using the contracted-out security firm that were usually responsible for these things. The sergeant was too busy to put up any resistance.

Harry headed out towards the hospital with Joshua handcuffed in the back. As they reached a quieter stretch of the road leading out of the city, they pulled into a lay-by. Matthew and Caroline followed in his car and pulled in behind them. Louise was elsewhere, organising the really crazy part of Matthew's plan.

Matthew tried to ignore the smug look on Joshua's face as they bundled him out of the police car.

"Right. Here we are. Now take me to the professor."

Joshua took a sharp intake of breath. "I think we're getting ahead of ourselves. The first thing we need to do here is to remove these."

Matthew eyed the others. He didn't want to do this,

but he knew he had to play along. He gestured for Harry to take the cuffs off.

Joshua rubbed his wrists. "Right, now I need to frisk you. If I find any sort of tracking device, your friend is as good as dead."

Matthew opened his arms out in a gesture that said *go for it*. Joshua took great pleasure in patting him down and lifting up his shirt to check for wires. He looked in both ears. He got up close and personal, so that Matthew could smell his breath. They stared at each other. Neither flinched.

"OK, I'm happy you're clean. Now, let these good people toddle off and we can get on with it."

Matthew nodded to Harry and Caroline to go. He hoped that the tiny GPS tracking device that he had put where the sun doesn't shine, was secure enough under the sticking plaster. It had been a tricky manoeuvre but the fact nothing had dropped out when Joshua was patting him down was a bonus.

Matthew decided to put the freed Joshua in the front. He didn't fancy the risk of a rear seat attack. At least with him sitting next to him, he had a greater chance of spotting any sudden moves that Joshua might make.

Before they set off, Matthew gave him the mobile phone he asked for. Joshua's fingers immediately danced over the screen.

"I've turned the location and GPS tracking off, just in case you were relying on that to track me."

Matthew tried to ignore the patronising smile on Joshua's face. "Where do I go?"

Joshua held a finger up in a *wait* gesture. He dialled

a number and put the phone to his ear. The call was answered immediately.

"We're on. Get the professor to the agreed location. We'll be there in about half an hour."

Half an hour. Matthew pondered the possibilities. He had a feeling wherever they were going was somewhere remote. The problem was, there were plenty of remote sites half an hour out of the city. He would just have to play along for now and hope the tracking device was working.

Joshua got the mapping on his phone, tilting the screen away from Matthew. He didn't want to give him any idea where they were going. "OK, keep heading south on this road until you meet the A720."

Matthew started his car. The engine of the 52 plate Volkswagen Golf spluttered into life. He didn't do cars. He would rather walk, but he had the car out of necessity. If it got him from A to B and didn't give him hassle, that's all he needed. The Golf had proven to be just that. A reliable workhouse. Just like him.

He pulled out of the lay-by and drove south. He was surprised to see Joshua close his eyes, like he was on some journey to go on holiday. Matthew wriggled in his seat, conscious not to dislodge the tracking device. He hoped the team were monitoring their progress.

Harry and Caroline had to be seen to go to the hospital so that anyone looking at the vehicle location system would think they had delivered their prisoner. Thereafter they were back to the station to start tracking Matthew's progress. He had instructed them to leave a half an hour gap before following them. He hoped that was a good judgement call. Wherever they ended up, Matthew needed whatever charade Joshua was planning to take at least that long. Otherwise... well, Matthew didn't like the odds. As he drove, he wondered how Louise was getting on at Joshua's house. This part of his plan was crucial.

As they neared the junction for the A720, Joshua seemed to instinctively wake up. "Go right until you see a turn left for the A701." He closed his eyes again.

Matthew drove on, his mind full of possibilities and doubt. Had he made the right decision? Could he really expect his loyal team to follow this crazy plan? What if DCS Alexander suddenly appeared in the incident room wanting to speak to him, just as the team were about to set off on their rescue mission?

He sighed heavily and shook all the thoughts away. Whatever madness had made him follow this plan didn't matter if he saved the professor.

"You OK?" asked Joshua.

Matthew ignored the faux concern and drove on. They turned down the A701. Five minutes later he told Matthew to take a turn onto the A703. Joshua sat up straight. *They must be getting close*, Matthew thought. The surroundings steadily began to change from semi-urban to full-on rural. Farming land began to appear on each side of the road. Tree-covered hills and rocky crags could be seen in the distance. Traffic was sparse as they carried on heading south. Matthew had been right. It was going to be remote.

All of a sudden Joshua gestured for him to take a right turn down a narrow single-track road. The tension in Matthew's stomach began to rise. They drove on, navigating the twists and turns of the bumpy road, masked on both sides by high hedgerows. Matthew had no visible markers to keep his bearings. Wherever this road ended up, he was fairly sure it was their final destination.

They seemed to be driving forever but eventually the road widened. A small hamlet appeared. They passed a couple of farmhouses. Two minutes later Joshua told him to turn left. As Matthew drove slowly down the lane, the track widened out to a small parking area. A black 4x4 was parked outside.

Matthew couldn't believe what he was looking at. They had arrived at a small, rural church.

58

Caroline and Harry parked up outside Joshua Billington's flat. They had been back to the station to pick up the tablet that was tracking Matthew's progress and had avoided any difficult conversations with senior officers, sneaking in and out of the incident room in haste. There was no time to lose. The tracking device had Matthew and Joshua heading south-west out of Edinburgh into a heavily rural area. They were in Caroline's car to avoid any chance that they would be tracked themselves. They bundled out of the car and banged on the front door. The door opened and Louise stood in the dim light of the doorway.

Caroline gasped. "Oh my! You look…"

Louise cut across it. "Come on. Let's get moving. I don't wanna be in this get-up longer than I have to."

Harry stifled a laugh as they rushed to the car.

Louise sat in the back with the tablet. As soon as she looked at the tracking map her heart sank. "Oh shite, the tracking device has stopped moving. They must have reached their destination already. Come on, Caroline. Get moving. We just can't…" Her sentence drifted off as she fought back tears. *Why had she agreed to this crazy plan?*

Matthew stepped out of the car, closely followed by Joshua who held his arms out in a ta-da gesture. In front of them was a small, weathered, grey-stoned church. Despite its size it was split into two levels with the lower roofed portion at the front and the higher roofed part at the back. There were a couple of Gothic stained-glass windows at the end and on the sides. There was only one entrance, framed by a covered stone archway. The building was finished off with a small conical tower at the back end of the building. Apart from the small parking area, the church was framed on all sides by dense trees, making the whole vibe eerie and unsettling.

Matthew huffed incredulously. "What's this?"

Joshua pulled a confused expression. "It's a church, obviously. Appropriate, don't you think, that my final act should be staged in her house of God? I've completed the devil's work. The sinners have been punished and now I'm ready to be accepted into her heaven. To finally be with her again."

Matthew shook his head. "Where's the professor?"

"He's inside waiting for you. Come. Come."

Matthew baulked at the patronising hand gestures coaxing him towards the church but fought back the rising bile and started towards the entrance. The vehicle worried him. He assumed it belonged to Joshua's lackey but there was no sign of another person. The hairs on the back of his neck began to stand up.

Joshua stood to one side as Matthew approached the entrance. The door was shut. Joshua gestured for him to go ahead. Matthew approached the door slowly, trying to hear anything that might confirm that someone was inside. It was silent. He grabbed the large circular handle on the door and turned it. As the large wooden door creaked open, he saw a figure slumped against the altar at the end of the short aisle that dissected the small space. A pained, gravelly voice shouted out, "Matthew!" It was the professor. As Matthew went to rush to his aid, he was poleaxed by a sharp blow to the head. His world went black.

*

"Take the next left." Louise was barking orders at Caroline as they sped towards the dot that was showing on the map. It flashed on and off like some sick countdown to their doom.

"Where have they stopped?" asked Harry.

"It's not anywhere. Right in the middle of the fecking countryside, miles from civilisation."

Harry nodded. "I guess that figures. He wasnae gonna make it easy for us."

Louise said no more. Her heart was pounding as they made good progress towards the final destination. She tried to eliminate the negative thoughts that were rushing through her brain. They had to get there on time. They had to.

*

Matthew winced as his vision began to return. His head was throbbing. He went to rub the offending spot but realised he was tied up. As he cleared the fog, he realised he was sitting down, leaning against the altar. He gasped as he saw the professor's face staring at him. "Hello, old boy. We seem to be in a bit of a predicament here."

"Are you OK?"

The professor laughed. "I've had better days."

Matthew looked around. He could only see the entrance door, the aisle and the few pews either side. The altar they were leant against was masking any other view they might have. Joshua was nowhere to be seen.

"Where is he?"

The professor shrugged.

As Matthew's senses began to return, he realised the area around where they lay was wet. The liquid formed around both of them and was doused on their clothes. It was a smell that haunted Matthew. The skin on the right side of his body prickled in some phantom post-traumatic sympathy reaction. The scars from when he jumped into that inferno to save Joshua were barely visible now, just red blotches in the worst affected areas, but psychologically the scars were deeper than he cared to admit. Matthew hoped he would never have to deal with anything like that again. The smell of burning skin was not something he cared to relive, yet here they were, covered in petrol.

As he looked back at the professor, he tried to hide his fear. This madman was setting up his final act. He was going to burn them alive.

59

DCS Alexander thundered into the incident room. A busy morning followed by a barely adequate lunch had not improved his mood. The call from the chief constable in the early part of the afternoon had made it much worse. The press was not letting the 'Edinburgh Devil Killer' story rest and the apparent lack of any progress in finding the madman was not helping. The shit was hitting the fan and if the chief was feeling the pain, she was going to make damned sure that everyone else below her was going to feel it too.

He looked around at the empty desks. He moved towards the side office where DCI McCallum was usually holed up. It was empty. He took a sharp intake of breath. The anger was rising. As he contemplated where his DCI could be, the door to the incident room opened. He swung around, ready to unleash his anger at whoever was standing there, but he stopped when he saw a face he didn't recognise.

"Oh, who are you?"

"Um, sorry, sir, I didn't mean to disturb you. I'm DC Morag Williams."

"Are you on this *devil* case?"

Her heart sank. "Er, yes, sir. Can I help you with something?"

"Where are DCI McCallum and the rest of the team?"

Her stomach was churning. She'd said she didn't want anything to do with the DCI's stupid plan, but she had agreed not to say anything. The chief super's angry eyes bore into her.

"I asked you a question, DC Williams."

Morag sat down. She wasn't going to lose her job over a DCI she barely knew. She looked up at the chief super, trying to supress tears. "They've gone, sir. DCI McCallum has taken Mr Billington out of custody. He said it was the only way to find the professor. He asked us all to help him, but I refused."

"So, the others are with him?"

"Well, sort of. DS Cookson, DC McDonald and Caroline Fleck, our profiler, are tracking his progress with a GPS tracker that DCI McCallum placed on his person."

DCS Alexander rushed out of the incident room and ran down the stairs to get to the control room. He marched towards the duty inspector's desk. "We have a major incident. Can you tell me where DCI McCallum is? He apparently has a GPS tracker on him."

The inspector didn't flinch at the interruption to his afternoon and immediately tapped away at his screen.

"Er, no nothing, sir. We haven't been asked to track him by a standalone GPS device and both his phone and radio are turned off."

"What about DS Cookson or DC McDonald?"

"Err, aye, sir. Both their radios are pinging together. They seem to be moving down the A703 towards Peebles."

"Get every available unit towards their location. NOW!"

*

Matthew tried to ignore the smell of petrol and his rising fear. His arms and legs were well tied, making any movement difficult, but he began to shuffle his away along the side of the altar. Just as he began to get a rhythm going, inching slowly towards the edge of the altar, he heard footsteps. It sounded like they were coming up some stone steps behind him. The lower part of the church building, he surmised. The figure soon appeared.

"Ahh, you're awake. Good. Now we can really start the final ceremony."

Matthew righted himself as he stared into the evil eyes of Joshua Billington. The smell of petrol intensified. Joshua was covered in it as well. The lighter he mindlessly fiddled with in his hands confirmed Matthew's worst fears. Joshua had played with fire more than once, the scars on his face a chilling reminder of the most recent encounter. Matthew shivered at the memory. He had jumped into the circle of fire to save Joshua Billington's life. He wasn't at all sure he wanted to take that risk again. The only thing Matthew could do to stop it was to keep Joshua talking.

"So, what's your plan here? Why am I not surprised that you lied to me? Again. You have no intention of letting either of us live. Have you?"

Joshua moved his head from side to side in a gesture that suggested he was thinking about what Matthew had said. Eventually his head stopped moving and he changed his attention to the professor.

"I rather think we have a lot to talk about before your final fate is decided. I mean. I've waited fifteen years to confront this piece of shit about what he did to me."

The professor was still slumped against the altar, tied up in a similar way to Matthew, making any movement difficult. "Don't engage with this madman, Prof."

The professor pulled a face. "I don't know, old boy. This man has obviously got something to say to me, so let him chunter on if it will help him get it off his chest."

Joshua frowned. "You really are an old windbag, aren't you, Professor? Even now, you don't have anything original to say. Stifled by your own narrow mind and petty prejudices. It's why you couldn't see my dissertation on Dante's Inferno for what it was. A masterpiece."

The professor grunted incredulously. "A masterpiece. Hah. That was one of the most disturbing things I ever read in my life. I have never come across anyone that interpreted the poem in the way you did. Dante is not guided to kill the sinners in that poem. It's a poem about spiritual understanding. About how hell exists as a spiritual realm alongside heaven and how he comes to appreciate this as he finds his way to his lost love Beatrice. It's a poem about love, not hate and murder."

Joshua leapt up and got right up to the professor's face. "I know it's about love, you piece of shit. When Mother died, it all made sense. I have been obsessed with that poem for a long time. I realised that when she left me, the poem was my guide to be with her again. I hated her God, but I realised that, to atone for my heresy, I had to show her my undying love by navigating through every circle of hell that Dante had travelled. The devil was a construct I could understand. He existed to hold the bad people to account for their actions. The sort of people who made my life hell. The sort of people whom Mother tried to protect me from all my life. The bullies, the sluts, the greedy bastards. The poem confirmed that all these people were sinners and had to be punished. It was the only way I was going to be with Mother again in her heaven. And here we are. Ready to meet her."

The professor didn't flinch at the tirade. Like Matthew he guessed their best chance of getting out of this thing was to keep him talking and the professor had a feeling that Joshua had fifteen years of hurt to deal with. "A very passionate speech, Joshua. I guess in your own way you really believe that madness."

Joshua backhanded him across the face. The professor ignored the blow. Matthew tugged at his restraints. Joshua didn't take his eyes off the professor.

"Did you even think for one second what impact expelling me would have on my mental health, Professor? When you university knobs sat in your grand halls sipping brandy, did you ever think about me and my future?"

The professor shook his head. "We couldn't let you continue spouting that rubbish and making the rest of the undergraduates uncomfortable. We had a duty of care to everyone else."

Joshua snorted in derision. "A duty of care. Hah. What a pile of shite. You hated the weirdo, just like everyone else. But what made it worse, was the way you treated Mother when she tried to make you see reason.

Ignoring her pleas. Sidelining her. Treating her like some second-class citizen. That is why you are here, Professor."

The professor sighed. "So, I guess you think I'm your ninth circle?"

Joshua cackled with excitement. "Oh yes. Clever boy. If ever there was someone that epitomises treachery, it's you."

"What about me?"

Matthew had remained silent during the exchange, grateful to the professor for prolonging the time they had. He had made little progress on getting out of his restraints, but every second should help his team get closer. He'd intervened because he had a feeling Joshua was heading for his final act. The question had the necessary effect. Joshua turned back to look at him.

"What about you?"

"Yes, what about me? If the professor is the one you want, why have you dragged me into this?"

Joshua pulled a fair point expression. "Hmm, the thing is, I really like you. You proved you were a worthy adversary, and you saved my life so I could complete my full journey. For that, you have one chance. One chance to prove that you aren't a treacherous bastard as well."

"What does that mean?"

Joshua laughed. "The thing is, I know you're not stupid. I know you probably have a backup plan. The problem is, that was your one chance to show me that we can be friends and that you are not going to break our bond. If any of your team turn up here in the next fifteen minutes, I'll know you are a treacherous sinner, like this poor excuse for a man. And, if that happens, I think you know the outcome."

60

Caroline was gripping the steering wheel so tight her knuckles had turned white. She could think of nothing else but getting there on time. "How long, Louise?"

"About eight minutes. There's a right turn coming up. It's a minor road so don't miss it."

As the turning came into view and Caroline swung the car down the single track, Louise's radio crackled. "DS Cookson, this is DCS Alexander. What is your status? Over."

"What the?" Caroline almost crashed the car with shock.

Louise looked at Harry, who grabbed his radio. "Oh shite. I forgot to turn mine off as well."

"DS Cookson. Report in. Over."

Louise turned the volume on the radio down so that she could not hear the increasingly annoyed tone of the chief super's voice. Harry followed suit.

Caroline was trying to concentrate on driving, taking each bend far too fast. "Do they know where we are?"

"Yes, Caroline. Just concentrate on driving. We can't be worried about that now. We need to save Matthew and the professor. Keep following this road."

As they ate up the miles between them and the flashing dot on the screen, Louise smiled to herself. She had left her radio on deliberately, hoping that this crazy plan would be rumbled and the cavalry would be despatched. The problem was, she knew it may all be too late.

*

Matthew fought back uncharacteristic tears. He had just sealed everyone's fate. They were all going to die. Joshua was a clever man and had worked out that Matthew would not expose himself like this without some form of backup plan. The problem was that in Joshua's disturbed mind, Matthew's actions were a direct vindication of the madness he had been playing out in his sick game. *The Devil's Code*. The ninth circle. *Treachery*.

Matthew was glad they had at least fifteen minutes, but Joshua's constant thumbing of the lighter was terrifying. Joshua had stopped talking. The exchange with the professor was done and Joshua confirmed his role as judge, jury and executioner. Now it was a waiting game. If his team turned up, they would all go up in flames. Joshua would see his journey as complete. He would join his mother in *her heaven*.

Matthew continued to work against his restraints. He didn't have a better plan.

*

Eventually the twisting roads ended, and they pulled into a wider area next to a couple of farmhouses. "We're nearly there, Caroline. Go about fifty yards up the road and see if there is somewhere we can park up."

Caroline did as she was told and crept slowly along the next bit of road. There was a small grass-covered lay-by to the left. Just enough space to pull in and leave enough space for other vehicles to pass, not that they'd seen another vehicle for nearly ten minutes.

Louise looked at the tablet. "There's a track up here on the left. Come on."

They walked swiftly but quietly up the road to the track. They turned down it. The area was overgrown with large trees on either side and the low afternoon sun was casting eerie bolts of light through small gaps in the foliage. They emerged into a parking area in front of a small church.

Louise whispered. "This is it. They're here."

*

Joshua was getting restless. He turned the lighter over and over in his hands. He checked his watch. Two minutes until he either let McCallum go or included him in the human sacrifice that was laid out before him. The professor had closed his eyes seemingly resigned to his fate. DCI McCallum had shuffled away, not wishing to engage Joshua any longer.

He inhaled deeply. It was fine. His journey was done. His worthless life was over, but he had achieved his aim. People had heard his story. He had been someone that people would finally talk about and now he would be with Mother again.

He checked his watch for the final time. The fifteen minutes was up. He was about to untie Matthew and let him go when the church door creaked.

He spun around to see who it was. Framed in the light of the door was a figure. A short, hunched figure, wearing a long dress and... Joshua could barely believe it. His mouth was dry, his heart began to race.

"*Mother*!"

61

Joshua stood staring at the figure in the doorway. He couldn't process what he was seeing. Mother was back. How was this possible? He had seen her die, hanging upside down in the crashed car. He had seen her zipped up in the black body bag. He had watched her coffin go into the flames. She was dead but... he shook his head to refocus. His mind was playing tricks on him. It was a vision. She wasn't really there. He closed his eyes and counted to five. She was still there when he reopened them. The figure spread its arms. She was speaking. The words barely audible. *Come to Mother*. Was that what she was saying?

Joshua glanced back at the professor and Matthew, who were also staring at the figure. "Are you seeing this?" Joshua exclaimed, a sense of panic in his tone.

Matthew played along. "You see, Joshua, your mother's not really dead. She's come back to you. You can stop all this madness."

Joshua looked back at the figure. "*No, no, no,*" he muttered. The figure still had her arms wide open. She was saying it again. *Come to Mother.*

Joshua's brain was running a hundred to the dozen. His mother was dead, but she was standing in the doorway of the church and... suddenly it all made sense. He was in his mother's house of God. It was one of those miracles that he read so often about in her Bible. She had somehow come down from her heaven to guide him home. To guide him to their final destination. It was a sign. It was time to go. He let out a squeal of excitement and turned to look at the professor and Matthew. He flicked the top of the lighter open and rolled his finger on the thumbwheel.

*

Chief Superintendent James Alexander stood in the control room, watching the screen that was showing the police assets and where they were located.

"Inspector. What's the latest?"

"Five units despatched to the area. Your team seem to have stopped in a remote location. The nearest unit is still twelve minutes away."

"What about the helicopter?"

"Just about to lift, sir. At least nine minutes flying time before they get to the area."

James cursed. He was going to throw the book at DCI McCallum when he got his hairy arse back to the station. Wasting resources like this. Putting everyone in danger. But first he had to make sure his DCI was alive to receive his rage. He watched intently as the assets that had been despatched moved slowly towards the flashing dot that was DCI McCallum and his team.

*

"No, Joshua. Don't hurt those people. Mother's here. Everything will be alright now."

Joshua stopped what he was doing. The flick of the thumbwheel had not worked the first time he did it. His second attempt was interrupted by his mother's voice but... Joshua turned around to look at the figure, which was now slowly walking down the aisle. The voice. It was wrong. It was too pure. His mother's voice was gravellier, a symptom of seventy-odd years of wear and tear. The figure continued to walk slowly towards him. He tried to focus in the increasingly dimming light, as the first signs of evening darkness appeared in the sky outside.

"I'm sorry, Joshua. I'm sorry you felt you had to do this. I don't know why they said I was dead. I've been in hospital, recovering from the crash. But I'm here now. Come to Mother."

Joshua's breathing became laboured. He couldn't process what he was seeing and hearing. The voice was wrong but...

"I saw you die. Hung upside down by your seatbelt in the car. Taken away in a black body bag. I watched your coffin go into the flames."

"They lied to you, Joshua. Like everyone in our lives. Constantly let down by people's lies and deceit. Don't you see that? It's only ever been you and me. Against the world."

Joshua shot a glance back to Matthew and the professor. "If that's true, Mother, then these bastards deserve to die. Their treachery needs to be punished. It's what Dante has been telling me."

"No. I love you with all my heart, but your brain is

muddled up with this one. God does not want you to kill the sinners. That stupid poem is nonsense."

Joshua's stomach lurched. Why was his mother suddenly being so horrible? His brain was racing. The voice was wrong.

The figure spoke some more words, but Joshua wasn't hearing them. He knew something was wrong. The voice. It wasn't Mother. He stared at the silhouetted shape as the backlight from the church door continued to frame whoever this was. His brain was processing it all slowly. It was a trick. He shook his head. McCallum had shown himself to be a treacherous sinner after all. He wasn't surprised. As the figure came into the light, still twenty yards away, the full spectrum of the treachery became clear.

The dress was right. One of his mother's favourites. The blonde wig. One of a number she wore as her own hair had begun to fall out. The stooped manner was a nice touch but as the figure came into view, he could see the police issue boots, sticking out from underneath the full-length dress. As the face of his 'mother' appeared, he knew that he had been tricked. The face peering back at him was DS Louise Cookson.

The reaction was instant. Joshua frantically flicked the ignition wheel on the lighter. It wouldn't spark. In the second he took to do that Louise moved towards him as fast as the costume would let her. Joshua's brain was torn. He needed to die but he had to punish the sinners. As Louise got within a few feet he launched a kick straight into her belly. She fell back, falling unceremoniously on the floor by the last of the pews. Harry and Caroline rushed in from the doorway. "Get the professor and the DCI," Louise shouted. Joshua grabbed the professor and dragged him behind the altar.

Harry got to Matthew first and helped him towards the door, frantically pulling at his restraints to free him from the shackles. Louise and Caroline ran towards the aisle, one running either side of the altar to block off any escape route. As they rounded the altar they stopped instantly, frozen at the scene laid out before them. Within a few seconds, Harry had got Matthew free, and they joined the scene.

Joshua was sitting against the wall, with his arm around the professor's neck, a manic smile spread across his face. The ignition wheel had finally worked. His other arm was outstretched, holding the lighter like a trophy as the small flame jumped and flickered in the gloom.

*

Chief Superintendent Alexander paced the room. "How long?"

The inspector remained calm, unfazed by this growling senior officer in his control room. "The nearest asset is seven minutes away."

"What about the helicopter?"

"Five minutes out, sir."

He paced some more, his chest heaving with deep, angry breaths. He watched the screen as the nearest police car moved slowly towards the target. It didn't really matter how much ire he reserved for DCI McCallum. If this went south, his job was on the line.

"I'm sorry. I'm sorry. Please don't hurt the professor."
Matthew's stomach was doing somersaults, but he had to
try to stop Joshua moving the flame towards their bodies.

"I know I let you down and I'm sorry. I broke our bond.
Our friendship, but like you I did it out of love. The prof is
my friend and, like your mother, I wanted to do everything
I could to have more time with the person that meant most
to me in the world. You can understand that, can't you?"

Matthew stared at Joshua hoping that his speech
might have some effect. Joshua still held the lighter out
in front of him, the flame still flickering menacingly, but
he said nothing. The scars from his previous pyrotechnic
encounter were still visible in patches around his head
and neck, creating a macabre backdrop to the flame that
commanded everyone's attention.

"Come on. Let the professor go. If you want to die to
meet your mother, then we'll let you do that, but spare the
professor."

The other three gasped at what Matthew said. Was
he really going to let Joshua set fire to himself? As they
turned to look at Matthew, questioning looks all over
their faces, he subtly turned his head, his eyes moving to
the right, urging them to follow his eyeline. Louise was the
first to pick up what he was trying to tell them. Standing
in a corner by the small pulpit was a fire extinguisher.

Matthew kept on talking as Louise slowly moved
towards the extinguisher.

"Where's she going? Tell her to stop or the professor
becomes Guy Fawkes."

Matthew pushed out an arm to stop Louise. "Let him go and this is all over."

Joshua's facial expression hardened. "The sinners have to die."

"OK, take me instead..." the gasps returned, "...I've proved to be a treacherous sinner, just as much as the professor." Inexplicably, Matthew started to move around the side of the altar, glancing quickly at Louise. Her eyes pleaded with him to stop as she picked up on his crazy plan.

"What are you doing? What are you doing?" Joshua's voice rose in panic. Matthew continued to move slowly towards him, hands outstretched, trying to show an unthreatening persona.

"Come on. I'm here. Let him go."

Joshua drew the lighter towards him. "No. Don't do it. Take me."

The next few seconds felt like they were played out in slow motion.

A commotion at the entrance to the church was followed by the loud *thud thud* of helicopter rotor blades, hovering above the building. Everyone turned to look at what was happening, away from Joshua and the professor. A fatal mistake. The next thing they heard was a whoosh as the petrol ignited.

62

ONE WEEK LATER

"I love you. You do know that?"

Matthew pushed the last of the peas round his plate as he tried to take in what Louise had just said.

"Er... thank you. I think."

Louise flushed. "Oh God, not like that, sir. I mean the kind of love you have for a family member. You know, like a father."

Matthew grimaced. *A father.* It figured. Any mid-life crisis fantasies he may have had about Louise and him becoming more than work colleagues were dashed with that phrase. *A father.*

Louise rambled on, unaware of Matthew's inner turmoil at what might have been. "I mean, my father was an absolute bastard. He left me and my mother when I was really young. I never knew him. We got through life without a significant male influence in my life. The more I worked with you, the more I realised you had been playing that role for me. When you kept risking your life for this case, I felt a pain I'd never felt before. The pain of seeing someone you love, nearly being taken away from you."

"Yes, I think I felt a bit of that in the church."

"Oh gosh. I'm sorry. How is the professor?"

Matthew rubbed his face. "You saved his life."

He could see the mention of that awful day caused tears to well up in Louise's eyes, but she fought them back. "I didn't know what to do. I've never seen anything like that in my life. Watching two people screaming from the pain of being on fire and... oh, the smell of burning flesh. It was horrific. When you jumped into the circle of fire on the hill, it was all done by the time I caught up with you, sparing me that horror, but this time... I was frozen in fear. One fire extinguisher and two burning men. I mean, what was I supposed to do?"

Matthew grabbed her hand. "You did the right thing. You saved the man who deserved to live. Joshua Billington had a death wish. As much as I wanted to bring that bastard to justice, I would have done exactly the same."

"How is his recovery?"

"Thankfully your actions minimised the degree of burn damage. He suffered the same sort of burns that I had. He'll be over the worst in a few weeks and back in his study drinking brandy, smoking cigars and talking rubbish."

"What about Joshua?"

Matthew sighed. "They have him on life support but there is no chance he will wake up. Don't forget his original burns were far worse than mine. They hadn't healed properly, and his body was never going to survive that level of additional trauma. He looks like a cross between Freddy Krueger and the Mummy, wrapped in all those bandages. At the end of the day, he got his wish."

"Why are they keeping him alive then? If there's no hope."

"The hospital lawyers are getting all antsy because he has no next of kin. No one who can agree to turn the machines off and let him go."

Louise put her hand to her mouth, fighting back the urge to scream out in frustration. "Why didn't we stop him? All those poor defenceless people that he sacrificed to satisfy his sick fantasy. He was always one step ahead of us, which is why I was so determined to stop him completing his journey. I really thought your idea of me dressing up as his mother would do the trick but of course, we didn't account for Morag blabbing."

"You can't blame her. She did what she had to do. I didn't want anyone else risking their career for me. Don't forget they wouldn't have found us if you and Harry hadn't left your radios on."

Louise's face fell and she averted her gaze. "I'm sorry. I guess I just didn't want your crazy plan to end in tragedy. Like you I wanted a backup plan."

Matthew once again placed his hand over hers. "Look at me..." he waited as she slowly turned her gaze back towards him, "...you've got nothing to be sorry for. Like you said, my plan was reckless and in the end the actions we all took contributed to the outcome."

Louise let out a frustrated grunt. "I know, but why did the chief super come in all guns blazing? We were seconds away from taking Joshua down."

Matthew drew in a deep breath. "Yes, the chief super's

timing was impeccable... but you are right. I should have been clever enough to get ahead of our Mr Billington. He outfoxed me and outthought me at every stage."

"It wasn't just you, sir. We all failed."

Matthew shook his head. "I dunno. Anyway, what about catching his accomplice?"

The deep frown appeared on Louise's face. "Harry's chasing down the leads through the bank and the car you saw outside the church, but it doesn't look good. He may have been a nutter, but he knew how to cover his tracks. This whole investigation has got me questioning my abilities as a copper."

"You're a brilliant copper and an amazing person. You need to shake this off and get on with your career... without me around."

Louise frowned. "What do you mean?"

Matthew pulled an envelope from his jacket. "This is my resignation. I'm supposed to have the first of my disciplinary interviews with Alexander and the professional standard boys tomorrow, but I'm not going to give them the satisfaction. I only have a couple of months until I've done my thirty years and with all the leave I'm owed, I think I can stretch it out so that I can resign before I'm pushed."

This time Louise couldn't stop the tears, punching him lightly on the arm. "Don't you dare forget me, will you, sir?"

Matthew leaned over and tenderly brushed a tear from her cheek. "I'll never forget you. You can come and sing with me, drink beer, drink brandy with the prof, listen to some Mahler, walk the hills, enjoy the fresh air and all the while calling me Matthew. No more, sir."

Louise sniffed back the tears and wiped her eyes. "You're going to live up to your nickname then. I presume you know what they call you?"

"Oh aye. McMorse. I guess there are worse things to be called."

63

A month had passed since that traumatic day. Matthew's resignation had been accepted. It seemed the senior brass were glad to brush it all under the carpet and avoid a PR circus. He had got used to being a civvy. Getting up late, eating a leisurely breakfast, going down the pub for a pint whenever he wanted. But today, he was readying himself to pick up the professor from hospital and help him settle back into his university apartment.

As he locked his front door, he almost bundled into the postman. "A special delivery for you, Mr McCallum. Looks all important, like."

He signed for the thin envelope, turning it over and over in his hands, trying to work out what it was. He glanced at this watch. He was running late. He jumped in the car and threw the envelope on the seat.

As he reached the ward, he could hear the professor from halfway down the corridor. He was sure the nurses and doctors were going to miss his jovial antics and his constant storytelling. One of the reasons they had become and remained such amazing friends.

"Come on then," Matthew exclaimed as he turned the corner into his room, "let these poor people get on with their jobs. It's time to get you home."

The professor smiled, wincing slightly at the healing scars left on his face. "Matthew, old boy. Thank you so much for doing this."

As the professor bundled his stuff together, giving Matthew some bags to carry, he embraced the nursing staff. He waltzed down the corridor announcing his departure, shaking hands and kissing cheeks as he went, like some famous person holding court.

They reached the car park and as the prof went to get in the passenger seat, he spotted the envelope. "What's this?"

They got in the car, the envelope now in the professor's hand.

"Oh, I dunno. It came this morning as I was walking out of my door. Some special delivery thing. I haven't had time to open it."

As they drove on, the professor eyed the envelope. "It looks official. Do you want me to open it?"

Matthew glanced at the professor. He seemed unusually disturbed by what he was holding. "You can if you like."

The professor tore the top of the envelope and pulled out a couple of pieces of paper. Matthew had a quick look, whilst trying to concentrate on driving. It looked like a solicitor's letter. "What is it?"

The professor said nothing for a minute, taking in the words. "Oh my. I can't actually believe what I'm reading."

Matthew couldn't stand the tension and quickly pulled over, grabbing the letter out of the professor's hand. As he read it his heart sank, looking at the professor in horror. "What is this?"

*

Matthew had settled the professor back into his apartment but made his excuses to leave as soon as he could, without seeming rude. The letter had poleaxed him. He sat down with a neat malt and read the final rantings of a madman.

Dear Matthew,

It's been a blast... ha, ha... sometimes literally!

If you've received this letter and the enclosed power of attorney, it seems my life hangs in the balance. You see, I planned for everything. Every scenario, every twist and turn in our dance with the devil.

It seems my life is in your hands. I've instructed my solicitor to give you the legal right to decide if I live or die. Kind of poetic, don't you think? You see, despite what you may have thought, I did respect you. You were a worthy adversary and I guess I'm not surprised that you messed up my final act. Which is why there has to be consequences for your actions.

Can you bear to watch me in that hospital bed for the rest of your life, haunting your waking hours? Maybe I can hear you. Maybe my body is dead, but my mind is agile. Wouldn't that be a thing.

What will you decide? Do you really think you've solved The Devil's Code?

I'm waiting.

By the time Matthew had read the note, over and over, the whisky bottle was almost empty, and the effects of the alcohol took their toll. His eyelids drooped and the letter fell on the floor.

64

Matthew had slept in the chair. His head was pounding, his mouth dry. His drunken sleep had been disturbed by the face of Joshua Billington, sneering and goading him. He looked around wondering where the letter had gone. He winced at his aching back, the chair offering no support for someone of his advancing years. As he leant forward the morning sun caught his eye, making him squint. The brightness too much for a whisky hangover. The letter was on the floor. It hadn't been an awful dream. The nightmare was real, lying on the floor in the scrawly handwriting of the man who turned his final days as a copper upside down.

He picked the letter up and placed it on the dining table, choosing not to indulge in the psycho's words anymore. He made a coffee and fried some eggs, forcing them down despite his stomach threatening to rebel at any moment.

A shower, another coffee and some toast, eventually began to take the edge off the hangover. He picked his phone up and scrolled through the contact list. He needed Louise. She may not be his trusted sidekick anymore, but he needed her more now than ever. His finger hovered over her name.

A minute passed. He couldn't call her. It wasn't her problem. They had him secured in the hospital. If he did wake up, they would put him in prison. If he didn't, well…

He stood up, grabbed his coat and his car keys. He made a decision. He was not going to let this bastard hang this over him for any longer than he needed to.

After a short trip to the hospital, Matthew stood in the side room of the ICU ward that Joshua Billington was in. He watched as the ventilators manipulated the rise and fall of his chest. He watched as the drips slowly kept his fluids up. He watched the numbers on the monitors go up and down, recording his vital signs.

Matthew wanted nothing more than for Joshua to wake up so he could look him in the eye and tell him he failed. Failed to complete his sick journey. He wanted him to know that he had ultimately solved his so-called *Devil's Code*, but as he stared at the half-bandaged face of the man who had made his life a living hell… ironic… he knew that would never happen. Ultimately, Joshua had won. Even though he was lying in a hospital bed, being kept alive by a myriad of machines, his brain was dead, his soul had moved on. A scenario Matthew thought Joshua's mother would probably approve of.

He sat down on the soft visitor's chair and read the letter again. It was like a dagger in Matthew's heart. A final act of vengeance.

Matthew wasn't sure how long he'd been sitting there, reading the letter and agonising over what to do, when the door to the room opened. Three faces appeared. Louise, Harry and Caroline. Matthew's heart leapt, especially at seeing Louise. He'd decided not to call her but somehow, she was here, along with his old loyal team. He gestured them in.

Louise spoke first. "Er, sir... crap, sorry, Matthew... I'm never going to get used to that... we heard what happened. The professor phoned me."

Matthew handed them the letter and they all read it in turn.

"What a wee bastard he is," exclaimed Harry. "Seems like he ne'er wants this to end."

Caroline sighed. "He may have had some serious mental health issues, but you can't deny he more or less planned everything to perfection. I said from the start of my profiling that we had a highly intelligent person behind all this, and I think with this final act he has proven just that. I agree with Harry. He seems determined to finish whatever game he thinks he's playing. The mention of consequences is a bit disturbing."

"I know. I think he means that if I don't agree to these damn machines being turned off, he's going to haunt me for the rest of my life."

Caroline screwed up her face. "Maybe. I guess he always said this journey should end with his death, so he could meet his mother again. I suppose if you are stopping him from passing over, he sees this as a further betrayal of what he wants."

Indecision hung in the air. Matthew caught Louise's eye. The stress was evident in her pinched expression and the worry lines across her brow. She suddenly stepped forward and gave Matthew a huge bear hug. As she pulled away, she fixed him with a firm stare. "You have to do this. Tell them to turn those machines off and move on with your life. He's not going to recover. We are not going to get the satisfaction of looking him in the eye and telling him he's going away for life."

Matthew sat back down and looked at all three of them. "I'm so sorry I got you involved in all this. I didn't want any of you to risk your careers for me."

Harry responded first. "Och, yoose didnae force us to do anything and anyway we only got a wee rap on the knuckles."

Matthew tried to hide his embarrassment and refocused on Joshua Billington. The rise and fall of his chest. The beeps and whooshes of the machines. He thought of the professor, relaxing at home, his scars improving every day. He subconsciously put his hand up to his own face, feeling the slight roughness of the faint scar that was just about visible from his own brush with the *devil's inferno*.

He thought back to what they had found out about Joshua's life. His overbearing, God-fearing mother. The bullies, the taunts, the injustice he suffered because of how he looked and how he was. The sexual abuse by his own mother, to satisfy some hypocritical need for carnal relief. Caroline had said that the concept of nature or nurture was a falsehood. Joshua's psychopathic traits had been moulded and nurtured by his mother, and yet despite this, he had worshipped her every minute of his life. Her death and his obsession with Dante's Inferno had been a powerful trigger for a troubled mind at a highly emotional time. Matthew agonised over whether he should be showing sympathy for Joshua. The guy didn't have a chance at a normal life but... there was no way he could condone him taking so many innocent lives to satisfy his sick fantasy.

He looked back at Caroline, Louise and Harry. "I don't know what to do…"

As the sentence trailed off, the door to the room opened and the doctor walked in.

The doctor nodded respectfully at the gathering before turning his focus to Matthew. "Mr McCallum. There is no rush here, but I have been asked to check whether you have made a decision."

Matthew looked from face to face. They gave a subtle nod. Encouraging him to do what needed to be done. He looked back at Joshua.

"I'm sorry, I can't do it."

65

Matthew didn't know why he did it, but the next day he found himself walking up the Crags, eventually arriving at Whinny Hill. The spring sun was out but the wind was still whipping up the loose grass and leaves. He zipped up his coat a bit further.

As he reached the brow of the hill, he stopped as the visions of that night came back to him. Joshua Billington sitting in a ring of fire. He shivered at the memory. He walked towards the spot where it had happened. Nature was having a good go at erasing the physical signs of the fire. Small shoots of grass and other plants were beginning to make their way through the scorched surface, but the scale of the burnt ground was still very much in evidence.

Matthew stared at the ground. He agonised over whether turning the machines off, that were keeping Joshua alive, would somehow give him closure, but as he stood on the hill he didn't feel it would. There was something still nagging at him. Something that was still haunting him. He couldn't work out what it was, but as he began to walk back down the other side of the hill, his gut tightened. He was scared. Something still wasn't right.

It took Matthew about twenty minutes to get off the Crags and he decided to walk round the edge of the hillside back towards the university. It had been a few days since he'd seen his old pal and he knew he was one of the people that could sort out his addled mind.

The professor was in his apartment and welcomed Matthew in, offering him coffee. They sat catching up about everything and nothing, the caffeine hit a welcome boost to Matthew's tired limbs. After a while the conversation inevitably turned to Joshua.

"You seem distracted, old boy."

"I'm sorry. For some reason I can't get Joshua Billington out of my head."

"It's not easy, old boy. Being forced to decide whether to turn off someone's life support is a difficult situation, regardless of the person lying in the bed. Give yourself some time."

"Maybe, but the whole situation still leaves me uneasy."

"Why?"

"I don't really know. I hope that if I turn his machines off it will give me some kind of closure, but I'm not sure."

"Don't be too hard on yourself. That boy was disturbed. He manipulated all of us with his silly games and it's pretty much all you've thought about for the last month. You can't just flick a switch in your head and forget about it. Give yourself a break and go enjoy your retirement."

Matthew pulled a pained smile. He knew the professor was right. The conversation turned back to matters of the university and the upcoming concerts that they were due to sing in. Talking about these things calmed his angst, but deep in the recesses of his brain, Joshua Billington was still there.

They were surprised when the grandfather clock in the apartment struck 5pm. They had sat and talked for almost six hours. The grumbling in their stomachs told them that food was the next priority, but as Matthew started to gather his stuff to leave, there was a knock at the door.

The professor answered, exchanging enthusiastic banter with the person at the door. He came back into the living room, a broad smile on his face.

"Look at this, old boy. One of my students has bought me a cracking bottle of brandy. Now sit yourself back down and have one with me."

"I really need to go."

"Oh, stuff and nonsense. You've got time for a quick snifter."

Matthew smiled as the professor started to unpack the bottle and arrange the brandy glasses. "Is that a card attached to the package?"

The professor picked up the now discarded package. "Oh yes. Here. Open it and tell me what it says."

The professor had the bottle open and poured two glasses, handing one to Matthew, who was struggling with the tiny envelope the card was in.

As Matthew pulled the card out and turned it around to see what it said, the nagging concern that would not go away, the fear that had seemed to be ever present in Matthew's mind suddenly came to a horrific realisation.

Matthew instinctively shouted for him to stop as he

saw the professor take a large mouthful of the brandy, but he was too late. The instant the professor swallowed the liquid he collapsed on the floor.

Panic gripped him, but he grabbed his phone and dialled 999.

"Ambulance. Quickly. Possible poisoning. Churchill Apartment, Upper Quad in the University of Edinburgh. Please hurry."

When the paramedics arrived, Matthew had been doing CPR for just under ten minutes. He was exhausted but they told him the professor was still alive and rushed him onto the stretcher and out to the waiting ambulance.

Sitting on the floor, trying to recover from the physical exhaustion and mental trauma, he picked up the card again. The horror of it all once again consumed him. Under a symbol of an inverted pentagram there were three words.

IT'S NOT OVER.

66

The professor was alive but unconscious. The doctors had flushed the worst of the poison out of his system but were concerned about damage to his major organs. Matthew sat by his bed watching the rise and fall of his chest, tears never far away.

It's not over. He could not believe that Joshua Billington was still playing his sick game. Matthew realised that being forced to make a decision about Joshua's death was all part of his plan. He always said the game would end with his death, to satisfy the morbid fantasy he had that this would somehow allow him to meet his mother in what he called *her heaven*. But, of course, he lied. His death wasn't the end.

The niggling doubt that had been playing in Matthew's mind had finally come to the fore. Joshua had planned everything meticulously. He had somehow considered every scenario and had someone still doing his dirty work, even while he was on a life support machine. Matthew finally realised why he was scared. They had thwarted his final act. Neither he nor the professor had died in the church, as Joshua had planned. The ninth circle in his *Devil's Code* had not been completed. In Joshua's eyes, the *treachery* had not been avenged. The sinners had not been punished.

Hundreds of thoughts raced through his head, the most concerning being the realisation that he may still be a target. As he tried to calm his nerves the door to the room opened and Louise walked in.

She rushed towards him and hugged him tightly. She pulled away and looked him in the eye. "I heard what happened. Are you OK?"

Matthew sighed deeply. "I'm fine but it's not me you should be worrying about."

Louise looked at the professor. "How's he doing?"

"The docs say we have to wait. They seem to have treated him for the poisoning, but they are worried that the time it took to get him to hospital may have caused damage to his major organs."

"Oh Christ. I'm so sorry. When will they know for sure?"

"They said the sedation they've given him should wear off by this evening. We should know more then."

The emotion in the room was palpable but Louise cut back to business.

"The chief super's agreed to get the team back together to investigate how this happened."

Matthew gave a contemptuous snort. "Not all the team. I assume you are not back here to rerecruit me to the investigation."

Louise looked a little embarrassed. "Um, no. That would be a fair assumption. I don't think the chief super is quite ready to welcome you back."

"Who's your new guvnor?"

"Actually, he's given me a temporary promotion to Inspector and asked me to lead this one, plus a few other cases he's thrown my way."

Matthew felt like he hadn't smiled in days but couldn't help but be delighted at the news. "I'm so pleased for you. So thoroughly deserved and maybe now this old fossil is out of the way, you can blossom into the shit-hot detective inspector I always knew you could be."

"Well, thank you, but I wouldn't be half as good as I am without your guidance. We all miss you."

They talked some more, Louise outlining the lines of inquiry they were pursuing. Each step she outlined gave Matthew some hope that whoever Joshua still had pulling his strings would be caught and the nightmare could end. Eventually it was time for Louise to go and he walked her out so he could grab a coffee and a sandwich.

It was several hours later when Matthew came to, having fallen asleep in the visitor's chair. The professor had woken up and was calling his name. He leapt forward and grabbed the professor's hand. "How are you feeling?"

His voice was croaky, but he managed to utter some words. "I… I've been better, old boy."

Before they could exchange any more words, the doors opened and the medical team came in, ordering Matthew to leave so they could do their assessment.

Matthew paced around outside for what seemed like an eternity. When the doctor came out, he pounced on her. "What's the verdict, doc?"

She looked at him quizzically. "Are you family?"

"Why? Do I need to be?"

Her face told him all he needed to know. "Just tell me,

doc. He doesn't have any family. I'm the closest thing he has."

She obviously believed him, adopting the stern expression that doctors always have when delivering bad news. "I'm afraid it's not good news. We've treated the poisoning, but it seems to have done irreparable damage to his heart and kidneys. I don't think he has that long."

The words came crushing down on him like a landslide. He grabbed a rail to steady himself, his legs threatening to give way. He didn't know how he was going to look his friend in the eye, but he knew he had to do it.

He gingerly opened the door to the ward. The professor was lying there, his eyes closed. As Matthew approached the bed and took his hand, the professor stirred.

He forced a smile. "Matthew. You're still here."

He fought back the tears. "Of course, I am."

The professor adjusted his position. "Seems like I'm done for, old boy. My ticker was never that good and it seems the brandy has finally got to me. Ironic really."

"It wasn't the brandy. It was poisoned."

"I know. I know. Just rather apt that I should meet my end drinking my favourite tipple."

Matthew couldn't hold the tears back any longer.

"Hey, hey. Enough of that. My time has come and maybe my death will give that lunatic the end he was looking for. My so-called treachery has been punished."

Matthew couldn't speak, the pain of seeing his friend dying in front of his eyes was too much. His stomach lurched; he fought for breath as all the while the professor gripped his hand.

"Come on. I've had a good life. Let me go, old boy. It's

the only way, and if it stops anything more happening to good people, then it will be worth it."

Matthew wiped away the tears and looked at the smiling face of his friend. So noble, so kind, even now in his last moments. All of a sudden, the firm grip he had on Matthew's hand loosened.

His vitals flatlined.

67

In the month that followed the professor's death, Matthew felt like he was on autopilot. He spent a lot of time writing the eulogy for his funeral. He sang with as much gusto as his body would allow at the university memorial concert that was arranged to honour the professor's years of dedicated service. He was heartened to be involved in discussions with the dean and faculty about naming one of the new buildings the Professor Roger Mountfield Wing. All of which distracted him from the pain of losing his friend and the uncharacteristic loneliness that he now felt.

He walked the hills; he went to the pub, increased the number of times he went to sing at the university and read some of the books he'd been promising himself to devour. But they didn't fill the void, because apart from missing his friend, he realised there was something else he was missing, which was why the knock on his door on a sunny afternoon lifted his spirits. It was Louise.

She followed him inside and then out into his small but tidy garden. They sat on some garden chairs arranged around a small round table.

"How are you?" she enquired.

He didn't say anything to start with.

"Are you alright?" she prompted.

"Yes, yes, sorry. Still finding it a bit hard to adjust to all this."

She leant over and stroked his arm. "I know. Losing such a dear man like the professor must be hard to take, but I might just have something that will cheer you up."

Matthew frowned. "Oh. Really?"

"Yes, we got him. The accomplice. Harry finally managed to gain and execute the warrant with the bank, and we managed to track the transactions. The twenty grand that was paid out to abduct the professor was followed by some further payments, which we think were linked to the poisoning. With some good grunt detective work and some payments to our informant network we tracked him down. Another lowlife living off his criminal gains, who is now banged up and ready to go down for a long time."

Matthew grimaced, fighting back tears. "I would have liked to have been there for that. To look that scumbag in the eye and show him the pain he caused by killing my friend."

"I can arrange for you to see him. If you think that would help. You know, with closure or something."

Matthew looked at Louise and shook his head. "I can't ask you to do that. You're free of my maverick ways. I don't want to ever again put you in a position where my actions jeopardise your career. You're too…"

Louise looked at him, expectantly. "Too, what?"

Matthew grabbed her hand. "You're too special. Too brilliant. Too everything. Remember that. You have the potential to be Chief one day and I ain't gonna get in the

310

way of that. Just thank the team for me and make sure he goes down for a long time."

Louise rode the embarrassment at Matthew's uncharacteristic emotional outburst. "Thank you. That's very kind of you to say. There is one more bit of good news."

"Really?"

"Yes, the guy admitted that the instructions he got from Joshua Billington were that the professor had to die. You weren't mentioned. I think Joshua saw the opportunity to avenge your perceived treachery at the church but had not told this guy that you were part of his murder plan. You can forget about that awful note. It's over. No one is coming for you."

They sat in silence for a few moments, watching the birds jump on and off the feeders. After a few minutes Louise broke the silence.

"Did you hear that Alexander has got an ACC job in Yorkshire?"

Matthew grunted. "Hmm, the shit always rises to the top. Who's taking his post?"

"Kristen McNally."

"Oh wow. I like Kristen. Well deserved."

"Yes, and she likes you."

Matthew allowed himself a brief smile as he looked at the mischievous expression on Louise's face.

"What are you up to? I can see you're plotting something in that brain of yours."

"She's promoted me to a permanent inspector position and wants me to lead up the new cold case team. Harry and Caroline are going to be working with me too."

Matthew nodded. "That's good. You three will make a good team and I'm sure the victims' families will appreciate you reopening their cases and finally getting them some justice."

"Actually, it's a team of four."

"Oh. Who else have you got?"

"You. If you want it. I'm not quite ready to let go of my maverick."

"What?"

"Kristen wants an ex-detective to fill a civilian investigator role in the team and she told me to do everything in my power to convince you to come back."

Matthew rubbed his face. "Oh, Louise. I don't know."

"Look, Alexander is gone, and she's got your back. The chief's got better things to worry about than having you back in the fold. It will be great, as long as you can handle me being the boss."

Matthew avoided answering the question by going into the house to get some cold drinks. As they sipped at the welcome coolness on an increasingly humid day, the question hung in the air.

"You're not going to start calling me sir again, are you?"

Louise smiled. "No. I told you. I'm the boss. You need to call me ma'am and I'll call you Matthew or McMorse."

He laughed. "People still calling me that then?"

"Oh aye. You'll never shake that one."

They sat, enjoying the sunshine, listening and watching the industrious birds and finishing off their drinks. Eventually, Matthew looked over to Louise and smiled.

"Thank you, ma'am. I'd be delighted to accept your offer, but…"

"But what?"

"There's something I need to do first."

*

Matthew walked into the ICU. His gut tightened as he once again had to look at the man who had made his life a living hell. The machines still pumped and beeped. Joshua being kept alive, like some freakish Dr Frankenstein experiment.

He so much wanted for Joshua to wake up so that true justice could be served, but weeks had passed, and nothing had changed. Joshua Billington was clinically dead, and there was nothing he could do about it.

He had to move on. He knew the professor was right. In some sick way, letting Joshua go would end his journey, however much Matthew hated to concede defeat.

The doctor walked in, a sympathetic expression on his face.

Matthew took one last look at Joshua Billington. He turned to the doctor.

"Turn them off. Turn every bloody machine off."

Acknowledgements

As always my first thanks must go to my family for their amazing support with my author career and to my alpha readers, Hannah Wade, Jacky Wade, Karen Warner and Anthony Cooper who read all my drafts without complaining.

A big thank you to my friend and fellow author Tony Guntrip who has become my go-to editor. His in depth review of my work undoubtedly makes my final story much better.

A huge appreciation to all my readers, especially those I have been able to meet at the numerous craft fairs, events and author talks.

Thanks to my publisher, The Book Guild, for all their support in getting a quality product out to the market.

Finally, a massive shout out to the local independent businesses in Oxfordshire that help me to sell my books – Mostly Books in Abingdon, Coles Books in Bicester, Crafters Emporium in Oxford and Root One Garden Centre in Wallingford.